The Color over Occam

The Color over Occam

Jonathan Thomas

Hippocampus Press

New York

Published by Hippocampus Press
P.O. Box 641, New York, NY 10156.
www.hippocampuspress.com

Cover art and design by Daniel V. Sauer, dansauerdesign.com.
Hippocampus Press logo designed by Anastasia Damianakos.

First Hippocampus Press Edition
1 3 5 7 9 8 6 4 2

ISBN 978-1-61498-451-1

Of all men's miseries the bitterest is this, to know so much and to have control over nothing.

—Herodotus

One

For years, people had complained of the tap water's "Gorman taste." Not exactly swampy, not exactly salty. A vague but chronic impurity. Monthly testing by the state Water Resources Authority always came back negative for various microbes and pollutants. The state tried blaming any taint on clogged or rusty municipal pipes, and local government, hard-pressed to cover the routine demands of infrastructure, sidestepped liability by blaming homeowners' antique plumbing or fussy small-town imaginations.

From where I was sitting, the water seemed fine, but we had only compass, stars, and full moon to steer by, and no instruments to measure contamination. Somewhere below us, in black depths beyond range of my camcorder's night vision and zoom lens, crumbled the stone walls and cellars of Aylesbury, Clark's Corners, Pocumtuc, and Whately, in fact all the valley enclosing Gorman County, submerged during the Depression to safeguard a water supply for its burgeoning neighbors.

At thoughts of all those Yankee and Native spirits, lo these many decades, who might object to a lake atop their old haunts, it puzzled me that rumors were spreading only now of corpse lights in the Gorman County Reservoir. Our informants were a romantic couple who shouldn't have been anyplace along the after-hours shoreline of high-security "public property," and a motorist on the ring road that skirted wooded acreage around the reservoir. Not much to navigate by, but Wil, manning the outboard, claimed those meager sightlines were enough.

Wil (in militant preference to Wilbur) Rice was the ideal, if not only, man for this job. Permission to overnight out here was a moot point because he was a ranger for the Department of Parks and Recreation, and Gorman was his workaday turf. For all I knew, he was on the clock right now. Not that I cared. He'd never earn a cent in the organization where he and I were

100% of the active membership. In most clubs, I surmise, deadwood surrounds a diligent individual or two. Anyway, Wil referred to this excursion as a few hours' getaway, maybe his last, before fearsomely pregnant Lucinda had the twins.

We couldn't have asked for nicer weather. The midsummer day's heat had gentled without the help of any breeze. Except for the rippling wake from our motor at low throttle, the surface was smooth as lacquer, and its reflection of too many stars and rising, swollen moon brought the sky imposingly close. Wil asked if I'd noticed the occasional flash of meteor and I nodded, although I hadn't. The undulant hilltops, of a drabber black than the cosmos above them, were foremost on my mind, with vagrant curiosity at how mountainous they might have loomed before the flood. A diffuse strip of light rendered the southern rim marginally more distinct. The wan glow from our woebegone little burg! As if the punchline to all the expense and sacrifice here had been written in electricity.

At the outset, submerging a county for the primary benefit of our expanding hometown had seemed logical, albeit callous. But in the twenty years before the reservoir filled to capacity, factories flourishing during World War II went bust or sought lower overhead in Dixie. The town completely lost its economic footing a quarter century later, when reckless yuppies mismanaged its ivy-mantled university into dissolution. What campus halls the wrecking ball spared became office space or condos, in common with the sturdier defunct mills. Due to these and more shadowy associations from which the town strove to distance itself, it resorted to the dramatic but impotent step of changing its name to "Occam." This simply amounted to a phonetic New England respelling of its old name, and the town's baffling new identification with a medieval philosopher monk, if anyone beside myself had even heard of William of Occam (especially after the university folded), did nothing to turn it around. Bucolic Gorman County had been demolished in the service of postindustrial blight.

So why would the indignant souls of the valley wait till this late stage to act up? In the best-case scenario, Wil and I, representing *OGAM*, were going to amass clues, and air them on the next *OGAM Chronicles*, the public-access cable digest of the Occam Ghostly Anomalies Monitors.

The motor cut out and Wil announced, "We're in the ballpark." I smiled at visions of antediluvian ballplayers directly below us, batting ectoplasmic homers through the murk. An obscenely plump Jersey mosquito whined by, which I ignored because they were supposedly fructivores. Then it looped back and dove at me. What the hell? I squashed it between loudly clapping hands, and winced at both the echoes from the hills and my bloodsoaked palms. Wil hadn't seen the attack and cast peevish doubts on my description of goliath insect menace. Grossly bad form, to make impulsive racket in our painstaking business.

I doused my hands clean in the lake, toweled them dry, and transferred my minidisk recorder from plastic pouch to the shelf across minutely nodding bow. I clicked on the mike to catch any electronic voice phenomena (EVPs to the cognoscenti), and peered into camcorder LCD display while slowly scanning back and forth, to catch activity hidden in the infrared range on or under placid surface. Into a ringbound notebook Wil scribbled moment-to-moment updates about wind, temperature, humidity, and rare traffic on the snippet of road exposed between two hillsides. Embarrassing to admit how often experts confuse headlights for more cryptic orbs! After fifteen minutes, we secured the equipment and proceeded elsewhere in our "ballpark," and mutely watched and documented for the same duration. We were anglers in a rarefied sense, biding patient hours on the off-chance of reeling in prize data.

Twice more Wil reoriented us, and accustomed as we were to wasted vigils, getting the fidgets in the thick of all-night monotony was only natural. Poor Wil! About to burst with the need to talk, judging by furrowed brow, and lips shaping silent words. Much as he deserved a break from Lucinda's hormonal bouts of temper and distress, guilt still ate at him for leaving her in the company of mere friends. Never mind that she'd dragged him to the fertility clinic, despite his philosophic acceptance that after three years of normal efforts, offspring were not meant to be. On second thought, maybe just as well we honored the ghost-hunter's code of silence.

When iridescence streaked the water a stone's throw from our prow, I was, sorry to say, incredulous, and had to verify it wasn't the reflection of a car, and aimed the camcorder too late. Wil was likewise dumbfounded, but blinked his astonishment away and scrawled rapidly. His notes affirmed we'd both felt initially topsy-turvy during that and each succeeding "corpse light," as if on the underside of a surface, looking up rather than down, into someone else's world.

We made for the brightness, nice and easy, afraid to rev the motor and disturb something that, for once, was discernible without aid of frame-by-frame or audio-filter scrutiny. We were too excited and focused for any anxiety about supernatural encounters. No investigators worth their salt fear harm from ghosts, and to be fair, a well-respected theory discounted will-o'-the-wisps as methane gas and oxidation from rotting plants.

Whatever this was, it winked out before Wil killed the motor, but re-kindled, right beside our port stern, a minute later. My viewfinder revealed that the coruscation only seemed to lie on the surface through some trick of refraction. It was actually fathoms below, and whenever I adjusted the zoom within a hairsbreadth of clarity, it retreated deeper again. Was I, or my lens at least, really chasing a classic will-o'-the-wisp? Wil broke our vow of silence. "Why do you keep futzing with that? The light's two feet away from you."

"Is it?" My tone may have come off as snide, but it did the job of nipping talk in the bud. Better that than marring any minidisk or camcorder EVPs. Obviously the view from where Wil sat was distorted. My figurative descent, meanwhile, had grown more frustrating and more mesmerizing. I dismissed a silly impression that the light was coercing me, or my mind anyhow, to follow it. According to his notes, Wil had also expected to meet transient, flitting orbs at best, and didn't know what to make of something so persistent and shapeless. He didn't mention the problem of its color, which I found impossible, between infrared vision and dark water, to specify. From second to second, my eyes registered white or violet or beige or silver or one that never lasted long enough to name. And further inspection proved me wrong about the anomaly's lack of form. I had a steep, almost vertical perspective on a translucent plane of irregular outline, that hovered a while, then instantly tilted to another angle, at a lower depth, and with a different outline.

My breathing, it dawned on me, had become hoarse and labored, as if my lungs were battling the pressure at the depth pictured on the LCD. One more refocus, and the glow of planar section intimated a circular structure below it, holding out amidst the choking silt. A farmer's well? Had my humble camcorder delved straight to the bottom? Peripheral motion I took to be fish, and then a curious trout bumbled up to the wall of color, which shifted to embed the fish halfway through it. The dismayed trout sped away, and a patch of brightness went with it, like a badge on its flank. Whether or not I was watching signs of ghostly sentience or the supernatural at all, I'd never heard of corpse lights hitching a ride on a fish. I wanted to pan away from the phenomenon, to record any manmade context of walls or foundations, but couldn't bring myself. The trout was putting on a better show of free will. My hands were clenched fast around the camcorder, as if stuck in a trap. Was this how the onset of panic attack felt?

At a tap on my shoulder, I drew a wheezing, convulsive breath. I whipped around, primed for an emergency. Wil's eyes were darting sidelong left and right, and the air whistled anxiously through his nose. He'd never acted cagey like this on previous outings, and didn't explain himself in his notes, but it had to concern more than the compass in his outheld hand. The needle pointed toward the stern instead of north, and was bouncing wildly up and down, clicking like an insect against the glass cover. Magnetic flux was typically welcome as a calling card of the otherworldly, and did help rule out the influence of swamp gas. Which was also good news in terms of our water quality, I reckoned. Reservoirs weren't supposed to belch luminous methane, were they? I nodded at Wil, who pocketed the compass and dug out his cell phone. Was he getting jittery out of worry for Lucinda? My attention had returned to the LCD. Had to blink, and ogled over the side. The seam of flexing brightness lay on the surface again, and its image in the display was sharp, as if I'd never touched the zoom.

This place was unsafe. I couldn't articulate why. Nor could I ignore the urge to decamp. Wil and I were rattled, and to put a more dignified face on it, I persuaded myself we were recoiling on an instinctive level, where discretion overruled valor. The mysterious light faded, and reignited a dozen yards off the starboard bow. Its scintillations may have tried beckoning us, but we were in tacit agreement that this expedition was finished. We hurriedly stowed the equipment, and Wil broke the useless silence. "The wife called. Didn't leave a message. So it might be nothing. Or else she takes for granted I know it must be important or she wouldn't phone at all." And I had relegated playing "mind games" to the dustbin of the '60s!

Thankfully, Wil changed the subject, and apologized for doubting me about the bloodthirsty Jersey mosquito. He'd flattened a couple that had landed on him, as well as three that were battening on my back and shoulders. Hadn't I felt him slap them off? I hadn't even flinched, he informed me. I could only shake my head and josh lamely about my dedication to videography.

Then Wil yanked the outboard motor into roaring life, and conversation was suspended. As we gained some distance from the anomaly, I relaxed and wondered if we'd let creepy ambience get the better of us, if we'd seriously overreacted. If we were further than we thought from being hotshot ghost hunters.

Two

After we'd hauled the boat into the Parks Department shed and hit the road, I asked brooding Wil if he didn't want to phone home for an update. Let Lucinda know he was coming. He shook his head, staring morosely out the windshield. "Whenever I get there, it won't be soon enough. If I reach her now, that'll just give her more time to get worked up. Trust me." I was reduced from colleague to chauffeur for the rest of the drive. A barely perceptible shrug and faint grunt rewarded efforts to engage him on the evening's findings. Quite a switch from the Wil who'd been dying to talk when we couldn't.

The Rices occupied one of several third-floor condos in Dyer Hall, named after a long-deceased teacher or benefactor of the former university. The name was all the developers had retained beyond the Eastlake masonry shell when they gutted the classrooms inside. A swath of lawn and a couple of uninspired petunia beds separated the hall from Ellery Avenue. Over the avenue, a quarter mile back, arched the florid, grandiose gateway in what few sections remained of a wrought-iron spear-top fence that had surrounded the former main green. Dyer Hall would have been one of the historic jewels in a prospective gated community, but granite drums from the columns of a less fortunate building guaranteed the gates stayed wide open, because retailers and dentists and other leaseholders down the avenue raised hell about restricting public access to customers. Bad enough that the gate's low clearance forced delivery trucks onto alternate routes. Most of these angry businesses also operated in rehabbed campus structures. At work I often processed applications from Wil's neighbors in so-called "Dire Hall," and in deference to their seasoned judgment, I always addressed return correspondence with the same misspelling.

I was all set to wish Wil luck and drop him off. Not so fast! He paused halfway out of the Taurus and fairly pleaded, "Can you come in a minute?"

I was gearing up to demur, with legit excuse that cops were quick to ticket on-street parking after 1 AM. But Wil had the drop on me, damn him. "Lucinda's been having trouble getting around lately, even with my help. I might need a hand if we have to go to the hospital."

I heaved a sigh direct from my stricken conscience. Wil's gratitude was effusive as I hid OGAM's equipment in the trunk and locked the car, but he reverted to brown study as we entered the lobby. Behind classy Victorian façade lurked '80s institutional bleakness, smelling of hard rubber and synthetic carpet fiber. Trudging upstairs I mused, not for the first time, how a stranger might have decided we'd each ended up in the other's proper niche. Here was Wil the forest ranger and diehard outdoorsman, consigned to tacky condo in the treeless middle of town, while I, a nerdy little clerk in City Hall, enjoyed a woodsy acre of elbow room around my cabin in the sticks. Well, each to his anti-stereotypical own, and to me, a condo was the hateful worst of college dorm and mortgaged money pit. A hive culture. Wil and Lucinda had damn little freedom to alter home sweet home to their taste, but when the pipes froze they had no landlord to pester, and they might be stuck with any boors in adjacent units for life. Too late for my sage counsel, though! And here we were. With weary resolution, he scraped caked mud off his soles into the welcome mat, motioned me to do likewise, and twisted his key in the dull steel knob.

"Right behind you, pal," I whispered. Just don't expect me to say anything.

The developers, I had to admit, knew their soundproofing. Only when Wil's index finger poked the door open did the uproar spill out. The wild-eyed Norwegian elkhound was yapping nonstop behind a baby gate across the kitchen doorway. From the bedroom barged Lucinda, getting around fine at the moment. She flung a cordless phone at the floor. It bounced across ersatz Persian rug, and was still emitting a dial tone. She squalled, "Where the hell were you? I tried your cell two hours ago! I came this close to calling 911 for an ambulance!"

She paused for breath, and her eyes homed in on me. "And what the hell is he doing here?" Reminded myself, don't take this personally. It was the hormones talking. And the pain and the stress. Tonight, anyway.

Wil had become well-versed at deflecting negativity. "You're not due for a few days yet. What are your contractions down to? Every other minute?"

"It fucking hurts all the time!" she wailed. "Why the hell did you have to go out with this idiot tonight?"

"I thought Tracy and Anne and what's-her-name were supposed to stay with you." Wil had turned to me with a doleful, apologetic grimace.

"Those assholes went to a nine o'clock movie! And when I got your voicemail, I tried to talk but I could hardly breathe!" Her last couple of words wheezed out between sobs.

"Okay, off to the hospital then. You all set?"

"My suitcase is on the bed. I'm nauseous. Give me a minute." She gripped the squeaky back of a brown leather sofa and leaned into it a little.

I wanted to be helpful. And to speed my departure from this bedlam. And to get away from that barking! "I'll go fetch the suitcase. Can I turn on a light?" Apart from a table lamp in the kitchen, these rooms were as dim as the moonlit reservoir.

"Please don't," Wil implored. "Lucinda's been photosensitive this trimester."

"What? Is that normal?" Maybe not the most tactful inquiry, but I was getting punchy from absorbing Lucinda's bad vibes.

"The doctor said it was rare." Wil seemed to let slip a hint of defensiveness.

"Okay." I advanced three steps toward the bedroom, squinting floorward for any obstacles. Lucinda noticed, and made a face that would have done a gorgon proud.

"Stay the fuck out of our bedroom! There's blood and gunk all over!"

I threw up my hands and backed off. At least I understood why the poor dog was agitated, even if I couldn't smell it myself.

Lucinda sidled from behind the couch. She stalwartly waddled forward and bellowed, "Wilbur, get the goddamn suitcase!"

A sound arrested us all, as of an awning full of rain giving way.

Lucinda's water had broken. A cascade struck the varnished hardwood floor, inches from the red carpet. Lucinda cried Wil's name repeatedly. I fought the temptation to bolt. What steadied me was amazement at the puddle on the floor. It was luminous. Bluish, or silvery, I couldn't say for sure.

By now, Wil had stumbled into and out of the bedroom, had trodden on a squealing dog toy, and on banging his shin on a bedpost or bureau leg, yelled "Shit!"

"Your water's glowing," I couldn't help but tell Lucinda as Wil took gentle hold of her arm and asked if she could make it to the garage.

At him she nodded, and at me she scowled. "What the hell are you talking about?"

Then Wil supported her weight as best he could with her suitcase in one hand, as the dog yapped with the persistence of a tape loop, and I followed at the Rices' heels, which left flickering prints after crossing the shiny pool.

At the threshold, Wil half-faced me and blurted something about the door locking if I slammed it after me, which completely muted the dog in midbark. From there, we forged on in opposite directions. Lucinda I couldn't blame for spewing abuse under the excruciating circumstances. I was rather more miffed at Wil for conning me into the role of human buffer zone.

Three

No telling how long Wil would be tied up at the maternity ward with Lucinda. Spent my Sunday in basement studio, reviewing reservoir data. This month's *OGAM Chronicles* was due Friday, with or without Wil's input, and if it wasn't about corpse lights, I'd again have to solicit ghost-chasing anecdotes, often pretty lame, from camera-shy OGAM members.

The audio on my minidisk and camcorder duplicated one another. An abrasive hum, with sporadic piercing crackles. The soundtrack, I hypothesized, of rogue magnetism. If these were recordings of equipment glitches, why would bursts of static spike at the same time in different devices?

To Wil I e-mailed QuickTime clips of typical anomaly footage, for him to digest at leisure. Here, I wrote him, was textbook example of good evidence that looked bad. As long as I had aimed at the surface, the shot was in focus, but even then, the streak of luster read as a blank, like a hole in the screen, devoid of color or brightness. And as the video progressed, the emptiness retained its stable, sharp outline, reprising none of its shifts in depth or angle, while the rest of the image grew grainier and grainier, till the end, when the surface snapped back into clarity. Whatever I'd been shooting, whether supernatural or mundanely electromagnetic, had excised itself from the record. Along with the fish it had frightened.

The camcorder manual contained some fine print about limited color resolution, distortions resulting. Yeah, okay, but swamp gas couldn't explain what I was seeing, or not seeing, in the frame. Here, in the guise of lousy videography, was footage whose apparent flaws were telltale signs of something esoteric. And there I had it. My preface to the "Eye on the Unknown" segment on the next *Chronicles*.

Monday and Tuesday plodded by without word from Wil, and my enthusiasm for our blockbuster new episode was cooling. Two days steeped in numbingly inane data at City Hall were taking their toll, despite one blip of excitement when an ornery codger singled out my window along the counter, because I had soaked him that for that fishing license in June. He'd hooked a nice fat trout in the reservoir, but it fried up rotten and stank him and the missus out of their RV all evening. I had the temerity to ask how long the filets had been sitting around raw. "They went straight in the pan the minute I got home!"

A chill hit me then, as the trout with attached corpse light leapt to mind. I further riled red-faced pensioner by pursuing the irrelevant detail of when he'd gone fishing. "Last Friday, dammit!" Ah, relief. Not the same trout. "What the hell did I pay you good money for? The fish was rotten while it was still swimming, I tell you!"

Diseased fish boded no good, but they weren't, I didn't mind informing the crotchety duffer, my department. If he'd saved any samples of tainted fish, he should bring them to the Bureau of Game and Fisheries or the Parks Department. Made a mental note to send Wil a heads-up about this customer. "Of course I didn't save the fish! It was putrid! Stank to high heaven!" Assured him I was sorry, but that was the best I could do for him. And really, it was.

I did recall how much he'd groused about the fee during our June run-in, when I mentioned that licenses might be cheaper in Houghton, Hoyle, Chapman, or Armitage, the other towns that drank from the reservoir. They all had the right to issue hunting and fishing licenses as they saw fit, which was how the state forestalled jurisdictional squabbles among the several towns (in different counties, yet) sharing one body of water. In June the curmudgeon had grumbled I wouldn't be rid of him that easily. That he wasn't wasting more gasoline on comparison-shopping all over creation. So he knuckled under and paid up then, and today he was tromping out of the office, spewing omnidirectional vitriol. Definitely, let Wil know this character might come knocking!

But still I shied from follow-up contact with my one day-to-day pal, during work hours and beyond, based on overwhelming odds he had his hands full with newborn twins and didn't need me pestering him. Was also loath to phone at a bad time and provoke Lucinda further. And when was a good time? Wil's fatherhood amounted to another sticking point. How to acknowledge it? The standard, facile, mealy-mouthed course would involve feigning a hearty "Congratulations!" No, that felt doubly inappropriate, considering his long-standing indifference to "blessed events" versus everything else of interest to him. To be realistic, though, best I get used to hosting most of our *Chronicles* solo, without holding a grudge against Wil, who had as little choice in childcare as he had in Lucinda's pregnancy: a classic marital "deal-breaker" if ever there was one. If he could swing a change of scene from shitty diapers and hourly feedings, then he would, wouldn't he?

During my slow Wednesday at work, I had to shake a recurring sentiment that dusty varnish and yellowing paper and overheated PC monitors were, and would remain, the smells of real life for me. Tried rechanneling my thoughts into the mystery of why people, and Lucinda in particular, would prioritize parenthood above everything else they could be doing. And didn't "women's libbers" ask that too, in a less blinkered decade? As if childbearing rendered people unique and exalted, instead of lumping them among the fertile billions comprising the genus *Homo* for the last two million years? I entertained no delusion that the world was poorer without my contributions to the gene pool, or that those contributions would be doing the world a favor. As for the motivations of Wil or Lucinda, or anyone else for that matter? I once knew a junkie who was wont to say between rounds of detox, "You'll never make sense of anything unless you know the he and she of it." In which case, barring a far-fetched tête-à-tête with the prickly Lucinda, the motives of this he and she to start a family would remain a mystery forever.

On the drive home, outlined how to wing a half hour of tv journalism without Wil. Open with a thumbnail history of Gorman County and the reservoir, cribbing online text and photos. Broach the topic of corpse-lights, likewise plundering the internet, and play up local angle by paraphrasing my informants' accounts. Recap our foray across haunted waters, with accompaniment of establishing shots from on shore and at intervals as we went. Roll footage of negative space where will-o'-the-wisp should have been, and explain why it meant something. Do not harp on feeling nervous and insecure in presence of anomaly. A responsible, professional, scientific quest for data had to disregard the subjective, or else we'd always travel with a psy-chic. Wrap up the show with "Occult Community Announcements," mostly of OGAM members' birthdays or church cake sales. Nearer Halloween, dramatic readings by a Poe impersonator at the library or a Haunted Occam tour might spice up the listings.

Through my back door, in the benign chaos of my kitchen, the red light on the answering machine was blinking. I brightened at hearing Wil's voice, but then he said, "We had the funeral today, finally. Just for immediate fam-ily. You hate that kind of emotional overkill, so please don't feel slighted that I didn't let you know. Anyway, listen, can you come meet me at the Aviator at 7:30? Thanks." End of message.

Funeral? How could I beg off after hearing that? And requesting my company at a bar? Almost as troubling. Splitting a six-pack on home turf was our usual modus operandi. A cornerstone of our friendship. In prefer-ence to paying double for drinks out in noisy, crowded public. But I under-stood the need for a space apart sometimes in which to deal with the worst, away from the influence of everyday associations. Like "going walkabout" without going anywhere. The sign of a desperate hour. Back to the Taurus, and back to damned Occam after eight grueling hours there.

Thank God it was the Aviator. Courteous Wil was in the booth nearest the door, to save me from scouting up and down the dusky length of the premises. I was early. He'd been earlier to the tune of two empty glasses plus the half a beer in his hand. Ten-ounce drafts for a dollar, including a half-decent local IPA, made for the basic draw here.

For the sake of catching up, went up and ordered two IPAs at once from the strapping old barkeep, sailorlike in tight striped t-shirt and scarlet do-rag, but rumored to be the Vietnam-era ace who lent the place its name. Threw culinary standards to the wind and got a microwave burrito as well, to cushion the alcohol. Offered via sign language to treat Wil, but he shook his dour head. Set my two ales on the black walnut table, rife with whittled names and initials from enough generations ago to be "quaint." Sat across from Wil on a high-backed blond maple bench, with Art Nouveau carvings of curly vines and foliage and perching finches.

Thanks purely to its location in a *terrain vague* between downtown and the tool-and-die quarter, the Aviator had evaded the urban renewals and civic improvements and redevelopments that would have blithely steamrollered a turn-of-the-century bierstube. In essence, the one vintage neighborhood bar in Occam had survived to make the Historic Register because it wasn't in a neighborhood.

Took a sip, and cast about for tactful opening sentence. What to avoid was pretty obvious. Since Saturday night, my thoughts had often drifted to Lucinda's glittering water on the floor. But alluding to that could serve no constructive end. Nor was it an observation I could make anything of, or do anything with. Not yet, anyway. "Four days to learn the autopsy results," Wil intruded on my thoughts. A good start, insofar as maybe he just wanted a sounding board. "Four days. And you know what they figured out? Nothing."

"Wil, I'm really sorry, but I don't know whose autopsy you mean." Half-afraid to admit it. Unsure of how fragile, how close to meltdown, Wil was.

"No, of course not." Was his expression clouded with grieving or brooding? "It stinks of malpractice anyhow. If those slippery schmucks at the hospital weren't so good at giving us the runaround, we could sue. Lucinda wants to, regardless. I need to regroup first."

"Uh-huh." The barkeep plopped a paper plate an inch from my elbow on the table. Ah, my burrito, with plastic knife and fork. "You got any hot sauce? And a napkin, please?" Had to ask fast, or supper would be cold before I could catch his attention again. He grunted noncommittally and barreled off. Wil was staring at my burrito as if it might move. And not with understandable mockery. Nothing at all humorous in his demeanor. I was glad when he went back to studying his glass, as if his words were in there.

"They struck me as completely ill-prepared in the delivery room. And it was something like a ten-hour labor, so they had plenty of time to think ahead. I kept my mouth shut and let the alleged experts do their jobs. Now I wish I'd stuck my neck out and fuck 'em if they didn't like it. Both twins were breech birth. We'd agreed on naming the older twin Warren. It was plain from what I saw of him coming out feet-first that he was blue, but they didn't give him oxygen, and I was too distracted to speak up because Morgan was born a minute later. The nurse wouldn't let Lucinda touch Warren and only let her look at him a few seconds, probably to stop her squawk-ing." Our bartender plunked a bottle of Tabasco between us like a center-piece. No napkin. Wil asked for another beer. I had to snatch a bunch of cocktail napkins from the bar. Wil pursed his lips, and found more words inside his glass.

"Morgan was also blue, and they ran off with him. One of the doctors said they had to run some tests and treat him like a preemie, in light of the stillbirth. Lucinda was groggy as hell but roused herself to demand why they were racing to treat Morgan if he was stillborn. The doctor said no, the sec-ond twin might pull through. It was the first who hadn't made it. Please ac-cept our big sincere condolences. But wait, don't tell me that baby's dead, I see him moving, Lucinda said. No, the doctor insisted, there are no vital signs. 'Then what am I seeing?' Lucinda practically screamed, and the doc-tor said he didn't know exactly, and I could see it too before the doctor shooed the nurse holding Warren out of there." The bartender set Wil's fourth beer beside his three empties and stood patiently. The policy here was pay-as-you-go, on a stool or in a booth. My wallet was out before Wil could protest. Least I could do, and a paltry gesture at that. Tipped the man a dollar to forestall even worse service.

"It must have been the lighting, but in those few seconds I stopped be-ing positive Warren was blue, and couldn't decide if maybe he was grey or purple. And I wondered if it was also the harsh light or if all newborns are like that or if it was part of what was wrong with him, that his skin gave the illusion of being translucent, although I'm sure it wasn't. It must have been my eyes working under stress, but I had to ask myself if anyone else there noticed anything like that, or if they only saw one more oxygen-starved miscarriage. But the rest of it they couldn't deny, and that's what made me question if they were telling us everything, and if maybe they were too cocksure that Warren was already dead. Or maybe they'd seen something like this before and had instructions on blowing it off."

A gleam of fixation in Wil's eyes was making me more uncomfortable. He'd strayed into a labyrinth of details built on one meager glimpse, beyond the stage where I could gracefully, or safely, interrupt him. If I tried, I had the distinct impression he'd shut down or storm out. And by no means, obey that perverse urge to blab about Lucinda's shining amniotic fluid.

"Maybe I'll never know what I was looking at, but I can tell you what it wasn't. Warren's blanket was displaced from the waist up, and not from squirming or flailing or anything deliberate, or spasms or some kind of reflex, or lolling around or tossing. He wasn't quivering, exactly. That would have been one overall movement. This looked more like bubbling in some way I can't explain. Like each muscle was straining independently, reaching out on its own. Like it was in danger of pulling apart from those next to it. And there was more that wasn't possible, the fine hair on his wet scalp lifting like it had a static charge. Thank God his eyes were closed. And wherever the umbilical was, thank God I couldn't see that either, because I started getting insane ideas about it."

Wil had been through a marathon trauma. That I could take at face value. How luridly he'd embroidered the details while ruminating and ruminating, I could only guess. So far, treading softly on the thin ice of Wil's psyche had taken the form of fleeting eye contact and nods between Tabasco-enhanced mouthfuls of a burrito that contained mainly rice, followed by pinto beans and traces of beef. Sawing through the tough tortilla underside with plastic knife, I kept hacking into flimsy plate and antique tabletop. I paused in my vandalism. High time to play a more proactive role, and lead my friend, as best I could, away from memories of the delivery room.

In my experience, Wil had always been level-headed, and Lucinda had been high-strung and high-maintenance. How could she not be a basket case if Wil was this close to the edge? "I'm a little surprised you were able to get out of the house with everything going on, but I'm glad you did."

"We agreed it might be good to spend a few hours apart. Maybe defuse some tension." Just like that, Wil was channeling his calm, rational self again. Very gratifying! And very stupid of me not to realize that's when I should have been especially on my guard.

"The other twin? Morgan? He's okay, then? Is he still in the hospital?"

I checked Wil's face, and could hear the thin ice crack under our table. "Morgan's color improved, and he stabilized. Or as they so modestly put it, 'We stabilized him.' But he still goes through spells of the same involuntary movements Warren had, and those clowns have no idea what's going on, so they sent him home and gave us some crap about 'Let's see if it passes,' which is as good as saying nothing. Maybe they had to free up some cribs on the ward and couldn't be bothered with us anymore, since we were outside the limits of their expertise. Who knows? If 'it' doesn't pass, we might have grounds soon to sue those negligent bastards after all."

"Let's hope it doesn't come to that." Right. That rang about as true as my congratulations would have, under better circumstances. Here, let's give the metaphorical steering wheel a nice hard wrench and see if it puts us in a better place. "If you felt like it, and you wanted another break tomorrow, or tonight even, it'd be great having you co-host the show due Friday."

Wil's brow creased and his expression grew searching and distant, as if he were already delving into a past life. He chugged half his beer. "I better say no. Might be a problem getting out two nights in a row. It's tough planning ahead, with the situation at home. That's something I meant to bring up, actually. In terms of helping on the show, it's going to be touch-and-go for a while." Was I oversensitive, or did Wil's gravitas imply he'd become a man who had to "put aside childish things?"

"That's fine. I was kind of expecting it." Shit, I had to cut this meeting short and work fast if I wanted to beat the deadline. But this minute, I needed something to fill the expansive awkward silence. "I'm guessing you're on paternal leave, or whatever they call it, this week, but when you were last on the job, were you hearing anything about inedible fish? In the reservoir?"

Wil shook his head as if few topics were less germane.

"Okay." To an uncertain extent, he was here to give me the brush-off, so why did I feel compelled to prove the depth of my friendship? Maybe it was guilt over wanting to clear out and contend with my own issues, which were nothing compared with his. In fact, nothing in my 35 years had been half as serious as what he was weathering nowadays. "If you two ever wanted to catch a movie or something, I could babysit. I don't know how much Lucinda trusts me, but I'm offering." Naturally I hoped they'd never take me up on it. And supposing they did? I'd have to grin and bear it to uphold my self-respect, kicking myself all the while.

"Thanks. That's really big of you, Jeff." He didn't have to sound so damn astounded that I'd propose an unselfish deed. "And Lucinda likes you, all right? You just have to cut her a little slack these days."

A startling white commotion came to rest beside my plate. Aha, the napkin I'd given up on, of heavy two-ply paper, half-unfurled, and scarcely marred by a coffee stain at one corner. "Almost forgot it," the barkeep gruffly confessed, and proceeded to load our empty glasses onto a tray on which I narrowly discerned "Falstaff Beer" and a fat cavorting Elizabethan amidst the rust and missing paint. "Did I hear you guys a minute ago say the fish in the reservoir were no good?"

I commended his finely honed ears. Not easy to eavesdrop on us, through the two dozen or so new voices crowding the air since I'd sat down. "I never drink that water," he continued. "And my dad didn't, and his dad didn't either. Grew up on bottled water. Third generation. Every-one drinks that bottled stuff now. Guess we were trendsetters, huh?"

Had to hand it to the Aviator, the last refuge of what I termed the "old Occam" attitude, where our bartender might not give a regular customer the time of day for years, and then buttonhole him like they'd been best pals forever. Or like what happened on my one and only date here with an art-history teacher who should have been wowed by the décor, but who hence-forth stopped returning my calls because a fiftyish barfly, who'd never no-ticed me before, had to lean over our table and make us feel how smooth her face was, and palaver at length about how she owed her youthful skin to a daily scrub with her own piss. To this day I wonder if she was on the up-and-up, or laughing on the inside at the thought of us going home and dunk-ing our heads in the toilet. And that's the kind of "old Occam" place the Aviator was and always would be, I reckoned, God bless it.

"Why didn't your grandfather like the water?" Wil seemed genuinely interested, which I assumed was a well-bred show of courtesy. "What kind of reason did he give?"

"He never said. But from the way he never said it, with the same look someone has when he won't say what he did during the war, it was obvious he knew what he was talkin' about. If the fish in there are bad, I'm only surprised it didn't happen a lot sooner." Arms folded, feet firmly planted, our bartender stood as if braced for dispute. A Colossus of Rhodes in the manner of Charles Bukowski.

Wisely, though it must have rubbed against his evidence-based grain, Wil replied, "I think your grandfather may have had something there." Or was he speaking sincerely, based on Parks Department info that he was declining to share with me?

Meanwhile, at the bar, someone I recognized from work was trying to glare holes into us. His path and mine often crossed on the City Hall stairs, but my echelon, I surmised, was too low for him to acknowledge. Except now his casual, listing posture on chrome-ribbed stool marked him as tipsy, and inadvisably eager to converse. "You people never shut up about that water, do you? The hell you know what you're talking about!"

The bartender was picking up the tray of glasses from our table. He slammed it down again, and all the glasses clinked into each other. "What do you mean 'you people,' you goddamn little elitist?"

As goddamn elitists went, this one was less than dapper in pumpkin-colored sportsjacket and big rectangular tortoiseshell spectacles. And worse, prominent teeth and cheeks gave him the air of a portly, balding woodchuck. He pushed his plastic frames back up his sweaty snub nose. "The state tests that water every month! It always gets a clean bill of health. Will you please read my lips? There's nothing wrong with that water!"

"You wouldn't know what to test for, you ignorant fucking hack!" The barkeep was still holding up his end of the shouting match from our booth. Wil's face mirrored the angst in my heart, though he too must have realized that if the barkeep stepped away from us, it could only signal hairier unpleasantness. Everyone else, from boozers to hipsters, kept their heads down and pretended nothing was amiss, but they were all ears, make no mistake.

"The next words out of your mouth better be an apology, or I'll have your liquor permit pulled so fast your head'll spin!" Frequent slurring badly undercut patrician diction. "Who the hell do you think you're talking to?"

"I know exactly who I'm talking to, Mr. Big Shot Recorder of Deeds. And I got friends on the Licensing Board, and they'll jeer you out the door. They also have more class than to come in here and start any shit. Now you can get out and stay out." The bartender's hand swept regally over our heads. "In front of these witnesses, I ban you for life!"

"I'm not going anywhere, you guttersnipe!" Guttersnipe? I'd have laughed out loud but was afraid it might be received the wrong way. I was also pretty confident that a recorder of deeds was in no position to pass judgment on water quality.

Argument was getting them nowhere. The bartender's jaw clenched combatively, and he looked his opponent up and down. Estimating his weight? Stubborn bureaucrat had barely bawled out his next syllable when he became part of a blur in transit from the bar to the door. And just like that, he was out on the sidewalk. A puff of fresher air from outdoors wafted into our booth. Did that even qualify as a scuffle? The instant before slamming door prompted the hushed clientele to shudder as one, the bartender shouted, "You oughtta be run outta town! The whole guilty lot of you!"

With a new spring in his step that put nobody at ease, the barkeep fairly swaggered back to our booth. "Sorry you gentlemen had to be at ringside for that. Beers are on me from now till closing."

We thanked him profusely. He cleared away the tray full of glasses. The flow of conversation had resumed around us. No sign that the evening had ever been other than serene. We indulged in a couple more rounds before the effort to chat about nothing became too much. Each of us had said what he'd come to say before the contretemps, and had that not happened, we'd have adjourned an hour ago. Out front, Wil promised to try watching the *Chronicles* premiering next week. He'd arrived on foot, and thought the walk back would do him good. I assured him I'd be fine on the road. Wouldn't be my first drive home one or two sheets to the wind. Or the first program I'd cobbled together in that condition. Behind the wheel, realized I should have asked Wil, or the bartender, or myself why some schmo from City Hall was so incensed at a "guttersnipe" talking trash about the reservoir. Or what they were "guilty" of over there. But of course I hadn't, because I was a sheet or two to the wind.

Four

Qualifying as what my fellow citizens call "eccentric" would be okay if I didn't have to deal with them Monday through Friday. I swear, some coworkers watch *OGAM Chronicles* just to give me grief about it. And in accordance with New England village mores, not even to my face. Or maybe I set myself up for abuse by concluding eerie reservoir footage with the rhetorical question, "We've cast our eye on the unknown, but will we ever decipher what it means?"

The first broadcast was Wednesday night. After Thursday midmorning break, I sat back down at the wobbly desk where I'd been processing change-of-address notifications. On a memo pad, below "While You Were Out," was penciled, "Will we desipher what it means? It means you are a fuckup you loser." Any number of ill-schooled critics could have scrawled that. With well-rehearsed pokerface, I detached top sheet from pad, gently crumpled it, and dropped it in the dented green wastebasket beside the desk. My standard procedure.

Why waste energy getting upset? My voiceover explained clearly and cogently the underlying significance of superficially poor video. A thankless effort, and more fool I when, in my experience, John and Jane Q. Public were most often hidebound, unwilling to see beyond the obvious or even pretend to listen. A much bigger letdown were the several e-mails from *OGAM* colleagues, who chided me for not getting in touch if I needed material for an episode. From them I had expected more faith in my judgments on occult evidence. Moreover, I wasn't sure why they assumed I'd routinely call them, when they were seldom available to do anything when I did.

While taping the show, I fell prey to a beery urge and solicited viewers' spooky stories and family lore about the reservoir and Gorman County. No phone messages or e-mails followed, but within a couple of weeks, three handwritten replies showed up in the *OGAM* PO box, which was not a bad rate of return. The moral? I had to start gearing content to an over-70 audience.

The first note arrived on St. Joseph's Indian School stationery, a scurrilous "charity" that used to send my grandmother plastic kachina dolls as tokens of gratitude:

> Dear Mr. Slater,
>
> Like they say about the apple I have never rolled far from the tree and have lived in Pickering my whole life. But when you asked on your program about Gorman County where the lake is now it got me to thinking about my grandfather who moved here when he was a boy. If I can recall he said it was because his father sold the family farm to some Canucks, and that was in Gorman County, near a place where the people went bust after some blight attacked their crops and it drove them crazy to lose everything. My great-grandfather was afraid the blight would spread, so as I said, he shifted to the outskirts of Pickering instead. When he was toward the end of his life, a few years before my time, he heard about them building the reservoir, and he was glad not to be in one of the towns that would of used it, and he called it a damn fool idea, or so my grandfather told me. I hope I have not bored you with this little remembrance from way back when.
>
> > Good luck to you,
> > Earl McGregor

The letter was most surprising for its revelation that *Chronicles* was on public access all the way out in Pickering, halfway to Pittsfield. As for the rest of it, plenty of Yankee farmers around then had given up on rocky soil gone fallow from overuse, and the feeble crops must have been easy marks for whatever was going around in that era of chestnut blight and Dutch elm disease. Only peculiar to me that clan McGregor hadn't moved a lot farther West.

A second note had a Paralyzed Veterans of America return-address label on the envelope. Another charity my grandmother favored. The message was somewhat pithier:

> Dear Sir:
>
> I am 97 years old. I never lived in Gorman County. My dad grew up in Aylesbury, however. He said that some woods down the road were haunted. They were where the water is now. I was born in Houghton,

where he was a foreman in a textiles mill. He refused to drink from the faucet after the reservoir opened. He said it was something about the woods that were down at the bottom, but he was not more specific. I don't know if he thought the water would be haunted or what that would do to somebody. It was about then he started getting bad in the head, which he was for many years, God rest his soul, so maybe that was why he was that way about the water.

That's all I can recall for you,

Luther Corey

I made a mental note to find out the bartender's surname at the Aviator, to see if he was near kin to either of these correspondents.

The final response fit on a blank USPS postcard, but in script so crabbed I had to rest my eyes three times before the signature:

If this can please be forwarded to the person that does the show on ghosts, I am answering your request for stories of happenings in the valley that was flooded. Round about the Great War (or WWI you call it now) my father and some others moved down from Quebec because the farming was too hard up there. They bought a great parcel of land cheap that had been seized for taxes and they divided it. Well my father's dream to make good on his own was not meant to be. At the edge of his fields there was woods on the top of a ridge. He and my mother and two brothers had not been working their fields a month when a cloud of grey dust blew over from the other side of the ridge. It was during a terrible windstorm, so bad it became my first memory, when I was only a year or two old. The dust got into the furrows and in the feed bins and the troughs, and it was easy to see against the soil and the cast iron which were both darker. I also remember my father was mad as a hornet after the corn stalks and the squash vines turned every color but green and then became black and died. After that the livestock took sick and he started to slaughter them but the meat was black, and at that he got scared and moved us away and let the devil have his own, as he always said later. We were lucky, though, because it was a boom time during the war and by winter my family had jobs at the burlap factory in Houghton, where I worked for 50 years starting at age 10 as a bobbin boy. Some people were leery about the reservoir at first but the water tests say it's okay, so thank God for something good. I've never had any problems with the tap water and I'll

be a hundred next year. Write to me if you have any questions and I'll see
what I can do,   Gerard Heroux

What I should've done was pen a few lines of thanks to each informant, but
with a mild twinge of self-denigration, doubted I'd ever get around to it; blaming even an uneventful life like my own for chucking too many roadblocks between me and basic etiquette.

   Gerard's was the only communiqué to raise a question, and a disturbing
one at that. Unfortunately, writing him about it would have availed me
nothing. The meat of his father's butchered livestock was "black," was it?
Had it stunk like the irate codger's rotten trout from the reservoir? A tenu-
ous connection to weave across the better part of a century, but that made it
no less unnerving as I dwelt on how that fish I'd seen with corpse-light attached might taste. What kind of anomaly could exert baneful effects then
and now, in dry earth or lake-bottom mud? I needed more dots to connect
into a clear picture.

Five

I sat listening in my Adirondack chair on the back deck of my shabby little bungalow. On my lap was a bowl of the bachelor's archetypal supper, refried spaghetti, the second of several this week. I loved the din of cicadas and crickets from the woods beyond my weedy yard, and tried to let it soothe me in the wake of an insane blowup at work.

Sneering history had seemed to repeat itself. After midmorning break, another memo sheet stood waiting between the rows of dingy computer keyboard at another wobbly desk where I'd been posted for the day. This note purported to be "From the Office of Humphrey Westcott," and stated simply, "See me." No time, no reason. Westcott was the City Collector, and a notorious grinch, and someone with whom I'd had the pleasure never to interact. That misspelled hazing memo from two Thursdays ago sprang to mind, so I dismissed this one as a hoax, a bid at luring foolish me into the den of a lion who seldom suffered fools gladly. What could Westcott possibly want with me? I disposed of this imposture as casually as its forerunner.

Within the hour, to my shock, the formidable Ms. Lathrop was looming over me, scanning my pitted desktop in vain for something. The memo sheet? She was one of those secretaries upstairs who knew the administrative gears and pulleys better than any elected official, and without whom the city would stall like an obsolete lawn mower. Cross her at your peril! "Mr. Westcott wants to see you right away." Borderline scolding me. "Didn't you get his message?" Best to slowly shake my befuddled head. She traipsed off, mission accomplished. Why squander valuable time on me? In a few more keystrokes, I finished what I was transcribing. Followed her lilac trail to the third floor. Still more perplexed than apprehensive.

No receptionist, Ms. Lathrop or otherwise, at the City Collector's anteroom desk. I lightly rapped on frosted-glass inner door. "What?" I could have been anyone, but the inflection imputed I was a fool till proven otherwise. Grasped the brass doorknob. Into the breach!

Westcott's office boasted oak wainscoting and substantial bolection moulding and gilt-framed mayoral portraits from the heyday of sideburns and ascots. Most impressively, it boasted air. It had sash windows that opened. Westcott, striking an imperious stance behind his massive desk, arms folded, was a WASP among WASPs. His linen suit matched his opal-blue eyes. He had a basset-hound nose and a mouth carved of flint and a dose of Grecian Formula 16 in his thinning hair and impeccable goatee. Despite the ventilation, a scent of cigars lingered, in disdain of the rules for everyone else.

"I heard about your tv show," he greeted me. Aware of who I was by other means than actual viewing, apparently. Dispensing with friendly preamble, he affected a tone that wavered between fatherly and domineering. "Now don't you agree it's on the reckless side to go stirring up old rumors and falsehoods? Why would you want to reignite baseless fears about the water we all have to drink?"

Wow, had I done all that? "I'm just collecting folklore, Mr. Westcott. No harm intended." Fretted inwardly that it was impossible to sound conciliatory enough with some autocrats. I also saw no need to mention that my household water came from an artesian well and ended up in a septic tank. "We" didn't drink the water.

"Eh?" I gathered he was too busy staying on-message to listen. And that he really didn't wish me to repeat myself. "Don't you think it would be the responsible thing to edit out any defamatory statements about the reservoir? Or add a disclaimer that the drinking water is perfectly safe?"

Since this was conspicuously not a frank exchange, I dared not imply my "superior" was overstepping his bounds. "Once I submit a show, Mr. Westcott, it's out of my hands. Sorry. The cable provider doesn't want to hear from me again till they've broadcast the show four Wednesdays in a row, and then they want a new one." Of course I could've phoned the company and had the episode pulled and replaced with a rerun, but this arrogant patroon was rubbing me the wrong way. "I don't know who told you about this particular program, but I guarantee you there's nothing derogatory about the reservoir, and I never get any feedback or indications that people are watching, anyway." Aside from my detractors and those three retirees, that is.

"I hope you're right. And I hope we won't have to discuss this again." His look bore down on me. As if he were appraising me through a jeweler's loupe.

"I hope not too. Sorry to have caused you any concern." I dearly wanted to take my leave, but an intensity in his expression held me there. I wished he'd say something, then wished he hadn't.

"I know bullshit when I smell it!" he erupted, smacking his palms against mahogany desktop, thrusting his face forward. His bulbous nose was reddening like an ember. "You don't think I can deal with fucking pipsqueaks like you? Consider yourself warned. You better be careful who you piss off around here. Now go."

After Westcott's roaring escalation from snide wheedling to almost transparent physical threat, I had difficulty moving. On the verge of tears. Outraged, indignant. And buried deep under the smoking emotional rubble, pitiful seeds of defiance.

Ms. Lathrop sat typing at anteroom desk. Hunched over glowing monitor, which tinged her doughy face a grayish green. I slunk by as if invisible. Or as if she'd overheard nothing out of the ordinary.

The bad vibes were still going strong as the sun set on dinner hour. Didn't want stress to increase my odds of indigestion. Detoured my thoughts onto the high road toward understanding why that bullying s.o.b. had made so much ado over nothing. Went no further than blaming August. Maybe summer, in a less plainspoken fashion than winter, also wears out its welcome. Too hot for too long, and tempers combust with impatience for relief. In the 1950s, wasn't this dubbed the "silly season," when level heads lost ground against credulity? And moodiness? I chewed it over. Nope, that didn't excuse the bullying s.o.b., though it did add a potential extenuating dimension to Lucinda's late-term temper.

Days were appreciably shorter. The one universal regret about summer on the wane. Dusk had already dissolved into a night rank with stars. Back here, I faced away from the brightness of Occam, and from sprawling development, and from the reservoir. That Saturday in the boat, Wil had seemed enchanted by a smattering of meteors. A shame the city light pollution wouldn't let him savor the Perseids in full swing. The northeastern sky was swarming with silver streaks, like minnows crowding a dark aquarium. I spaced out on the spectacle, and on snapping out of it, wasn't hungry for the half a bowl of cold supper in my lap. Scraped it back into the iron skillet on the stove, and slid skillet back into fridge. More for the rest of the week! The phone rang. Speak of the devil, it was Wil.

Please, would I come meet him in front of the house? He had no one else to turn to. Elsie had run away. Elsie was the elkhound, I presumed. Yes, I'd help him shout the dog's name around the neighborhood. Might even be salutary immersing myself in someone else's awful day, to divert me from my own.

As the woods on townbound road thinned into suburbs, my headlights revealed several more strays trotting purposefully in the breakdown lane. A golden retriever, a bichon, a boxer, among others, all heading for the wilderness. No Elsie. Normally I would've stopped and corralled the more tractable pets for their worried owners, but had to put Wil's anxiety first.

He was sitting on the granite steps of Dyer Hall, and sprinted over while I parked. Had Lucinda already hit the streets? Maybe in the family Outback? No, she was up in bed. Sedated. Way too agitated for any part in this. Or for driving under any pretext lately. Wil led us toward town center, which was 180° wrong according to my gut, but this was his gig. Without result, and meeting no one, we circled block after block of tacky tripledeckers, funeral homes, daycare centers, convenience stores. We had to shout twice as loud to compete with barking that bombarded us from porches and windows and yards, but which wasn't directed at us, because it was also audible from afar during quiet interludes.

Meanwhile, plenty of meteors were visible in spite of milky urban sky, but Wil, like the dogs, seemed too distraught to take an interest in cosmic spectacle. Or were the roiling Perseids somehow inciting canine unrest, unlikely as that seemed?

We'd reached the periphery of Commercial Street, where half the facades were boarded up. And stapled to the plywood and to telephone poles, and taped to mailboxes, were upward of a dozen different flyers for lost dogs and cats, and only now did it hit me that we'd been passing these all along. Was this an epidemic of runaways, or merely the average number, to which I was more sensitized tonight?

Since I wasn't a father, I was pretty hoarse before thinking to ask if anyone was minding Morgan. Wil chose words with scrupulous care. "He's a sound sleeper. I don't foresee any problem staying out as long as we want." An undertone of reserve dissuaded me from prying deeper into family matters.

Wil was less reticent about how the dog had gone AWOL. "After supper, Lucinda let Elsie out front as usual. People are indoors, and it's getting dark, and the streetlights aren't on yet, so the dog can take a quick dump on the lawn with nobody the wiser. But this time she just sniffed the air and bolted. In the foyer Lucinda screamed and screamed at her to come back till I coaxed her, my wife I mean, back in and sent her to bed with some meds. We love that dog." If they did, they could've done better than flout leash laws because they were too lazy to escort her to the curb, but why pick an argument now?

We plied back lanes to either side of the main drag. On these subsisted more marginal businesses that lent Occam its aura of "Salem West." A botánica, New Age herbal pedlars, Tarot readers, Wiccan accessories. Whatever attracted them here, I'd have been happier without them. As it was, OGAM rated precious little respect. We didn't need these charlatans and screwballs around for less discerning folk to associate with us. Wil and I had patrolled within smelling distance of the river, and within hearing of the traffic hum on the bypass, that demon brainchild of '70s city planners that had killed Commercial Street by rerouting everyone over the river and directly into the suburbs.

"I can't stand this anymore," Wil confessed. "There's too much ground to cover, and my voice is giving out. It's futile. We'll just have to notify the pound and put up fliers and hope people see 'em among all the others. Let's go home before this barking drives me crazy." I had tuned out the racket a while ago. And reckoned it hadn't entered Wil's overwrought consciousness, or he'd have griped about it blocks ago.

"Are the dogs usually this noisy around here?"

"Couldn't tell you. We're always inside with the windows down and the air conditioner on. Elsie was fine till this evening, to my knowledge."

Across the street, a dalmatian sporting a day-glo green collar glanced at us as it padded ahead. It was panting instead of vocalizing, and its spadelike tongue lolled straight out. Its eyes hinted at some impending crisis. A minute later, a bug-eyed, breathless blonde in shocking pink jogging suit and clutching a day-glo green leash caught up with us, and we both waved her in the fugitive's direction before she uttered a word.

"So what do you figure all this ruckus means?" I kept the blonde in my sights purely because she was the only moving object on the landscape.

"They say animals act up when an earthquake's about to happen. Or a tidal wave." Wil had adopted a disarmingly cool tone for prophesying disaster. Perhaps too much grim reality weighed on his mind to treat misery on spec seriously. "If you go in for that sort of thing, shooting stars are also supposed to presage calamity, and based on what's up there tonight, this ought to be the end of the world." Wil did have a talent for perceiving more than he let on. And maybe more than he was aware of. Whether in terms of barking dogs, teeming meteors, or domestic troubles that he swept under an ever more convex rug. A style of housekeeping with a very limited future.

We hiked back on as few of the same streets as possible, for all the good it did. Should I have told him about those several dogs fleeing town? Didn't see how it would have helped. Much as I hadn't seen how harping on Lucinda's luminous water would have helped at the time. After which, I didn't want to be accused of withholding information. The only word out of either of us till we stood in front of Dyer Hall was "Elsie."

The ponderous glass door flew open, and Lucinda, the antithesis of "sedated," raced out to us. She gripped a sheaf of 8 × 11 papers in one hand. She pulled Wil aside, and the only words I heard her whisper in Wil's ear were "Morgan" and "jelly." Wil imperfectly hid his alarm, and Lucinda skipped uncomfortably close to me. Within range of her hot, swampy breath. I tried not to stare as she thrust the papers upon me and blurted, "You have to put these up for us. You're the only one now. You have to help us." I nodded gravely, and she scurried inside.

Wil was thanking me, but his eyes were on the glass door. "I'll be in touch soon."

"What's going on with Morgan? Is he okay? What's his pediatrician been saying?" Wil was poised to bolt, but I felt I'd been too long in the dark and deserved a scrap or two of confidence if I were really "the only one" in the implied sense.

"No pediatrician. Not in the last month. They're a bunch of quacks around here." I'd sooner have expected that kind of telegraphic, disjointed verbiage from Lucinda. "We're not wasting any more time and money getting bamboozled. Nothing but misinformation."

"How about a specialist in Boston then?"

"Jeff, I'm sorry. I have to get going." And with that, he was off. Leaving me with a couple of dozen ink-smudged, hand-printed fliers about Elsie. She'd included no phone number or address on any of them, and a shaky hand had undermined every attempt at a straight line. All right, guess I could see my way clear to adding contact info and posting these before clocking in tomorrow. Probably just as well Wil had vamoosed before I'd plucked up the nerve to speak of one more oddity I'd never dare broach again. For as long as Lucinda was violating my personal space, I'd have sworn that her eyebrows were standing on end, quivering, as if prey to static electricity. I retreated to the Taurus. Somewhere down the street, a guy with a Latino accent was wearily hollering for his dog.

Six

An item on the local news at 11 scared me into committing workplace espionage. Tucked between perv kidnapper foiled by heroic crossing guard and a preview of Saturday's Civil War reenactment on Sentinel Hill was a breezy fluff-piece on hive collapse across the "Occam metro area." Blasé state official trotted out the standard suspects of virus or parasites, and a doe-eyed effervescent reporter trivialized the silence of white bureau-like hives around her as "a bitter blow to a sweet commodity." No apparent inkling of what this portended for agriculture. Or that bees were disappearing in the wake of dogs and cats.

Pushed the Mute button on my remote. Hard to concentrate while another doe-eyed correspondent nattered about Gettysburg with a husky faux Confederate whose Bluetooth protruded from one muttonchop. Hive collapse. Yes, absolutely, one more piece in a puzzle that included corpse lights and olden days' haunted woods and toxic dust from nowhere, and something that stampeded dogs and bees and had accumulated in Lucinda's womb and *ipso facto* her bloodstream. One additional piece, and I was positive I could correlate these mental contents into a theory of what was besetting Occam. I almost had it, and it was taunting me like a word unreachable on the tip of my tongue.

My roving mind came to fortuitous rest on a smarmy commercial for St. Mary's Hospital, a former Episcopal charity for the Victorian indigent, newly reconceived as a for-profit, state-of-the-art maternity clinic. Wil and Lucinda couldn't swing the insurance for it, and had to settle for Occam General. Had St. Mary's recorded a recent uptick in stillbirths? Had Occam General? Attrition among pets and bees I could make a case for, but not infants, not with Warren Rice as sole example. Yet nothing would be simpler to tally than perinatal death toll. What was it Wil had suspected? That his twins weren't the first with their symptoms? That hospital staff had instructions to separate such babies from parents? The tv took up the entire top of the squat dresser at the foot of my bed. I hit the Power button with the remote from my nightstand and sank the bedroom into darkness. Sat up with my back against the headboard and deliberated.

To compile who was dying of what, I needed death certificates, and what the hell, I worked in City Hall. Moreover, to avoid electronic fingerprints that online search might produce, I only had to abuse the trust of Mr. Marsh. Mr. Marsh, my immediate supervisor, had no first name as far as we subordinates were aware. He was Chief City Clerk, or officially, sole claimant to title of *the* City Clerk. From his third-floor sanctum, he issued one mass e-mail each 8:30 AM, listing every clerk and his or her day's assignment. Otherwise we'd have had no proof he was in the building, though he'd been as cozily entrenched some 40 years as an oyster in its shell. I attributed that staying power to a talent for divesting himself of personality, for absenting from his bodily presence all but the modicum of a self that went through the routine motions. There was too little of him on the job for monotony, office politics, or friendships to make any incursions. A model of "transparency" in government. But in the sense of virtual invisibility, rather than openness.

He indulged one passion in his high-ceilinged oyster shell of an office, and that was what impelled me to sneak upstairs during his dependable noon-to-one lunch hour. In drawers built into all four walls from floor to cornice, in row upon row of steel filing cabinets surrounding his desk like waves overwhelming an island, he had crammed decades of the documentation that municipal database had rendered redundant: building permits, assorted citizen grievances, expired union contracts, and a hundredfold other forms, including death certificates, of course. With everything in an ingeniously alphabetized, chronological system where garden-variety intuition functioned as 95% reliable guide.

The most recent death certificates were at convenient waist level, in an olive-green unit within pool-cue length of Mr. Marsh's spartan desk, but beyond sight of the door. With a pen and Post-its from out of my hip pocket, I started totaling "stillbirths" as bundles of four lines and a cross-stroke, but as I flipped back through the first half of August and into the folder for July, it behooved me to tabulate "miscarriages," "fetal deaths," and "neonatal deaths" as well. This was gobbling up unforeseen amounts of time, and at prospects of confronting Mr. Marsh, my hands grew clammy, and from my empty stomach rose acidic gurgling. I dared not consult my wristwatch, for then I'd feel constrained to check it again and again, squandering valuable seconds and, potentially, my lifetime allotment of heartbeats.

Unsure if my rapid scrawl would even be legible tomorrow, I felt obliged to fray my nerves further by jotting down each new cause of death. "Stroke," "heart failure," "seizure," and "spasms" all smacked sharply of pre-varication. The notation for Warren Rice read "umbilical asphyxiation." Right.

As of mid-July, I counted 30 maternity-ward deaths altogether. That couldn't be normal. Were Occam's doctors up against more than they knew, or more than they would say? By accident or design, did those separate headings of fetal and perinatal and infantile fatality disguise an underlying trend, a common mechanism that killed earlier or later? And how to tell when I, like Wil, was in danger of wading over my head into murky conspiracy theory? On the other hand, how could the brain trusts at two hospitals have failed to grasp such a glaring pattern?

Wait a minute. Hadn't one entry from a week ago been x-ed out except for "seizure"? I backtracked, and through the censoring ink, made out "crawling skin syndrome." A diagnosis I could safely bet would never surface in the *Physicians' Desk Reference*. Or in these files ever again. One or more practitioners had seen something in sufficient numbers to attach a name to it, informally at least, but had incurred second thoughts or higherups' disapproval. How'd that old saw go? Just because Wil was paranoid didn't mean he was wrong? Crawling skin syndrome. My emotive cogs stalled and overheated as I tried to process that.

"Are you about done in here?" I dropped my pen clattering into the drawer and turned my reddening face toward waxen Mr. Marsh's. He stood beside his desk, hands folded behind him. No malice or sarcasm or rebuke enlivened his speech or his expression. His feelings about my trespass were, I gathered, none of my business. Nor did his bland look demand excuse or justification from me. It was like being busted by Bartleby the Scrivener. Abandoning my pen, I shut the drawer and mumbled apologetically and cleared out. But if I'd insisted I wasn't quite done yet, would he have backed solemnly out of his own office?

As I clambered downstairs, trying to project an air of blamelessness, Mr. Big Shot Recorder of Deeds was lumbering up, with swaying steps as if the liquid content of his lunch were sloshing back and forth. True to habit, he feigned blindness at my existence, and may well have forgotten I'd borne witness to his disgraceful exit from the Aviator. That was heartening, as was the certainty that my intrusion would not be grist for Mr. Marsh's conversations, insofar as he never had any. All in all, a cloak-and-dagger mission commendably accomplished. But an overall picture of what hung over Occam still evaded me, even after adding and connecting that dot of "crawling skin syndrome" to the rest.

Seven

My lunch-hour discoveries joined the list of all else I'd withhold from Wil with mixed feelings. I foremost didn't like adding fuel to any of his destabilizing, obsessive trains of thought, even if (or especially if) they were on the right track. And whatever I did tell him at this stage might beg the question of what I hadn't told him previously, fraught scene resulting. All the same, when he phoned, I was almost conscience-stricken into opening up to him, until the purpose of his call threw my good intentions overboard.

I should've been used by now to hearing from him at suppertime, just as I was unwinding after work, and looking forward to staying put. Could I please come over within the hour and babysit, as I'd promised that night at the Aviator? They had to go out. With leaden emphasis on "had." Aloud, I acquiesced readily. Inwardly, I groaned like a soul in perdition. He imparted no further details before waxing lavishly grateful, as on that other night when I stopped in and Lucinda's water broke.

I heated up the last of many servings from that refried spaghetti, and let the skillet soak amidst a few days' cups and dishes in the sink. My hand was on the doorknob when the phone rang again. A reprieve? Please? Afraid not. The archetypal lilt of blueblood matron was requesting I announce the Occam Historic Society's rummage sale on that "local history program" of mine. She tossed off her name too briskly for me to intercept it. Sadly, her event was happening the Saturday after next, a week before the next *Chronicles* would air. At this late date, I advised her, she had best submit her info, tomorrow if possible, to the Community Bulletin Board that Pabodie Cable posted between shows. But it sounded like a great event for a worthwhile cause, I enthused, and promised to be there, and hoped it'd be a big success. Her cooler tone implied she didn't care what I hoped if I couldn't do what she wanted, and after perfunctory good-byes, I pondered how low the old money had fallen, for its Historic Society to go the Swamp Yankee route of fundraising.

In front of Dyer Hall, I opened the Taurus door and hysterical screaming assailed me. Where exactly was it coming from? Couldn't say. Somewhere in the immediate neighborhood. Dear God, let it not be Lucinda! On and on it went, as if expelled from lungs possessed or bottomless. A thirtyish citizen in baggy shorts and Izod shirt strode past, endeavoring to block the racket by riveting his eyes on the sidewalk. I, however, had paused too long, as if a Siren tune were embedded in the caterwauling, which on closer listen revealed semitone shifts in pitch, and gradual transitions between vowels, and barely perceptible staccato gaps, like rapid-fire Morse code. In my fascination, these nuances took on a semblance of exotic language. And when the voice abruptly ceased, breath caught in my throat while an echo, or possibly two echoes, lingered somewhere in the brownstone and aluminum-sided walls of urban canyon. Belief in unrealistically long echoes was less problematic to me than belief in one coded scream answering another.

I wagged my head free of trance. Wil buzzed me in, and a hush surrounded me up to the Rices' door, and it persisted after I knocked and Wil let me in. What hit me instantly was the condo's overripe, rancid, carnal odor, with a more pernicious element of death, sickening despite half-open windows. A lapse in housekeeping because baby came first could explain neither the odor nor the squalor that also surrounded me. And here I had agreed to babysit for how many hours?

Chic domicile was now the kind of lair where someone manic might have hoarded forty cats. Despair had found expression as disorder. Dirty laundry on the floor, dirty plates and cups on glass and wooden surfaces, spills and stains mottling the carpets and upholstery. And none of it, curiously, included baby bottles, clothes, or diapers. Dog toys, though, still lay scattered about, days after Elsie's getaway. The air conditioner was broken. Someone had punched in the touch-screen controls.

On the couch, Lucinda, in unclean yellow jogging outfit, blended right in, as good as camouflaged. She sat no less inert than the disarray around her, eyelids drooping under the weight of sedation, so that only black slits stared out. "Jeff's here, honey," Wil told her, to no visible effect. I couldn't define how, but would swear she was physically as well as mentally withdrawn. Literally not all there. Behind ashen complexion, a portion of her had been sucked inward, collapsed, disappeared. And what of Morgan, and where was he?

"Poor Lucinda's been up against a triple whammy." Wil's eyes pleaded with me to understand, and more importantly, to take him at his word. "The postpartum depression, and the problems with Morgan, and then Elsie escaping. It's come to where I think she needs a clinic for however long, and I was able to wrangle a bed for her even though they don't usually admit after 6." Overcoming malaise at her comatose look and the vile smell, I essayed a soft, compassionate smile, and vetoed asking if Lucinda had been screaming till a minute ago. Instead, I raised what struck me as a safely moot point, insofar as the die was cast and they were as good as out the door. How was it he trusted the psychiatric establishment more than the medicos?

"This place is holistic. I don't know if the insurance'll cover it or not, but the situation's out of hand, so we'll have to burn that bridge when we come to it." And if I read between the lines of that "situation" correctly, then yes, Wil had administered Lucinda something stronger than her wailing hysteria, and it had kicked in upon my arrival. A happy coincidence for me. "Some other new parents who've been dealing with the same issues recommended this facility. A lot of herbal and homeopathic therapies."

Desperate Wil really didn't want my opinion of "alternative medicine" or New Age anything, but I almost let slip that more new parents were in his boat than he realized. With so much on his plate already, though, why increase his burden with facts? Nor was I quite ready to draw full breath and speak again. Still growing acclimated to the odor, and inhaling shallowly. I also had to stop and consider Wil's talk of "other new parents." Since Lucinda's ills went miles beyond his armchair diagnosis of depression, were other mothers of crawling-skin babies "dealing with the same issues" of a similar condition, and were they harbingers of something bigger and worse in the offing?

"Anyway, the clinic's over in Armitage. Not too bad a haul, but we ought to get going. Jeff, I can't thank you enough for stepping up like this."

I only nodded, and crassly prayed the odor might ease up in Lucinda's absence. "And don't worry about Morgan. He won't need tending to till I get back. He's a good little sleeper, normally." I picked up the same overtone of equivocation from Wil as when we'd left Morgan alone with a tranked-out Lucinda while we hunted for Elsie. But let it go! The sooner they went away, the sooner Wil would come back.

"Honey, can we start heading out?" Wil leaned over and appealed to her affectionately, but stopped short of touching her. She reacted sluggishly: her mind remote, I intuited, within an Empty Quarter whose breadth encompassed her former self, and where words were slow to penetrate, and slow to make sense.

She wasn't overweight, in spite of recent pregnancy. Had always prided herself on her figure, in fact, and worked out religiously. Hence my twinge of cognitive dissonance, when each adjustment of her legs and torso for the sake of standing had the ungainliness of a zeppelin uncoupled from moorings. Her mass seemed too cumbersome for her. Her limbs, simultaneously, seemed flimsy and loose-jointed, and begged the question of whether she could cross the room without crumbling.

Wil was inured or oblivious, or both, to her fragility, and she poked forward unaided while he instructed me, "The sofa folds out, you know. I might be gone past your bedtime. Feel free to sack out if you like." I risked gulping foul air to thank him heartily for that. A raft of cleanliness in this unhygienic Sargasso. And that was before my eyes chanced to light on the sofa cushions, where flakes and dust lay like a tentative chalk outline where Lucinda had been sitting. Skin and flesh, precipitating off her brow, out of her sleeves? Was she truly crumbling, grain by grain?

At a polite distance, I followed the godforsaken couple across the room. She was still a step ahead, and struggling to open the door as if she'd never used one before, with left hand on the knob and right hand grasping the jamb. She tottered back, and Wil put a hand on her shoulder to steady her. As if prey to deep-seated reflex, she took a clumsy swipe at him, which he evaded easily and with no show of surprise. How often did she transform into a vicious stranger, lashing out at his good intentions? He had touched something in her that didn't recognize him at all, and that had distorted her face into malignant unfamiliarity. Wil turned and conceded sheepishly, "She's not herself right now." I reverted to calmly nodding. She shambled out, and he hovered beside her, and I locked myself in.

Their Outback was at the curb, and through filmy glass I watched him guide her into it with diplomatic phrases and gestures, as if she were some dim, unpredictable brute. Careful to avoid hands-on assistance. He seemed aloof to a further change in Lucinda that both frightened and baffled me. Was she vaguely luminous, emitting that same unidentifiable color as her amniotic fluid? Or had my tired eyes misread a streetlight or the moon beaming on her? I heaved the window all the way up, but a clearer view made no difference, and as they departed I opened every window all the way.

Next I swept the leather cushions to the floor and dragged a glass-top coffee table to one side and pulled out my fresher-smelling refuge of a queen-sized bed. In the process, a tv remote popped free of confinement in unfolding mattress. Perfect! The Rices had sprung for premium channels, and relative to mine, their screen was on a multiplex scale. Did a belly-flop onto the creaky bed, to rest my chin at the foot end, facing the tv across the living room. Unless nature insisted, I wouldn't budge for the duration. Wil would never begrudge me food and drink, from top-shelf down, but I wasn't about to set foot in what must have been a nauseating kitchen at best.

After losing myself in a flurry of channel-flipping, the sensation of being too alone here bothered me. I muted the set, and all was quiet as a vacuum. No infantile snoring or rustle of blanket. Had to take Wil's word for it that Morgan was asleep in a crib behind the door narrowly ajar, adjacent to the open door of parental bedroom. I was loath to go in and see, and upset him into squalling. What then? Sight unseen or not, I was profoundly averse to handling that baby. Then too, there were decent odds of a denser stench in that more confined space, sending me, gorge rising, to an equally disgusting bathroom. No, best leave well enough alone.

Lulled myself into switching, at commercial breaks, between a docudrama about the Trojan Horse and some '30s vehicle for William Powell and Myrna Loy. When ads ran on both channels at once, I pressed Mute and strained my ears, never to any purpose.

The loutish question arose of what the hell I was doing here. The baby was "dead to the world," as I indelicately observed, while I continued to mouth-breathe, with stomach aching, in that stubbornly abiding miasma. Of course, nobody with an ounce of responsibility would leave an infant to its own devices, and my presence "just in case" was mandatory. My tribulations tonight comprised only a paper-thin fraction of Wil's everyday own, but I was miserable enough. The evening was playing out as I knew it would, from the reckless moment I'd volunteered.

Or so I thought. Apathetic hours of viewing had dulled my wits, such that I made nothing of the news at 11 that the Canada geese were gone. A voiceover during before-and-after footage of a strutting flock and then of still waters touted this as cause for rejoicing, because the birds had been a perennial nuisance, chasing folks, fouling the shoreline, interfering with recreational craft. Presumably, it had entered their heads to migrate south, for once, and good riddance forever, with any luck. Now, the voiceover sighed, if only the swallows and swifts would do their job and eat this summer's oversized mosquitoes and horseflies.

I yawned. Harrumphed wearily at extra inflow of distasteful air. Killed the tv. Too drowsy to absorb any more. Or to keep my eyes open. I wallowed onto my back. With my shoes on, and no bedclothes or pillow under me. Didn't care. Falling asleep was a good way to shut out the odor, and as I drifted off, I mused that Wil might as well stay out till morning and let me get a restorative 8 hours.

What the hell? I awoke disoriented, in the stinking dark, in a cold sweat. The smell reminded me where I was, but why I was up was harder to fathom. And much more worrisome. I lay still, with exhalation stuck in my throat. Then a plastic dog toy squealed loudly on the floor. Something was squeezing a long, shrill, bending note out of it. A foolish sound to find so unnerving! It died away, followed by a hiss of indrawn air as the hollow plastic refilled, and as the room filled with the certainty of a furtive presence. Wil would be apologizing by now if he'd tiptoed in and accidentally rousted me, and it couldn't very well be Elsie. I reached out slowly and waved my hand to and fro till it bumped the lamp on the side table next to the sofa. My fingers brushed the cord and pulled, and I closed my eyes against the shock of brightness.

I sat up and scanned the floor in front of the bed while my blinking eyes finished adjusting. To my right, Elsie's toy, a coiled yellow snake in porkpie hat, stood out on red and black carpet, and grinned as if nothing was amiss and it had never, ever squeaked. In a filthy blue jumper, Morgan was on the move in unbabylike fashion, in deathly, unnatural silence, away from the jolly snake and toward the kitchen door. The jarring expulsion of darkness had made no overt impression. He heedlessly became entangled in jumbled yoga wear and socks and used Kleenex, and just as heedlessly cast them off, as he clambered hand over hand while lolling back and forth on spasmodically twitching belly. Chinese takeout cartons and pillows and yogurt tubs he flopped onto and over like a lungfish humping along a Devonian beach. His legs dragged limply, or kicked up and down to no effect. A swimmer out of water. On litter-free floor, his progress was still laborious, like that of an insect climbing a sticky wall. I began to tremble at the understanding that this was not a baby gone exploring. He took no interest in me or anything in his path.

I was in no state to guess at what had set the body in motion. Butting nursery door open with its head must have made the noise that spoiled my sleep. Nothing but inertia was maintaining it on haphazard course to the kitchen, where it had no reason to go. It had no reason to do anything. Nobody, in human terms, was piloting that flesh. Nothing remained of Morgan but a specimen of "crawling skin syndrome," whatever that really was.

My curtailed view of him from up on the bed counted as my one transient blessing. Only the back of his head, bobbing loosely at each exertion, showed outside of ratty blue jumper. In the stark light, through bleached-out hair fine and dry as flax, infant scalp was grey and porous like a barren moon. Or as if rot and regeneration were vying with one another in untenable deadlock.

Then fortune frowned and Morgan's lunging shoulder failed to clear the doorframe. Thumped into it, and tried to keep going. Inertia twisted him into profile. If Morgan were the vessel of something sentient, it was well disguised. Jaw hung open as if unhinged and forgotten. Glazed, bulging eye never blinked, and conveyed the blank indifference of a shark. Soulless energy goaded Morgan into repeatedly nudging the doorframe till he pivoted right around and was inside the kitchen, and without pause he scuttled mechanically into the shadows. My eyes and ears strained compulsively after him. A soft bump marked his collision with wall or stove or fridge. No further sign of activity emerged, all the while I kept fixated vigil, sitting up in bed as if catatonic, eyes steadfast on the kitchen doorsill. Sense of time deserted me. I may have been staring for hours.

From somewhere faraway and irrelevant, a key jiggled in a lock. Sometime afterward, Wil was bending over me, hand floating over my shoulder, as if wary that I might react to contact as savagely as Lucinda. "Jeff? You okay? You been up all night? It's 4 AM."

"Morgan," I croaked, and raised a cramping arm toward the kitchen. At a loss to say or do more.

He followed my gesture casually, as if humoring me. "Was he restless? I'm sorry. You really didn't have to concern yourself. And sorry I'm so late, but you can't imagine all the rigmarole we had to plow through." Why wasn't he in more of a hurry to deal with his wayward son? Moreover, what was Wil's very personal meaning of "restless"? The coherence to address these matters was still beyond me. Instead, I valiantly marshaled my wits to ask how Lucinda was doing.

"They're very compassionate over there." Uh-huh. Evasion had become second nature to hopelessly beleaguered Wil. Tending to the baby now lent him ample excuse to say nothing else about his wife. "Be right back." He ducked into the kitchen without turning on the lights.

After a hushed, oppressive while, he bustled out with Morgan wrapped in a threadbare dishtowel, with scarcely a sliver of grey, concave cheek exposed, perhaps for Wil's own sake as much as mine. The towel and its contents behaved as one lifeless bundle for as long as I squinted.

"Sometimes he gets restless in the middle of the night." Apparently "restless" was Wil's code word to help him cope with what I'd witnessed. It didn't help me, though, and on second hearing, convinced me I'd be crossing a line of ghoulish complicity unless I said something. Let the chips finally fall where they may.

"It's only a body, Wil. Has Morgan ever acted like a normal infant?" I was afraid of being too blunt, and of being too oblique.

"He's not like other kids. We accept that."

Wil's self-deception was beginning to make my own skin crawl. "He's dead. That's what you have to accept. I don't know what that so-called restlessness is about, but it's not life. You can't keep him here."

That did it! Wil was bristling, but inappropriately, as if I were cutting Morgan from the Little League team, or as if Wil could bicker away the reality of his plight. "Who are you to say? Are you going to report us?"

I wasn't, but didn't feel I owed him either a free pass or a straight answer. Without him, I had no friends in this town, no way to keep OGAM afloat, and no long-term future for the *Chronicles*. I couldn't stand idle while he sacrificed his sanity on the altar of a parenthood he hadn't wanted in the first place. He had to snap out of it. Be himself again. "I can't condone this. It's unhealthy on every level in the book."

"Whose side are you on?" Oh crap. Had I overplayed my hand already? Hard to tell without taking the full measure of Wil's paranoia.

"You have to do the right thing on your own. Might be easier while Lucinda's away."

Wil reddened and pressed limp offspring tighter to his shoulder. "Fuck you! You got a goddamn lot of nerve trying to turn me against my wife and kid. I think you better go now, and don't plan on coming back." He stalked to the door and flung it wide and glared at me.

Game over. I was in past my depth and couldn't have acquitted myself more competently, not against Wil's advanced pathology. Yes, just like that, our friendship was on the rocks, and I was in shellshock. Who'd have expected the chips to fall straight to hell? We eyed each other warily as I withdrew, as if we were newly capable of inflicting bodily harm on one another without a second thought.

At my nearest approach, he leaned involuntarily away and thudded against the wall, spreading protective hands across Morgan's swaddled, quiescent back and head. Over the threshold, I compulsively gulped relatively sweet air and braced for the door to slam an inch from my butt. To my amazement, though, after an anxious pause, Wil was entreating me from the doorway, "Do you think the water's at the root of all this? Am I to blame for spending so much time at work out there?"

I shook my head, but without taking my eyes off the corridor's hideous burgundy carpet. Inner turbulence, I reckoned, had briefly dredged a more lucid, pensive Wil to the choppy surface. Hemmed and hawed for some innocuous reply that his milder self could latch onto like a lifeline. Too slow! The door slammed, and from the other side I heard "asshole."

Eight

Poor Wil! Sometime during the groggy, spacey eon when I drove home and watched the sunrise and breakfasted and changed clothes and reported to heinous work, I realized that he, amidst Job-like trials, was now as friendless as I. Lucinda had implied as much by naming me "the only one" while begging me to post fliers for Elsie, when the Perseids were at their peak. And more was the pity, because I'd plucked a theory at long last, out of that mental fog where free associations thrived, to account for what was afflicting Occam. But I wouldn't be sharing it with Wil, and if not him, then with whom? By the same token, he'd never enjoy due credit for delivering the final dot that formed my theoretical picture.

Like it or not, I had to be thankful for my ordeal in babysitting. Otherwise I'd have been much slower to ascertain that something was infesting organisms, blighting them, and imitating the former life within them. Something whose behavior bore no relation to that of ghosts or anything supernatural. It infiltrated hosts via water, as did some parasites and pathogens, but nothing earthly, I felt safe in saying, would reanimate a corpse. Something utterly alien it must have been, and I envisioned a disembodied force or microscopic swarm or class of matter beyond human ability to sense or measure. Ornery decades of mistrusting the reservoir would be justified if its waters had ever previously served as alien conduit. And corpse lights fit within my scheme as eerie sign that cosmic portal was open, a portal whose opening may have been invisible without the water around it, and from which had also come toxic grey dust and rumors of haunted woods.

I jotted down these conjectures when I should have been drafting a letter to the City Council, outlining the agenda of their next meeting. A quick scan confirmed that no one was spying over my shoulder or sidelong across the room. Hurray. Not that passersby were common in this conference chamber of the mayoral suite. Gingerly I tore the sheet off the yellow lined legal pad and folded it into trouser pocket.

I was up here at the behest of Deputy Mayor Nathan Atwood. A regular guy among the stuffed shirts. Could've been my long-lost cousin or a more together version of myself. We had the same ski-jump nose and navy-blue eyes, and baseball-sized bald spot lurking in the premature grey. I shuffled Atwood's brace of scribbled notes on various index cards and napkins, but they wouldn't organize yet. Not till my vagrant speculations had crystallized into a plan of action. The invaders per se were impossible to detect. That didn't mean they weren't planting a signature, chemical or radioactive, in the water. A broader range of tests might vindicate me, along with every-one over the years who'd fussed about the "Gorman taste." The authorities wouldn't have to believe in aliens for them to condemn alien byproducts as a threat to public health. And if anyone in City Hall could pass for open-minded, it had to be Atwood. My best bet for an ally, and though I might have gone to Wil's employers or numerous other departments and organi-zations, City Hall was where I'd need an ally, where nasty opposition had confronted me before I'd even realized I was a whistle-blower.

I scampered out to the suite's reception area, and the sun shone daz-zling on the secretary's red-oak desk through the high, wide southern expo-sure. The secretary favored me with a bright smile. She projected a winsome girl-next-door charm, despite photograde lenses masking her eyes. I requested an appointment with the Deputy Mayor. To discuss some envi-ronmental concerns. She could pencil me in for 15 minutes at 10:30 Mon-day morning. I said that was fine. What a delightful change from the City Collector's grim domain!

With less divided mind, I assembled Atwood's letter, and attached it as a Word document in an e-mail where I refrained from alluding to our Mon-day meeting. Couldn't finesse how to do so without coming off as fatuous. And after punching Send, the daunting prospect of making my case with Atwood, without making an ass of myself, began to sink in. I needed more substantiation. Every bit I could muster. At least enough to get him on my side, and in a position to thumb my nose at Humphrey Westcott and his overreacting ilk.

If Lucinda's was genuinely one postpartum breakdown among many, even a rough idea of how many would be extremely helpful. The pertinent records, though, weren't in City Hall. Not that I'd dare court Mr. Marsh's deadpan displeasure again. The county Department of Health was down Ellery Avenue from Dyer Hall, in rehabbed Anthropology Department of the defunct university. Out and about with Wil, we had passed the building a hundred times, such that I remembered a Division of Mental Hygiene on the white-and-gilt sign looming over narrow front lawn.

Took the calculated risk of calling from the phone beside the conference room computer. A mayoral number on the caller ID box at the other end should have bolstered my pretext of official business. I ran the gauntlet of automated menu till the extension for Mental Hygiene came up. Someone whose name I couldn't catch eventually answered. Told her I worked for the city, and was researching healthcare delivery in Occam. With particular emphasis on the wellbeing of women. Decided I'd be more convincing if I stuck to true statements, fibbing only to the extent of connoting a link between my statements. Could she please give me information about any rise in the number of psychiatric admissions for depression or other causes among new mothers in the last 3 months?

She was sorry, but facts regarding individual patients were confidential. Yes, and rightly so, I chimed in, while suspecting her of deliberately misunderstanding me. Specified that I was only interested in monthly statistics for the last quarter.

Those figures would not be available until the end of the year, she claimed. Without bothering to sound sorry. Impatient with me already, after playing dumb from the get-go. The crummy attitude that gives us civil servants a bad name! This exchange, if I were any judge of sullen vibes, was over as far as she was concerned. Might as well press on for the fun of further annoying her. Okay then, had she observed any trends informally in terms of institutionalizations? Off the record? She wasn't rising to the bait, damn her. "What did you say your name was?"

"I didn't." I hung up. Her petulance had suddenly taken on a thornier edge, putting me on my guard. Making me wonder if friends in City Hall were instructing her to stonewall any OB/GYN-related questions. Or was her every interaction with the public steeped in reflex pettiness? Either way, I was already down one talking point for my presentation Monday, and had trod one slippery step on the descent into conspiracy craziness.

Fortunately, my fact-finding included a Plan B. I had yet to confirm that symptoms of invasion had spread beyond Occam. The forecast for Saturday was cool and cloudless. A preview of chilling fall, perhaps, but ideal weather to cruise the ring road around the reservoir, and stop off in those other towns that shared our "haunted" water. Houghton, Hoyle, Chapman, and Armitage proved as disparate as fingerprints, with one disappointing similarity. In whatever landscape I parked and strolled, whether of Georgian mansions and belfried church around an idyllic common, or a Main Street of moribund shops and derelict mills like an Occam in miniature, or a ticky-tacky sprawl laying waste our forefathers' pastures and cornfields, people were walking their dogs and pushing baby carriages and exhibiting no signs of the careworn or wary. Bees droned lazily in and out of hollyhocks and asters along white picket fences. The sun shone brighter everywhere, without that perpetual, subliminal filter of hometown drear, conspicuous now only in its absence. I had lunch at a blue and silver deco diner, and a happy-hour pint in a backstreet bar full of tiki junk and cracked red leather upholstery. No one started a fight, or expressed the slightest bother, about the "Gorman taste," though it was there all right. In terms of broadening the map of alien infiltration, this trip was a bust. I'd found nothing to further my cause, come Monday morning.

Not, at least, till I reentered the Occam metro area. Traveled many crooked miles down country roads, to avoid a more direct course home through tedious downtown. Filled up at a ramshackle gas station, with white tile walls and green trim. No self-service. A pocky lackadaisical youth with a Six Flags cap manned the pump, and I moseyed over to the pumpkin field beyond the blacktop apron. Gawked a minute, then whipped my head around toward the kid. He rested an elbow on the roof of the car and chewed gum with a slow, circular movement of his jaw, as if nothing was wrong. The pumpkins really didn't like the Gorman taste. They and the vines retained mere streaks of green and orange amidst a sea of withered grey and spinning irrigation sprinklers. I fetched digital camera out of the car and snapped a series from close-ups to panorama. I paid the kid and asked what had happened here, jerking my thumb back at the desolation. He mulled it over for three chomps on his gum and shrugged. "Sucks, don't it? For the kids, I mean. No jack-o-lanterns this year." I agreed and moved on. Hadn't banked on more incisive analysis from him.

I missed Wil's input that night, as I reviewed the day's findings. Felt a tad degenerate polishing off the 32 ounces of Sierra Nevada I would've split with him, but it was better than no liquid inspiration at all. He might also have disputed my musical selection of the Residents' *Duck Stab* as an aid to thinking. Well, it worked for me, and that's what had to matter from now on. My undramatic daytrip, on second thought, hadn't been a waste of gasoline after all. The putative normality around most of the reservoir did suggest limits to alien capacity. The submerged portal apparently opened toward Occam, and whatever it disgorged was bound by momentum or something more esoteric to continue in a straight line, and into the Occam water system. Alternately, the presence had arrived in insufficient numbers or amount to contaminate more than a modest area at once, till it could gain strength or reproduce. None of these speculations, of course, were intended for Atwood's ears, or for the *OGAM Chronicles*.

My mind wandered more productively in the dark, but guests usually objected to groping around by incoming starlight. Another reason to be glad I was alone. The dark was extra comforting tonight because nothing was luminous that shouldn't have been. I crossed the silent living room with tentative steps, ready to stop when my toes met with obstacles. Ejected the Residents from my CD player, and put in some Roxy Music. Returned, like an astronaut slowly traversing lunar surface, to couch and coffee table, and refilled my glass. High time I realized that today's dying pumpkin patch was a case of history repeating itself. With its parallel way back in the 20th century, when the Heroux family's corn and squash had been destroyed by windborne grey dust. I'd presumed the dust was part of hostile exotic environment that had wafted through the portal, or else the baneful traces of what had already fallen victim to alien influence. But suppose the portal was admitting sentient life that appeared to us as dust, and that spread invisibly as a solution in water?

Atwood would hear none of this either, though the poisoned pumpkins were nothing he could ignore, or fail to investigate, especially in conjunction with my data on infant mortality. And what, I wondered, would he hold responsible for "crawling skin syndrome," since space invaders could hardly figure among the candidates? Who cared, so long as he got the ball rolling with a ban on city water?

I killed the bottle and listened to the CD and stared into darkness and concluded, This has been a good Saturday, and an evening well-spent. To most onlookers it might have seemed dull and pathetic. How did I tolerate such a monkish life? As if a gym or a disco would have helped me shape tonight's insights! Hah. See what they thought of my pathetic life after I saved their precious town.

Why wasn't I at least on the lookout for a significant other? Truth is, I had been head-over-heels in love, during college, in Boston. The relationship burned hot for a year, then went into on-again, off-again tailspin for a second year, plus a messy, protracted breakup that ensured I'd never mistake that senior semester for the happiest months of my life. Afterward, didn't have it in me to pursue another soulmate, and risk going through all that again. A classic instance of once burnt, twice shy. Wasn't even sorry her name was buried in some synaptic pothole on most days. Like now. So why the hell was I dwelling on this water under the dam? Might as well blame the pale ale, since it wasn't likely to backtalk in self-defense.

Nine

Sunday I soldiered through a low-level headache, to print out images of diseased pumpkins and type up the stats I'd pilfered from Mr. Marsh's files. What a pity I could no longer bounce back with impunity from a night of drinking alone. On the positive side, navigating in a moderate fog all day kept me from overthinking what I'd say and wear on Monday morning. To quote Oscar Wilde, real life was too important to take seriously, and the upshot might be woefully serious if I continued acting the gadfly without any friends in City Hall. Maybe that was why I racked up four hours' sleep at best.

When the enchanting secretary showed me in at precisely 10:30, I was only mildly self-conscious in a powder-grey suit I usually unbagged for funerals. While crossing the room, had to admire a gigantic poster in a nouveau gilt frame, on the wall opposite Atwood's desk, for Méliès' *Voyage dans la Lune*, probably the coolest thing he could get away with putting up in here, and which blended right in with the Victorian décor. Atwood proffered a warm handshake and a brown leather armchair in front of his rosewood desk. "You had some information about environmental concerns? In regard to this building, or the city in general? You're on Mr. Marsh's staff, aren't you?" I sat down, set my flea-market briefcase on my lap, and opened it, lest I get tongue-tied at this rare collegial treatment in the workplace.

I was never prouder of myself, never more articulate or composed or dynamic, as I summarized hospital records in support of anecdotal evidence, a.k.a. the tragedy of Wil and Lucinda, minus its least naturalistic elements. Luminous amniotic fluid, yes, that made the cut. Morgan crawling postmortem, no. A fine line to negotiate! And to maternal calamities I cannily tied irrigated harvests wilting on the vine, and laid out my high-res illustrations. Ended with an earnest appeal for him to order more rigorous analyses of city water, targeting radioactivity, exotic trace elements, less common pollutants, and banning its use in homes and on crops, pending test results. Lives were at stake, and dealing decisively with an emergent public health issue could only cast him in a heroic light. I skirted the pitfall of listing corpse-lights and yesteryear's poison dust, with its supernatural overtones, among the more fantastic attributes of reservoir pollution. Remarkable how brightly I could shine when officials treated me as an equal, or when they resembled me enough to let me feel I was talking to myself. A flawless presentation, if I did say so.

Then why was moisture beginning to spread under my armpits? The first familiar trickles of flop sweat? Atwood's casual riffle through my photos, giving each the minimal polite once-over, didn't augur well. Nor did the searching look on his downcast face, as if he wished the desktop concealed an escape hatch. Still averting his eyes from mine, he extracted a folded newspaper from a well-oiled top drawer. He passed it over to me. It was the Town and Country section of Sunday's *Occam Advertiser*. "I appreciate your initiative coming in here, but I'm sorry you didn't come across this yesterday."

The headline above a quarter-page article proclaimed, "Bees, Borers Behind Bad Year on Farms." Alarming full-color close-ups of a honeybee and a bulbous white caterpillar enlivened the text.

"No, I didn't see this," I confessed.

"I don't mean for you to read it now, but it covers more extensive fieldwork than a single pumpkin patch. The writers build a pretty convincing case for a multifaceted impact on different crops all over the county. A perfect storm, if you like."

I didn't like. His recourse to one of those clichés beloved of newscasters set my teeth on edge, but I exerted myself to nod affably and rein in my grimace.

"A spike in the population of squash vine borers coincided with a spike in other insect pests," he went on. "And as you may have heard, hive collapse has been a problem this summer. In short, why go on a costly wild-goose chase after something bizarre and indefinite, when we don't need more explanations for crop failures than we already have?"

I knew full well why we needed to chase something bizarre, but was briefly dumbstruck at a co-author's name in the article's byline. Ephraim Atwood? Brother or cousin of Nathan? My inner gears froze till I gave up on phrasing a way to ask about family connections that wouldn't infer the Atwoods were in cahoots.

"As it stands, I'm persuaded these tribulations are temporary," Nathan Atwood declared in answer to his own rhetorical question. "Inside the credible boundaries of natural extremes. I'll even go out on a limb and say the bees will come back by themselves. Or people will reintroduce them, as they've done elsewhere. The situation is unfortunate but under control, unless you can show otherwise."

To his credit, Atwood was disputing me in a civil tone. Neither dismissive nor high-handed. Taking the time to spell out his opinion for me, when he could have cut this meeting short and pawned me off on the Department of Health or Environmental Management. I still respected him, but wasn't about to throw in the towel on his say-so.

"This involves more than agriculture," I reminded him. "There's also the abnormally high infant mortality rate. Don't you find that at all suspicious, happening at the same time as vegetation dying?"

"And many births still proceed normally. Just as some plantings have come along normally. How would you account for those, if everyone's using the same unsafe water?"

In terms of something alien that could encroach in only so many places at once? No, that wouldn't do. "Mr. Atwood, that's not a criterion you could apply in the context of any other disease. Some people, and some plants, are always more susceptible, and some are more resistant. Good genes, good nourishment, more fit in general."

The spring in Atwood's chair squeaked as he leaned back and considered me like we were old cronies with a cracker barrel between us. "Okay, I grant you that." He indicated my notes and photos on his desk with an easygoing gesture. "Before we tie up city resources in search of God knows what, though, you'd have to make me believe there's more in all this than a sheaf of random factoids."

"Maybe I can do that for you right now." And maybe my outbreak of flop sweat had been premature. "Some details in my presentation may not have received the proper emphasis. What we're dealing with is a congenital condition that the mother then acquires from the baby. Isn't that an odd enough twist in the normal course of events for you to drop everything and take a closer look?"

Atwood raised his line of sight toward the Méliès poster behind me. "I do feel sorry for the family. My heart goes out to them. As you just said, though, this condition has affected only one mother that you know of. A little too soon to call it part of anything bigger. I don't even see where the illness would necessarily have spread from the child to the mother. She could have had a preexisting condition that stayed latent until the stress of childbirth or a pathogen in the hospital or other triggers activated it, in which case, the mother would have infected the child with this mysterious condition prenatally, so it showed up in the child first, with his weaker immune system, and then the mother, as her condition deteriorated. Lead poisoning is known to follow such a pattern. Framing it that way, we don't have to posit some wild convolution of cause and effect."

This verbal sparring was costing me a lot of energy. Worse, Atwood's serene, relentless voice of reason was wearing away the underpinnings of what I knew damn well to be true, like gentle waves eroding granite piers. Time to sink or swim. "But your argument would fall apart, wouldn't it, if the father was also showing signs of the baby's malady?"

"Well, that would tilt the balance a little in your direction." His gaze shifted from Méliès to me. I'd finally delivered a salvo he hadn't seen coming. "Provided you bring me strong supporting material. Medical records, or a video diary comparing father and son." His sporting smile awarded me a point. "And we'll work from there."

Leather heels on hardwood floor grew audible beyond Atwood's closed door. They stopped and I held my breath, thinking nothing at that juncture except, This is *my* 15 minutes in here. Go away! Silence ensued for what may have been a mere heartbeat or two, though it seemed much longer. I was all ears, and lost track of whatever was in front of me. Then the footsteps receded, which all too briefly seemed the optimal turn of events.

Atwood smiled mildly on, as if nothing had impinged on his awareness, but the atmosphere chilled immediately. "In fairness to us both, don't misread me. I'm not trying to encourage you. This pure-hearted quest of yours might do a lot more harm than good."

His chair squeaked as he sat up straight again, ambled to the nearest in a row of bay windows, opened it wide, and beckoned me over. Did all the third-floor honchos rate sanctums with windows that went up and down? A draft of the nippy air that had lingered since Saturday made me shiver. "From here, it's normal as far as the eye can see." He was right, but the odds were stacked in his favor. Decaying Commercial Street was around the corner. City Hall fronted a glazed brick square, which it shared with the 1970s structures housing the *Advertiser*, the courthouse, the Occam Savings and Loan, and the Department of Motor Vehicles. The Victorian idea had been to buffer the town fathers from the loud nuisance of mercantile activity by placing City Hall's facade on what was then a side street, whereas now the building's placement buffered their modern counterparts from the main drag's desolation. Lawyers, bureaucrats, other "professional" types, and citizens across the demographic spectrum fostered a fine illusion of vitality, with the added vexation of contented moms expectant or with babes in arms, as if expressly out to refute me. "That normality isn't something to disrupt lightly. If it ain't broke, don't fix it, right?" My lips remained politely sealed, and he set his gaze upon the scene below. "I bet you're sick of hearing this, but the city, county, and state each run their own tests every month, and the water has always come back clean."

So soon after spouting the cliché "perfect storm," for him to parrot the official excuse for quashing debate about the reservoir was doubly disappointing. Annoyance rallied my flagging strength. "Then please, arrange for more exhaustive tests while we still have that semblance of normality, before it's too late. The standard battery can't be perfect."

Atwood was beginning to wear his patience on his sleeve, as if rubbing it in that our interview was proceeding solely at his finite sufferance. "You also must be aware that we're operating under a deficit. Cutbacks and layoffs are forcing us to plug holes in the infrastructure with Band-Aids and gum. Those of us still on the payroll are lucky." That couldn't be a muffled threat, could it? "The crux of it is, we can barely afford to keep doing what we're doing now, and what we're doing are the absolute essentials. More stringent water tests would put us deeper in the hole. There's no money to spare unless you build a case too powerful to ignore, that would justify our risk of adverse p.r. from coast to coast, and of a very angry, very frightened public here. As for everything you've shown me today, insofar as there's a kernel of credibility in any of it, it all might easily consist of disconnected blips that'll pass on their own. As all things must, sooner or later." With the informality fading from his smile, he shut the window, a clear symbolic signal that our meeting had also drawn to a close. "I'm sure you wouldn't want to be partly responsible for plunging your hometown into receivership." He extended his hand with a Prussian degree of warmth.

I took it with the spirit into which he had descended, and would have felt more crestfallen had I not completely run out of steam. As on those few other occasions when I'd been firing on all six cylinders, I crashed and crumbled all too soon. Wanted to hide somewhere and grab a nap, but before unhanding Atwood, fought to salvage one scrap to good purpose. "Until such time as I have more to divulge, could I please have your word that our discussion will be kept in confidence?"

"Sure." He nodded absently. Mind already on his next order of business, no doubt. With a dwindling pretense of enthusiasm, I let go of his hand and thanked him for sparing the time to listen and address my concerns. That's what he was there for, he quipped with a straight face, and ushered me out.

The bewitching secretary had her nose in an appointment book and didn't see me tromp through. After 15 minutes on the sunny elite mountaintop, I was down in the bog again. Resorted to black coffee from a machine in the basement to revive myself. By its bitter end, two rationales for City Hall's intransigence were vying inconclusively, with only a cover-up in common. On the one hand, the government of Occam, like any other organism, whether individual, collective, or corporate, was foremost dedicated to self-preservation, above and beyond creed or charter or professed ideals. Naturally, Atwood and Westcott and everyone else on the third floor would, as Atwood frankly admitted, protect their governmental house of cards from inconvenient facts that might unsteady it. Closing ranks for the sake of the body politic, and their own careers. Suppressing the truth, and deliberately blinding themselves to it, even to the point of criminal dissociation. And could I honestly say I'd have acted so differently from Atwood, had our roles been reversed?

On the other hand, if alien sentience had infiltrated politicians' bloodstreams and corrupted their minds, Westcott's gratuitous hostility became easier to explain. Moreover, I could forget about the cooperation of any infected officials, whatever my quality of forthcoming evidence, whereas their violent opposition was a cut-and-dried given. I thought again of those footsteps that had preceded the change in Atwood's tone, without a word aloud to influence him, and I glumly inserted quarters in the machine for another fortifying cup of coffee, despite its assertive taint of the Gorman taste.

I stifled an urge to merge with the shadows when a pair of high heels click-clacked into earshot down the cement-floored corridor. Maybe someone searching for the janitor. Maybe Ms. Lathrop keeping tabs on me. In any case, false alarm. Nobody entered visual range, but to my chagrin, I couldn't stop wondering, Was it one of us, or one of them?

Ten

I wrangled a personal day for later that week, and wasted a good half of it. In my kitchen, on the sea-foam green and silver grey Formica table, my whitish cudgel of an old portable phone lay next to a double shot of McClelland's. Lunch plate and saucepan were soaking in the sink. I was sipping at my Scotch courage every several minutes. Atwood, presumably a man of honor, had agreed, in so many words, to review my data with a less jaundiced eye if I recorded signs of "crawling skin syndrome" in Wil. Not the most enticing proposition. Wil was infamous for holding a grudge. The Occam General maternity ward and I might well languish *persona non grata* till doomsday. He'd never buzz me through the front door of Dyer Hall, and supposing he did, I didn't want to risk seeing what remained of Morgan. However, Wil might have to mount a veneer of civility if my camcorder and I cornered him at work. Assuming he could still hold down a job. I snatched up the phone and called the Department of Parks. Drummed my fingertips on the tabletop till the automated menu gave an extension for the "Gorman County Reservoir Control Center." Long shot or not, this was my one excuse to importune Atwood again. My one possibility of a friend in high places.

I was poised to jab the Off button should Wil answer, but no, it was a chipper Ranger Metcalfe. "Don't tear him away from whatever he's doing," I prefaced, "but could you tell me if Wil Rice is in today?" I couldn't tear him away if I wanted to, Ranger Metcalfe remarked, because Wil was a mile away on path maintenance. Any message? No, but could the ranger tell me if Wil was on one of the public hiking trails? Yes, he ought to be. Metcalfe came across as an enviably upbeat fellow, which I attributed in large part to his career choice. Too bad I hadn't grown up to be a forest ranger! Before heading out, I finished my drink with the biggest mouthfuls my cut-rate sophistication would countenance. No guzzling single malt faster than I could taste it, even the stuff within my budget. My one nonnegotiable concession to class.

The "Control Center" was a rickety whitewashed cabin with a corrugated tin roof. I parked among the few other cars, including Wil's Outback, in the lot out front. A silhouette behind the screen door was watching as I locked up the Taurus. In case the silhouette belonged to Ranger Metcalfe and he'd pegged me as the guy on the phone, I waved pleasantly, to defuse any fear that I was tracking down Wil to murder him, and with a camcorder, no less. The silhouette waved back. Nobody came out.

The cabin and parking lot lay within a widening of the paved road, like a meal in the belly of a python. The road no sooner narrowed than a padlocked cow gate restricted access to all but official business and foot traffic. Beyond the gate, where the tall trees grew denser and canopied the road, the tarmac ended, and my pace gradually relaxed on the hard pebbly dirt, despite inner churnings in advance of Wil's vividly foreseeable displeasure.

Off the road branched a trail, flanked on the left by a pin oak with a column of red, blue, and yellow dots at eye level, and on the right by a weather-beaten but newly repainted sign. The sign mapped where each color's path diverged and meandered. I hit the trail, calmer with each breath, lulled by the scent of evergreen needles and leaf mould, by the cool gleam of afternoon sun on foliage, and by the surf-like ripple of boughs in the breeze. Scanning no farther ahead than the next tree with three dots, I wished for this first solitary nature ramble in years to go on and on. But then I had to pause and choose between main red-and-blue trail or its yellow-dot offshoot, and once I stood still and more heedful, discussion drifted up to me from downhill on the yellow trail. Quality time was over.

As the yellow dots traced a leisurely, curving descent alongside a shallow slope, the gaps between trees on my right gave onto glimpses of sun glinting off the reservoir. These gaps became rarer as brambles and vines expanded from timid patches to a rising tide that bracketed the path on both sides.

I came around the bend and strolled up to a couple of rangers. The sight of me seemed to startle them when I cleared my throat. The day was dry and temperate, especially in the woods, but they were sweltering in beige uniforms as they chopped and pried up colonies of Queen Anne's lace and hedge mustard from the packed earth. Their movements had been cumbersome, as if their joints ached, and how much should I make of that? Were they out of shape, or under pernicious blood-borne siege?

"Sorry to bust in on you," I greeted them, "but am I on the right track to find Wil Rice? I need to talk to him a minute."

They both blinked daze from red, watery eyes and nodded wearily. As the more sunburnt and lankier of them raised his long-handled spade to point down the trail, a shovel slid out of the slick grip of the freckly, stockier one.

"He went off by himself," the sunburnt man volunteered. "Good luck getting anything out of him, though."

"Quite the Silent Bob lately?"

"Yeah." Then he had a coughing spell and spat into the bushes.

His colleague said, "Must be allergens or extra dust in the air. We've been stuffed up since we got here."

I tended to blame the dust, but kept that to myself. Both men were panting harder than the skimpy heap of weeds between them justified. I gestured toward their harvest with my camcorder. "Tough row to hoe today?"

"It's been like this all summer," the freckly ranger complained. "Every time we turn our backs the trails are overgrown, and it's impossible down near the water."

I vetoed a whim to video these guys. Nothing outright sinister about their appearance or their assertions. I bade them good luck, and brandishing camcorder at their day's work, added, "Thank God it's not poison ivy, huh?"

They seconded that with eyebrows lifted in unison, and frowned at the vegetation they were about to attack. I glanced at their campaign hats hanging on branches as I sidled by. Thorny stems were scratching at the brims.

From here on in, tufts of grass and weedy uprisings marred more and more of the trail, with blades and leaves that may or may not have been disproportionately wide and too brightly green. I didn't dare stop to investigate, and sacrifice my momentum. After a 90° turn, clumps of grass functioned as footholds as the trail cut a straight swath down a steep incline, putting me on increased alert. The breeze carried no birdsong to my sensitized ears. Was this the normal hush when a stranger came galumphing through the territory? Or were the more newsworthy Canada geese only one of many species contributing to an exodus?

The trail's beeline toward the shore continued on level ground, bisecting a boulder-strewn grove of black birch. Prickly, matted undergrowth flanked the path like hands about to clap, and made the woods impassable for anyone without foolhardy resolve and industrial-gauge hip boots. The tangle crested inches below trailside yellow dots.

I heard Wil sawing and hacking a minute before spying him a stone's throw ahead. Like his coworkers, he was deaf and blind in his world of toil until I coughed loudly, on the outskirts of highest-resolution autofocus. I'd been steeling myself to aim and shoot amidst raving verbal abuse, or turn tail if he charged at me. But unlike his more sociable coworkers, he merely lifted dull eyes toward me and kept sawing at a root protruding like an arthritic knuckle from compressed, stony dirt. He breathed huskily through open mouth. His hat was wedged on low and crooked. He was hunching over, knees acutely bent, as if striving for maximum discomfort and inefficiency. The angle of the saw allowed him the use of only its first several teeth, which repeatedly scraped across the ground. Based on lax expression, he cared as little about that as he did about seeing me. "Hello, Wil." I aimed for the kind of peaceable tone that wouldn't scare off wildlife. He nodded listlessly.

"Okay if I record you at work?" He neither acquiesced nor asked why I would, but prolonged his blank stare as he dragged sawteeth mechanically back and forth and into the dirt. I zoomed in on his face, anticipating eyebrows outstretched, scalp rippling, restless muscles distending his cheeks and temples. Nothing! Was the infestation somehow wise to me? Laying low? I went wider, for lack of a better idea, and sick at heart at my best friend's infirmity in close-up. A full-body view of his hapless efforts was equally depressing, and I shamelessly spaced out, and regrouped with my fickle attention centered on the less discomfiting root at Wil's feet.

Wrong again. Through viewfinder I distinctly observed that the root, at the touch of serrated steel, was moving. As best something embedded and insensate could, it was straining to press down, squirm aside, save itself, evade pain. Wil didn't seem to notice. I was about to berate myself for failing to video this anomaly, and with a disoriented shudder realized I'd been shooting all along.

At the edge of the frame was a smidgen of the messy sheaf of weeds Wil had uprooted. I zoomed back to encompass it, and needed a few seconds to resteady my hands. Stalks and leaves were writhing infinitesimally, just above the threshold of perception, liable to be mistaken for interplay of sun and shade, except that the sky was cloudless and no forest shadows overlapped the path.

My initial sense, that the loose herbage was snailing toward shelter off the trail, away from the indignity of being ripped up, proved false. The movements between plants and within each plant were totally uncoordinated, as aimless, as purposeless, as Morgan's had been. The reservoir, I speculated, must have fed into the groundwater here, or maybe something insidious had traveled this far via capillary action from the reservoir through moist soil.

With that thought, Wil's more static face seemed a less dreadful prospect than the unquiet weeds. He was still gazing dully at me while he labored, and he was beginning to drool. This had gone on long enough. I had to effect some change in him, by whatever means occurred to me. "Wil, how are Morgan and Lucinda doing?"

A spark of rancor gave him pause, and brought him upright. "I shouldn't be talking to you." The conspiracy theorist in me found ample room for interpretation in his choice of words. He shouldn't because he was mad at me and we weren't on speaking terms? Or because persons unknown had warned him off me?

"Okay." I stopped filming. What more did I need here? Anyway, the scent of whatever Wil had been pulling, mostly reminiscent of wintergreen and sassafras, had become cloying. Repellant. Identified in my overheating brain with the drooling stupor on his face. Yes, I had to retreat.

The urge for one last look at Wil won out only after I thought he might be out of view, and even then I had grave misgivings, as if turning into a pillar of salt were a real danger. Distance had reduced him, but hadn't quite swallowed him up yet. He was back at grueling work, a bobbing homunculus between shaggy green walls, with no outward sign that our interaction had ever occurred.

The path ascended toward Wil's two colleagues, whose conferring and cussing were intelligible already. I'd gladly have blazed a lengthy detour around them, had trailside thickets left any openings. I cringed before the fact at their inevitable questions. How was Wil? What had he said?

In fact, his body language had spoken volumes, and none of it suitable for their ears, or Atwood's. It told me that Wil's level of debility must have fluctuated according to pattern or purposes unknown, for this virtual zombie unfit to hold a saw couldn't have handled the morning commute. Nor did he act possessed, like Morgan and Lucinda, so much as consumed, worn down, resigned. By something that used certain bodies as hosts, and battened on others?

Relief was writ plain on the rangers' faces at my return. Keen on any excuse for an unscheduled break. They subjected me to the foreseen questions, right down to the precise wording, and had to make do with my off-the-cuff rejoinder, "He's a man of few words, all right." I pushed on, sorry to disappoint them. Their stack of weeds hadn't grown appreciably, and though I didn't mean to be critical, my eyes fastened on it and my pace slackened. When I grasped that I was biting my lip, waiting for limp foliage to move, I hurried along, bidding them best of luck again. Their hats lay upside-down on the ground, and a few twigs and crushed leaves had landed in the crowns.

Wait a minute. Why not recruit these guys to come see Wil's discarded greenery in action? Plus, perhaps, the extra treat by now of a severed root trying to crawl like an inchworm? Show them how lucky they really were. Yes, they were slaving away where the underbrush was rank and stubborn, but not where alien infusion had grown pervasive enough to animate anything. I was halfway turned around, ingratiating smile at the ready, when a piteous bellowing erupted from Wil's direction. His coworkers dropped their tools, and we all bolted in his direction. At the sharp right, elbows grazed the swaying briars, and we recklessly plunged downhill. Nobody said a word, while up ahead, the outcry repeated at odd intervals, and had come to sound like the belling of a wounded stag. Wil had seemed a good ways off before, but in our haste we covered that same ground in no time, and then we were skidding into the blood around him.

Where I'd been sick at heart, I was now sick to my stomach as well, and my companions' expressions doubtless mirrored mine. I stayed back to let ranger emergency training take over, and reflex made me operate the camcorder till sense of decency stopped me. Thrashing Wil had failed to disconnect the root, which I distinctly glimpsed twitching. But when I rewound and studied a freeze-frame, it showed how Wil had succeeded in misapplying the saw between left pants cuff and shoelaces, through his sock, and into his extensor tendon. I lowered the camera, and he was still rocking from side to side, back arching spasmodically, clutching his foot with both bloodsoaked hands as if to keep it attached, and roaring out to vent each overload of pain.

His coworkers strove to calm him, to examine him, but were shouting themselves hoarse penetrating his anguish, and were laboring with all their might to hold him down. They had also to beware his free leg's constant frog kicks. "I think he sliced a tendon!" I yelled at the top of my lungs, without any great faith that I'd be heard.

"We're on it!" the lanky ranger barked, while the other was bracing Wil's slippery red hands with his own and begging, "Let me see it, let me see it!"

As my announcement echoed from the reservoir, Wil stiffened from head to toe and focused on me, enabling the freckly ranger to roll down sticky sock and roll up the trouser leg. "What the fuck are you doing here?" Wil screeched, further distorting his masklike rictus.

"Just passing by." I felt obliged to make good on that. Slipped on past him and toward the water. Winced at briars snagging the back of my flea-market varsity jacket.

"Did you guys have an argument or something?" shouted the freckly man at me.

"No. He wasn't angry when I left," I maintained with qualified honesty, while moving along. They were too busy to press the issue, or, I wagered, to notice anything they'd never expect to see, like a flexing root or weeds. Self-inflicted injury had freed Wil from his trance in the worst way, or had willful flora somehow rallied against him? Were his colleagues going to bind the wound? Or improvise a splint or tourniquet or stretcher? Whatever the plan, he'd be less agitated in my absence. I stepped carefully over Wil's hat, with sweat darkening an inner circle on its broad brim, and his saw, on which a sheen of sunlight vied with a wet red sunburst pattern.

I didn't get far. Performed an about-face. Didn't want it said I had fled the scene of an accident. "Can I help at all? I don't think he wants me around right now."

The darker ranger waved me away. Wil was hardly tranquil yet. I forged on. Two last snatches of conversation carried on the breeze.

"There's so much blood!"

"Nothing's completely detached. His foot's not quite dangling."

Wil's hysterical shrieking overtook me for several more minutes. In that same span, expansive splotches of grass and plants joined up to carpet the path, which gradually narrowed as the thorny walls closed in. My earlier wish to prolong this nature ramble was coming true, though nature had lost its allure, and the reservoir was my least desirable destination. But where to go except forward?

I began to smell the water as the carpet rose knee-deep, with loftier spikes of goldenrod, Joe Pye weed, milkweed. Bridges of vines at shin level forced me to push resolutely till they snapped. Trailside yellow dots were a memory, hidden in the towering brush that guided my course by looming that much higher than the grass and trash greenery clogging the trail. I wanted less than ever to confirm whether that vegetation was misshapen or stirring with idiot volition.

And just like that, August succumbed to November. The foliage on path and off retained its imposing height, but was brown and dry and brittle. It rattled. Under my shoes, against my jean legs, it disintegrated as if it had burnt out. Carbonized. As if too much alien invigoration were like an overdose of fertilizer. Then I was crossing sand that fringed a snug cove. To gain some perspective on the damaged ecology, I scaled a flinty outcrop, roughly the shape and size of a beached whale, jutting from out of the woods to the water's edge. The band of dead brown girded the semicircular cove at a uniform, sharply defined width. The overarching trees still flaunted healthy leaves and needles. This must have been such a rapid, recent die-off that the "Control Center" had yet to learn of it, since one of the rangers had described the underbrush as "impossible down near the water" rather than blighted and crumbling. Here was a timberland counterpart to last Saturday's stricken pumpkin patch or last century's Heroux farm.

The slant of late afternoon sun cast a gloss on the reservoir, and pinpoint sparkles drew my gaze to the foreground. At water's edge and along the shallows floated a fine powder that had coalesced into a design like a series of festoons, and that hugged the curve of the cove as far as I could see. It foremost resembled the yellow pollen that formed sheets on puddles in springtime. But it beckoned me with a mineral glint as of quartz or mica, and its nebulous color shifted between gray and pink and cobalt with every rippling breeze. This modern resurgence of the dust that had killed the Heroux crops and livestock must have been spewing all summer from the lake-floor portal, propelled toward shore, insoluble in earthly H_2O. I whipped handkerchief from back pocket and over nose and mouth, petrified that inhaling fresh country air might lead to lungs polluted or possessed. Shuffled guardedly backward down the spine of the rock, as if the dust could home in on heedless movements. Deliberately or not, congestion had found its airborne way to the rangers, hadn't it?

I twisted aside to ensure I'd descend upon the sand, and not into the dead swath of tall thicket. Something in the woods balked at my abrupt maneuver, or coincidentally tripped and staggered behind its screen of crunching foliage when I turned to face it. Twigs and branches snapped amidst the thuds and tumble of unseen bulky body. And then nothing. I didn't dare puncture the restored silence to ask who was there. Yes, rangers might be searching for me. A deer might be foraging. Or a black bear. Or what else? Nothing that wanted me to get a fix on its whereabouts. On the bright side, for what it was worth, I couldn't imagine Wil had fought off his coworkers and was limping from tree to tree, ax in hand. But it wasn't necessarily anything friendlier.

Absurdly, I'd walked into one of the most shopworn scenes from the horror-movie playbook. Trapped and alone in haunted wilderness, at the mercy of a hidden menace. It would've been laughable had it not been happening to me. On top of that, malignant dust had been massing by the waterside, maybe poised for my next careless inhalation. And because I wore no wristwatch on my days off as a matter of principle, I could only measure time by the lengthening shadows and the increasing ache in my back and up-held arm, for I hadn't budged since beginning to bend over and climb off the rock. Camcorder in my other hand was putting on more and more weight, causing my hand to cramp and my shoulder to throb. Nothing broke the deceptive forest peace, and the absence of bird and insect song only wound my nerves tighter.

Did I want to be standing here after sundown, when navigating the over-grown path became a fool's mission? How long did I have before staying the night ceased to be a matter of choice? I let my stomach's first plaintive squeals of hunger persuade me that whatever had been around must have lost interest and slunk away. I quit playing statue. Lowered my arm and straightened my spine, with groans of relief. Clambered to the ground, holding my breath all the while, and jogged over to the weed-encumbered path. Waded in, wincing at the noise of brown leaves underfoot after ages of bated stillness.

Was my progress loud enough to echo off the reservoir? The crackle of trampled vegetation was converging on my ears in disconcerting stereo. I halted midstep but the crunching went on, and in isolation was resonant with the momentum of a rolling boulder, and it was certainly headed for me, even if I couldn't pinpoint from where. Something too powerful for the underbrush to hinder. My heart rate, already elevated, instantly skyrocket-ed, making me wonder if a coronary would kill me right this minute as I broke into a desperate scramble. Racing, for all I knew, into the jaws of whatever was on my scent. If so, control over my legs had gone AWOL. Panic wiped my mind blank, not that I had any choice of direction but for-ward or back. An animal fragment of awareness had rallied in my ears, as I listened helplessly for pursuit gaining on me. Whether this were hungry bear or human psychopath, whether alien intelligence had any role here or not, had become moot.

Fear had stupefied but not blinded me. I was cognizant of the border between brown and green thicket, of dashing across the bloody, defoliated ground where Wil had floundered in agony, where potent wintergreen odor had not abated. And it did sink in that his hat was still there, red fin-gerprints smearing the crown, though his saw was not. In the heat of the moment, I gave that no thought. With the same blunted response, I processed that my lungs were feeling scorched, and then the steep uphill grade was butchering my knees, and my eyes had to strain in the graying daylight. Camcorder was still locked in my charley horse grip. Handkerchief I had discarded, God knew when.

From over the top rang urgent hallooing. Had I been in a lousy horror film, this would've been too good to be true. I paused for the seconds it took to fill my chest and shout, "Over here!" For that brief interim I listened as well. At the voice of impending rescue, the lurking unknown had likewise paused. Though camouflage of leaves and dusky shadow still hid its physique, its heaving, whistling breaths, perhaps through nose or perhaps through snout, sounded appallingly nearby. After the newcomer called to me again, the whistling respiration slowed and quieted, as if trying to blend in with the innocent breeze. My legs, on their own initiative, resumed strenuous ascent.

I kept the booming dialogue alive, for want of other means to make the presence think twice about last-ditch assault. "Who's there?"

"Metcalfe! With the Parks Service!"

"I'm two thirds up this really sheer slope on the yellow trail! Where are you?"

"Almost in sight! Are you okay?"

Didn't want to jinx myself by saying yes. Vindictive stalker might yet pounce and do grievous harm in a flash. "Please hurry!"

"If you're okay, keep moving! Be right with you!" Was I picking up a pleading undertone? My cramping legs valiantly boosted me the final inches onto level path, and I witnessed my one-man cavalry at full gallop. I prayed to nobody in particular, Please let our shrill voices bluff the thing out of lunging at us! Hatless Ranger Metcalfe was stout and balding and sweating redfaced, and about half a foot shorter than me. A cheerful, intrepid public servant, yes, deserving of unconditional respect, I firmly believed that, but not a formidable specimen. On beholding me hale and intact, he stopped and crumpled slightly, panting, hands upon bent knees.

"Christ, am I glad to see you!" I exclaimed. "But are you okay?" My ears meanwhile were on alert for rustling herbage and ragged breaths. Nothing competed with Metcalfe's wheezing as he waved aside my concern and pulled himself together.

Discipline triumphant, his huffing and puffing subsided as he explained, "It gets dark fast out here. Well before the sun goes down. Saw your car in the lot, and didn't want you stuck in the middle of nowhere. The Center's closed for the day. Just you and me between here and civilization."

Not quite just you and me, but didn't want to correct him outright and maybe pique his curiosity into investigating. Tossing back an anxious glance, I asked, "Did you hear anything crashing around while you were en route? Have you had complaints about bears or cougars, or about hikers being harassed?"

Metcalfe gestured up the trail toward civilization and started trudging, and I followed, needless to say. "No, nothing's come to our attention lately. Could always be bears in the woods, you know. Or coyotes." Yes, fair enough, but bears that pilfered serrated implements? It didn't sit right that something "crashing around" didn't spark Metcalfe's interest, and his remarks struck me as a little glib, considering the potential disaster so recently at my heels. Or did he have his own official reasons to be imperfectly frank? In any case, these quibbles on my part felt ungracious. My nightmare was over, and he had effectively ended it. And perhaps he changed the subject as a further diversionary tactic. "You're Wil's friend, right?"

I nodded. Mortified at forgetting about Wil's genuine suffering while mine had remained in the speculative realm. "I hope he's gonna be all right."

"Those two guys you met got him to the emergency room. He didn't want to go. Argued till they were inside the hospital." We were halfway along the curving slope leading up to the main trail, and Metcalfe scooped up his colleagues' abandoned hats.

"What? Where else could he go?"

Metcalfe threw up his hands and shook his head. "He didn't seem to think the ER could do him any good. All we could do was stop the bleeding and bind up the wound. He needed a lot more than that."

"He's had some bad experiences with hospitals lately. Did he say anything about his wife and kid?"

"He said they were taken care of, and not to worry about them. I think his wife's laid up, isn't she?"

Is that what she was? If that was a direct quote from Wil, he still had it in him to invent extraordinary euphemisms. "Last I heard, yeah. I was hoping to find out more from him than he cared to discuss." And that was true, without putting too fine a point on my motives and his state of mind. "What did you do with his car?"

"Glad you asked, actually." We hooked a left onto the main trail of red and blue and yellow dots. "One of us returned it to his garage, but I ended up with the keys. You're his friend. Would you mind holding on to these for him?"

Wil might mind, but I didn't. One more opportunity for "crawling skin" footage. At my cooperative nod, Metcalfe fished key ring out of beige jacket pocket and thrust it at me, as if to beat any second thoughts to the punch. The ring was hefty with house and car keys and others. Better and better! "How long they'll keep him there is anyone's guess," Metcalfe said. "Overnight, if he's hurt himself really badly. Let the hospital know you have his keys, and they ought to tell you when they expect to release him." They could well hold him longer than overnight, I mused, depending on the upshot of bloodwork or physical exam. In any event, it was a safe bet that Wil wouldn't be driving to work or anywhere else for a week or two.

The head of the trail deposited us on dirt road again. "By the way, what do you make of that gigantic band of dead vegetation down the trail from where we met?"

"Nobody mentioned it to me." Metcalfe was looking me straight in the eye, but that was no guarantee of candor. "If someone had, we'd probably wish it was more gigantic, after all the trouble we've had clearing weeds this summer. It's been crazy. A banner year for 'em. But maybe where you were, there was a blight or a shift in the water table. These things happen." How simple to debunk any element of the fantastic, without half trying, anywhere I perceived it. At this remove, even the covert, snuffling menace was fading to figment status.

But then, as pavement resumed beneath our feet, Metcalfe casually shifted the goal posts of reality on me. "You and Wil work on that cable show about unexplained phenomena, don't you?"

I copped to it, without enthusiasm. I'd been through the wringer this afternoon, I wanted to go away, and I didn't want overlays of unrelated info to distract me from phoning the hospital when I got home. But that earnest, almost childlike glow on his face shone like a traffic light. He was dying to confide something pertaining to the occult, and I alone would listen without scoffing. What the hell, I brought it on myself, hosting *OGAM Chronicles* without wearing a disguise. "I can tell you about something you might find interesting." And there it was. The prototypical come-on! I politely begged off. We negotiated the cow gate at the edge of the parking lot, and I cited a need to deal with poor Wil post haste, but could we reconnoiter later?

Metcalfe appeared to be a good sport about being put off. Accompanied me to the car, where he cautioned me to check for ticks, to take off my jacket for inspection and lift up my shirt, roll up my trouser cuffs. "It's been a bad year for bugs as well as weeds. Scary bad. The jumbo mosquitoes died down early, but not the ticks."

Who was I not to humor him? The Jersey mosquito that had strafed me on the water some weeks ago definitely qualified as jumbo. Off with the varsity jacket then, and after giving my t-shirt the once-over, bunched it up to my collarbone. Was in the middle of asking Metcalfe if he was watching my back. The sentence stalled with an unintended click partway into "watching." In the jungle of fine, short hair above my navel was the distinctive brown and black raindrop shape of a deer tick. It wasn't engorged, but it was the size of my thumbnail, and upon exposure to daylight, was crawling in aimless zigzags, as if drunk or diseased. Mute with disgust, I brushed it off, located its anarchic gyrations on the blacktop, and stomped it. "What was I telling you?" Metcalfe chimed in. I raised my foot. Ticks were often sturdy enough to withstand a crushing heel, but this one, perhaps in consequence of its disordered biology, lay impacted in fragments like dry crockery. "Looks like you got him," Metcalf congratulated me, while acknowledging no more uncanniness here than in everything else I'd been through today.

"Thanks for seeing to it I didn't take that home with me." I flapped my jacket downwind before shrugging it back on, and bared pants legs past my knees in case of more stowaways, and promised Metcalfe I'd be in touch soon. My mental note to that effect was more committed than the one to send thank-you cards to Gerry Heroux and his fellow correspondents. Only out on the highway did it dawn on me that the reservoir, where Metcalfe spent 40 hours a week, may have been the subject of his supernatural anecdote. Dammit! I might well have blown off my most valuable informant. On the other hand, stay on track! I had to phone the hospital the instant I walked in the door. Hours had ticked away, and for all I knew, Wil and his bandaged leg were stewing in the lobby at Occam General, minus a ride home and the keys to his own building.

How many Wils were out there in the "metro area?" Isolated, in the dark about what was happening to them and why? By turns, deathly passive and hair-trigger belligerent? Going to pieces, figuratively if not literally, in their own bedrooms and living rooms, with no one the wiser, and if anyone were, clueless over what to do about it? Melancholy ruminations, but at least they kept my thoughts on track.

The last few miles called for headlights. In the driveway, I opened car door onto dim moonlight and nearby cacophony. This wasn't the first evening it sounded like an animal shelter had set up shop in the neighborhood. A dog pack was roving the formerly serene woods out back, and reasonable to assume it included some of the pets I'd seen fleeing town at the height of the Perseids. I slammed the car door, and the barking desisted a wary moment. Sometime when I had the energy, I planned to holler for Elsie.

Eleven

I was back at the kitchen table, where the day's travails began. Bottle and shot glass and portable phone were lined up and waiting where I'd left them. Poured a double, and crossed my fingers that the phone's battery hadn't conked out. Nope, good strong dial tone. Occam General was on the list of emergency numbers taped since 1990 to the grubby top of the phone. Savored a few gulps of McClelland till the extension for Admissions came up. The nurse on duty gave the impression she was at the end and not the outset of her night shift. There was no inpatient named Wilbur Rice. She transferred me to the ER, whose records indicated he'd been discharged an hour ago. Wherever he was, he had left the hospital.

Resorted to Wil's cell number. Had he cadged a lift from a coworker or another OGAM member? Was he stranded on the front steps of Dyer Hall, leaning with his crutches against wrought-iron railing? I wavered between preferring to reach erratic Wil or his safer voicemail.

"Hello?" Wil slurred, as if on powerful meds. I winced at painful interaction in the offing.

"Wil, where are you? I have your keys. I'll bring them to you as soon as I'm off the line." I decided not to say my name, lest it incite knee-jerk hostility.

"I'm home," he mumbled, followed by dead air. Which stemmed as much from my bewilderment as his sedation.

"Wil?" I finally ventured. "How'd you get inside?" That is, if he truly were inside.

"I'm home," he repeated. While I fumbled for a question that might draw him out, he hung up.

If I chose not to take him at his word, what then? Comb random streets for him till all hours, with no better result than when he and I were searching for his dog? Smarter to accept that he had a spare set of keys, plausibly with a neighbor, and to quit while I was ahead. Relinquish my key ring sometime when access to his apartment might benefit him or me.

In a positive light, my efforts had yielded new footage. Nothing to function as lynchpin for the next *OGAM Chronicles* due in a week, or of what I was supposed to film for Atwood, but with its own merits to boost my confidence when requesting another appointment from Atwood's fetching secretary. The 15 minutes she offered on Monday morning were on the daunting side of soon, which didn't mean I was about to haggle. I had the weekend to cull and rig close-ups of and loop the pertinent clips for a laptop presentation. As if anything else cluttered my social calendar.

No, there was something, and the upcoming *Chronicles* had some bearing on it, somehow. It pestered me on and off all Friday afternoon till the tumblers clicked of their own grudging accord. Aha, yes, on Saturday was the Historic Society yard sale that the brusque matron had asked me, too late, to announce on the program.

At the crack of noon, I was in the sale's environs and on a quest for parking. The earlier birds in their BMWs and Mercedes and 10-mile-a-gallon SUVs were hogging the curb three blocks away. Instead of wasting time and temper cruising for a closer spot, I pulled over on a side street, resigned to a few minutes' constitutional. This was the heart of the posh hilltop East Side of the river, where the last scion of those industrialists, scholars, and slave traders, the Danforths, had bequeathed the Society his ancestral Georgian mansion. The local concentration of colonial and Federal and Victorian elegance handily outrivaled Chestnut Street in Salem and Benefit Street in Providence, but architectural tourism had always inexplicably snubbed Occam's red carpet.

As for signs of present habitation, a pair of joggers sporting iPods may have been West Siders on a jaunt, and a Guatemalan girl chatting on a cell phone while pushing a stroller may have been some yuppies' nanny. None of the homeowners were out delighting in the August warmth or their flower-beds or other portions of their dearly mortgaged properties. The only proof of occupancy consisted of front-lawn sprinklers spinning water into sloppy spirals or swinging it back and forth like a lazy hand with a whip. Turning the hose on was evidently the lowest the aristocracy, old or nouveau, would stoop toward tending their own grounds. Hence I may have been lone witness to the grass rippling in multiple yards, not at the impact of periodic dousing, but afterward, as if individual blades had reflexes to shake off uncomfortably cold water. I'd have missed it myself had I not been watchful in those few seconds before the grass resumed its pretense of normalcy. I didn't bother examining more than a half dozen frontages. What did it say about me nowadays, when writhing grass altogether failed to raise goosebumps?

Among the earliest birds, to judge by optimal parking spots, were minivans and Japanese compacts with Wiccan slogans on their bumper stickers. What the deuce was that about? What could be less witchy than the majestic Danforth pile, a monument to the Age of Enlightenment? Its massive three stories were classic textbook Georgian, with brick walls fronted by a colonnaded portico and a pilaster-framed Palladian window, beneath a hipped roof and widow's walk that sported pineapple finials on the corner posts, and with two towering chimneys at each end.

In contrast to this opulence, the cobbled drive, wide as an interstate, that once conducted coaches to the porte-cochere and carriage house beyond, was crammed and chaotic like a trailer-park junkyard. Oh, some high-end detritus, to be sure. Initially I premised that members of the Society and generous friends had trawled their cupboards, cellars, and attics for worthy sales items, but most objects had a tag taped or tied to them somewhere with an accession number prefixed "OHS." Yikes! Bluebloods as well as "just plain folk," for the sake of posterity and safe storage, had long entrusted cherished heirlooms and treasures to this stately sanctuary in perpetuity. Yet decades of donations had been cast out, priced to go, expendable in the face of worsening recession. Some customers today, wittingly or not, may have been buying back the gifts of their ingenuous grandparents.

A pity, that, though I was more concerned about the spacious lawn, which I determined to be dry and inactive. What a smart decision to spare it wear and tear by selling antiques on the cobblestones, in case the grass recoiled at being flattened with furniture and trampled. How could that not put a damper on business?

Society matrons, gaunt and plump and statuesque, roamed the maze of jetsam, and gold badges with "OHS" in red enamel were pinned to the lapels of their designer casual wear. They hobnobbed with friends in similar pastels and with prospects who ran the gamut from three-piece suits to patchoulied (and Wiccan?) Goth youth to suburbanites in polo shirts to doddery retirees in the drab outfits of fixed incomes. Professional dealers must have cleaned out the best stuff hours ago. Nonetheless, trade was brisk.

Browsers swooped in on carnival glassware, mandolins, china sets, ladderback chairs, deco makeup mirror, wicker bassinet, sometimes from right under my nose, putting it out of joint even if none of these items was my cup of tea. The nerve of people! I plotted the rest of my route so as to minimize face-to-face interactions. Also didn't linger over anything of a bulk to inflict hernia while hauling it to my car. I'd finished one empty-handed circuit of the merchandise, and exercised my rule of thumb to save this trip from being an unalloyed bust: must-have purchases seldom leapt at me from this kind of teeming miscellany till the second go-round.

A wax-cylinder phonograph, replete with outsized green lily of a sound horn, had vacated its corner of an oak buffet table, to expose a stack of sheet music. Wow, the "$1" penciled in each upper-right corner shouldn't have stopped these from flying out of here. Hank Thompson, Ernest Tubb, Loretta Lynn, the Louvin Brothers, Webb Pierce, Red Foley, the hit parade went on and on. Vintage country with colorful, snazzy cover art. Not that I was in the market myself. I neither played nor owned a piano. If any of this eye candy came home with me, I'd admire it a day or two, stash it in some drawer, and forget about it forever.

All the same, no harm in ogling some charming graphics right now. But what was this? It was also marked a dollar as if it belonged in this lot, by someone who may have endured too much writer's cramp to care that it wasn't sheet music. In point of fact, it was a two-pocket folder, on slightly embossed stock like rough parchment, in a lime green that I associated with the '80s. And indeed, on a yellowing sticker, more or less in the middle of the front cover, had been typewritten, *Some Centennial Notes on the Gorman County "Aerolite," 1882-1982. By Francis Thayer. Submitted to Misk. Univ. Facult. Annu.* The left pocket held a sheaf of brittle foolscap in a florid, fading script. The right pocket held a draft of Thayer's article.

I felt giddy without understanding why, and clutched the open folder two-fisted with baffling intensity. A meteor in Gorman County? News to me. Its relationship to lake-bottom portal wavered beyond my reeling intellect, as did the occurrence of two unrelated cosmic phenomena within a few decades in the same penny-ante county. The abbreviations, I gathered, referred to a yearly journal of articles by the faculty at Occam's erstwhile university, on its last legs by 1982. It may have gone belly-up before Francis Thayer's contribution had seen print, making this copy rare if not unique. Not bad for a dollar. I clasped the folder against my chest as I foraged on.

I was feeling lucky. But with walleyed gaze full of the wide view, I narrowly avoided tripping over the paintings, one propped in front of the next, that jutted across my path like a peninsula. I stooped to thumb through the canvases, blocking even more of the way, and scowling daggers at everyone squeezing by who didn't mutter "Excuse me." The art was also trying my patience. It would've constituted a dismal sampling of the "thrift shop" variety, had thrift shops existed when these paintings were new. Terminally dull in terms of color, subject matter, technique, composition. Redeeming eccentricity was uniformly absent in family portraits, still lives of fruit in bowls or flowers in vases, historic tableaux. A puritan maiden at her spinning wheel occupied the lower right corner in a hall where only a dark, gaping fireplace and a diamond-lattice casement broke the monotony. Everything was brown or black or smudgy white. A Revolutionary War scene projected no less ennui, as a line of redcoats and a line of bluecoats at opposite edges of a green plain blasted their muskets at each other, without casualties on either side.

Next! My exasperated sigh stalled in midflow. Overwhelmed by gilt rococo frame was just another drab, mundane piece of hackwork, till my casual scan resolved crude strokes into forms. To label this landscape "primitivist" would be arch flattery. Disturbingly swollen tree trunks with leafless boughs dominated the field of view, under a sky the blue of diluted milk, out to a yardstick-straight horizon two-thirds up the canvas. In the foreground, roots of trees were awash in coarsely stippled grey sand that ended in an irregular, wavy shoreline of sorts, halfway to the horizon. The rest of the distance to the horizon resembled scorched earth. The artist, I wagered, had been operating *en plein air*, because multiple overlaps and overlays of paint bespoke an inability to tell if the alleged sand weren't really violet or pink or beige. As experience had taught me, the dust from elsewhere was of ambiguous color, where it could be identified at all.

My left hand still pressed Thayer's documents to my pulsating chest. My right hand lifted the painting by its scalloped frame while I stood up. A few white chips were off-putting, like bone, in the gilded plaster. My eyes were bugging out, weren't they? I didn't care. Nor did I care when my jaw dropped, after I swiveled the painting around and deciphered the penciled scrawl on one of the ill-fitting slats used for backing: "The Blasted Heath. 1926."

This picture was definitely good for the proverbial thousand words, and they came gushing into my head. Based on my fan mail from nonagenarians, I'd been thinking in terms of a temporarily open portal somewhere in Gorman County, circa World War I and again this past summer. But here was badly rendered testimony to the desolation wrought by continuous alien influx, conspicuous enough to attract Sunday painters, even earning a nickname out of *Macbeth*. Remarkable only that the aversion to reservoir water and the rumors of haunted forest weren't more firmly entrenched! How long had official channels been discouraging reservoir naysayers? How long had that suppression received input from whatever had been crossing the portal all along?

"Aren't those colors just incredible?" I flinched like I'd been busted. A statuesque OHS dowager in coral pantsuit, perhaps she who'd phoned two weeks ago, must have read me as an easy mark. I tried blinking my pop-eyes back into their sockets as she trumpeted, "These days, a gallery would hail something like this as 'outside art,' I guess you'd call it." Uh-huh. Humored her with a tentative nod. A sticker spanning most of a plaster chip in the frame's lower-right corner was asking $30. The dowager was beaming at me, as at a sure thing, prematurely.

"I don't know. Thirty dollars." I pursed my lips to simulate fading interest.

"Why, the frame alone is worth more. When we put this out, I imagined someone would buy it just for that and throw the picture away." That was some harsh subtext. Meet my price or this canvas is a goner!

The Yankee in me couldn't give up on dickering quite yet. I stopped hugging the folder and held it midway between us. "Okay then, thirty. And can you throw this in too?"

Her squint went straight to the price in the upper right, as if the rest of the item were invisible. "It's a dollar." Intoned with flinty finality. As if I needed her to demonstrate how the rich stayed rich. Even when they were crying poverty and dumping assets.

"All right." I produced my wallet, and she whipped out a receipt pad from jacket pocket. Hell, her polyester outfit was practically as historic as a lot of the inventory here.

Had to console myself that chances of any more Gorman County views among the unseen paintings were infinitesimal, because this outlay had eaten up most of my cash. Struggled for good-humored parting wishes as I accepted the receipt and pinned it against the folder with my thumb. "Guess every little purchase helps. Good luck making whatever it takes to keep the pipes from freezing this winter."

She declined to dignify that with the least change of expression. Turned on her heel, on the scent of bigger spenders.

I pondered the apparent lax security while seeking an exit from the labyrinth. Neither fence nor wall enclosed the sale. Did this gaggle of beldams seriously expect the honor system or their hobbling patrol to deter theft? Were they about to chase down perps at the end of the driveway, or even notice them amidst the commotion? On closer survey, however, the perimeter wasn't really so porous. Beefy guys in dark suits, rougher around the edges than the other attendees in formalwear, were strolling back and forth without straying into the clutter, ignoring it, but sizing up the clientele, especially anyone, like myself, heading out. A few of these watchdogs were somehow familiar. Yes, they were members of the plainclothes detail that upheld the peace at City Hall, whence someone from the third floor must have assigned them. Officialdom's sub rosa contribution to the event.

I looked none of them in the face lest that stir their suspicions, and made sure my white receipt was in stark high-contrast sight upon lime-green folder, till I was on the street. This guest shift, I theorized, was racking up overtime on the city's dime. The administration, on the brink of insolvency or not, could always scrape something out of the till to help genteel friends.

Twelve

Believe it or not, I didn't touch Thayer's notes that weekend. Too preoccupied pulling together Monday's make-or-break appeal to Atwood. And as often happens, I foolishly neglected my time-tested, if strictly personal, life lesson: the more effort I invested toward a goal, the more I wanted it, the worse the results.

The enchanting receptionist was less upbeat than previously. Marshaled only the thinnest modicum of a smile, and I tried not to read too much into it. Atwood was correspondingly less welcoming, less collegial. I thanked him warmly for his time and his open attitude. He shook my hand and bid me sit as if he had a train to catch. "Well, let's see what you've got." Today his poster for Méliès' *Voyage dans la Lune* seemed more symbolic of my far-fetched chances than of a kindred spirit in the wings. Best not pay it any heed.

My spiel was well-rehearsed. My laptop had new batteries. I aspired to the most compelling spin on what wasn't exactly the material as promised. The screen was positioned at a corner of the desk between us, ensuring I knew what he saw as I spoke. Opened with a couple of clips of Wil's sweaty, bedraggled face in close-up, to depict his pathologic lethargy, even though he wasn't mimicking Lucinda's squirming muscles or undulant eyebrows. I included the business of panning to the saw in Wil's hand, on the principle that it was better for my credibility than no context at all. Quick-fade to the root at its most agitated, and while that sequence looped for a minute, I emphasized the reservoir's proximity, and the virulence of a toxin that afflicted plants and people with the same freakish symptoms. And whose effects, in reference to footage of writhing uprooted weeds, continued after the host had been killed. Right then, thoughts of crawling, decaying Morgan pushed uninvited into my mind. Banishing them took some doing.

I stole a glance at Atwood, and instantly regretted it. Impatience was creasing his forehead and smoldering in his eyes, as if he were itching to interrupt me but wanted to give me enough rope first. That ill-will sideswiped my confidence into the gutter, but I rattled along to the bitter end, with an impassioned plea to wrangle more stringent water tests from state or federal agencies, if the city couldn't afford its own. A strong finish during dry runs, but in practice, it was whiny and, more damningly, inadequate. I wracked my brain for more to say. Something from outside the box, in Atwood's trendy parlance.

Yes, I had blanked out, inexcusably, on one incident till now. The grouchy codger's rotten fish, those many weeks ago, downstairs in Permits and Licenses! My first omen of malignity in the reservoir! In desperation I fairly babbled about it, ruefully aware that my delivery was reducing a valid postscript to a pitiful non sequitur. But how could Atwood turn a deaf ear to this easily substantiated warning about a public food supply, demanding belief in nothing more esoteric than bacteria or industrial leakage, regardless of the messenger's emotionality? Though as I recalled, I'd done precisely that to the old coot, hadn't I? Given him short, skeptical shrift. Couldn't get rid of him fast enough. I lapsed into mortified silence. Braced for karmic ax to fall.

Unsmiling Atwood pushed at the edge of his rosewood desk, and rolled his chair back on squeaking wheels, as if from too much on his plate. "Concerns about diseased trout might be better served by the Bureau of Game and Fisheries or the Parks Department." Ouch. My own advice to the codger, come home to roost in more urbane phrasing. "As for the rest…" A fraught pause conveyed his disappointment. He leaned forward. "You and I could both be doing the taxpayers some good right now, but I let you take up valuable time, with the understanding you'd obtained more evidence of a particular unnamed disease. Instead, you come pawning off this completely irrelevant sensationalism, something you might have rigged very easily with a few cg effects. I'm not saying that's what you did, but that's the first objection anyone would raise. And what is it you're propounding here? An even more grandiose, outlandish disaster in the offing. The vegetable kingdom is mobilizing? Really!" Atwood's diatribe sounded almost as well-rehearsed as my show-and-tell, as if he'd counted on me to exasperate him, and in that respect, I hadn't disappointed him at all.

I, meanwhile, was contrarily serene. Why not? No mistaking what kind of ride I was in for. Might as well batten down and coast along. "But that's the issue, exactly. The crisis is bigger than I'd guessed, and it's accelerating. So many disparate elements. The diseased fish, the crop failures, hive collapse, the abnormal weeds, the infant mortality. When you add them up, how can you ignore the implications?"

"Because they're only implications, and you can't keep handing me these bigger claims with evidence for them in inverse proportion. As you said, they're disparate elements. Apples and oranges. They don't add up to anything."

"But that's why you have to authorize more tests in the reservoir. To provide that evidence."

"No. Based on the quality of your presentation, I couldn't justify the time and expense."

"That's kind of a Catch-22, isn't it?" And more puzzling, why hadn't Atwood invoked executive privilege and kicked me out yet, as I might have if I were him? The one answer I contrived led me deeper into paranoia. Suppose that Atwood, and Westcott, and Mr. Marsh, and others in City Hall were under alien influence. They'd have to tread a fine line between low-key behavior that wouldn't attract attention, and callous suppression of inquisitive *Homo sapiens*. How else to explain Atwood's gross intractability? His about-face from cordiality into sarcasm?

"Listen, you're not the only observant person in town. What makes you so much smarter than newspaper reporters and hospital orderlies and county agents? If anything, they have more on the ball than you do, because they know better than to blow unrelated happenings out of proportion, and they shut up about them rather than incite public anxiety, and they don't embark on quixotic crusades to divert limited resources that can hardly prop up our infrastructure as it is." Or conversely, if the water were dispersing an alien fifth column throughout the population, maybe that explained the lack of outcry at everything going on, or the insistence by Wil, and God knew how many other parents, that nothing was wrong with an energetic dead baby.

"So please, take your laptop and get back to work and let's not hear about this again. I also can't imagine your sickly friend would appreciate a camcorder stuck in his face anytime soon." He stood up. Arms motionless at his sides. Handshakes would be inappropriate now.

Strange, but as I exchanged a parting nod with the more subdued, less fetching receptionist, I wasn't utterly demoralized. Conceivably I was in shock. Or it may have been the solace of an audacious plan in formative stage, whose germ Atwood himself had planted by suggesting I take my rotten fish to the Bureau of Game and Fisheries. As for why I hadn't been fired by now, alien intellect may well have subscribed to the aphorism about keeping friends close, and enemies closer.

Thirteen

Atwood had slammed the door on any cooperation from City Hall, but the lime-green cover of Thayer's folder amounted to a new door onto parts unknown, for me to open at will. I might even luck into refreshing new territory for the *OGAM Chronicles* due Friday. If my chutzpah held out, the episode might also function as testing ground for my theory that Westcott and his ilk wanted to maintain covert tabs on me, and therefore I could call their bluff to some extent. On the other hand, my chutzpah might not hold out. Or I might want to save it for that audacious plan Atwood had accidentally inspired, and that had miles to go before it gelled.

That evening, while nursing a single-malt aperitif and throwing together my usual inauthentic stir-fry of tofu, broccoli, and potatoes in a cast-iron skillet, I debated whether I maybe was in shock. Atwood's scathing denouncement of my "crusade" still wasn't bumming me out, though I felt it should have, even if I'd seen it coming. My ingrained cynicism may have been paying its rent at last, or was I in the process of falling apart in earnest? In any case, to make up for my lousy day, I resolved to pore over Thayer's folder tonight. After refilling my shot glass with a digéstif, I started on the yellowing notes in the left pocket, but there was scant reward in them. They were excerpts from a very technical report of 1882, rife with outmoded scientific jargon in a fancy but smudged, spidery script.

Sketchy narrative of a meteor impact in the barnyard of an isolated farm, and the ensuing 19th-century equivalent of a short-lived "media circus," and the meteor's annihilation in a lightning storm took up much less foolscap than the enumeration of results and values for "borax beads," "occluded gases," spectroscopy, "aqua fortis," "aqua regia," "Widmannstätten figures," and other oldfangled chemical analyses, if that's even what they were. I skimmed pedantic scrawl in vain for conclusive links to the reservoir's anomalies.

In right-hand pocket, Francis Thayer described those links galore, but instead of supporting what I thought I knew, they plunged it all into doubt. He obviously had recourse to primary sources beyond arid research figures, and flipping ahead, the lack of bibliography at the end was a letdown. But why should that negate his credibility? *Faculty Annual* articles must have undergone some vetting and peer review. Thayer also won points for using a Selectric with new ribbon cartridge, crossing out and revising text in neatly printed red.

His introduction fleshed out what I'd just read. The aerolite had crashed on the farm of the Gardner family, who marveled at its putty-like texture, amenable to gouging, and then at its overnight contraction, to about 80% of its original diameter. Fascinating in its own right, but nothing to bring on that constrictive prickling of nerves till Thayer rendered 1882's abstruse data in modern layman's terms, and began striking a series of familiar chords. Among the meteor's properties was magnetism, which made me flash back to the stubborn misdirection of Wil's compass needle during our midnight hunt for corpse lights on the reservoir. The spectroscope's revelations were good for a much bigger jolt, in terms of "eliciting bands of reputedly unidentifiable color." How like the shifting and finally mystifying pigment of the submerged anomaly, of stillborn Warren, of dust that gathered in reservoir cove and smothered forest floor in my painting of "blasted heath." Meteoric sample also glowed in darkness, as had Lucinda's obliquely tinted water the night it broke, and as Lucinda herself had, eventually.

Further traits were captivating, without any bearing on my personal experiences yet. Embedded in the malleable rock was a glossy nodule, like an impractically large Christmas tree ornament, that had miraculously survived its plummet to earth, but vanished like a bubble on being tapped with a hammer. I made no more of that at the moment than had the professor remiss enough to use a blunt weapon on a unique unearthly relic. Back at the university, none of the solvents in a Victorian lab exerted any effect on the samples, though contact with glass resulted, to quote Thayer's jesting Cold War usage, in "mutual assured destruction," and air per se caused slower but unstoppable disintegration. Moreover, the Gardners' cosmic debris was prey to electricity, as its obliteration one night by multiple thunderbolts attested.

Much more germane to me were developments on the farm after the storm, as compiled, according to Thayer's footnotes, from newspaper items, Gorman County records, and oral histories. Regional lore affirmed that the Gardner fields and orchards flourished beyond the family's dreams into September, in parallel with today's riotous growth of weeds and bushes toward the reservoir. Then like the crescent of plants around the cove or the pumpkins by the gas station, every single ounce of produce putrefied, and whatever retained a veneer of edibility was no less rotten inside. The following spring, Nahum, the Gardner patriarch, found the authorities as unreceptive as I had when he claimed the meteor had poisoned his soil. The *Gazette* (decades before its merger with the *Advertiser*) didn't scruple to ridicule him in print, and I sympathized with his pathetic attempt to persuade a smug urban editor into taking misshapen, discolored saxifrage leaves seriously.

What really wrenched at my heart from across the centuries, though, was the arrival of grey dust amidst the stunted crops and the livestock's bloated cadavers. As I'd already anticipated, the Gardners about that time succumbed to erratic behavior, and soon to caterwauling madness, according to the testimony of their neighbors' grandchildren. That tragic past was now repeating itself in the persons of Wil and Lucinda and unnumbered secluded others, wasn't it?

I was unused to thinking of the dust as a byproduct of fragmenting plants and animals, and not as the encroachment of an alien environment. But that begged the question of how a meteor's impact, or something in the meteor itself, was supposed to have created an otherworldly rift. Obstinately or not, I wasn't ready to scrap the idea of a portal, in view of the planar, doorway-like look of the so-called corpse lights, as well as the calamitous, if vaguely described, end of the Gardners' ordeal. In October 1883, family members who hadn't recently died at their own or each other's hands came to grief in a conflagration that eradicated every building and its contents, save for foundations and a well. Had too much admixture of alien environment with our own triggered an inferno? Affidavits by a coroner and policemen at the scene skirted any hint of supernatural or nonhuman intercession, unless I chose to read between those lines relating how "everything that had ever been living was gone." I chose to do so, and concluded that celestial trespassers had been purged, and the portal sealed off a while, at the cost of five acres under a residue of unearthly dust, whose epicenter was the farmhouse cellar hole.

Thayer traced evolving rumors and superstitions about haunted woods and blasted heaths and blighted homesteads to the meteor and the blame it had absorbed from the Gardners for their farm's undoing. Forty years carried the myths across and outside Gorman County, and fueled those lingering fears about impurities when the reservoir atop the Gardner place went into service. Thayer's collation of this folk material was distinctly flavored with a grain of salt, but to the insidious grey dust he attached more weight. He had requisitioned two phials of it from storage at the university museum, purportedly collected at the Gardner cottage an hour before its incineration. Therefore he could vouch for the reality of the dust and for the sad facts, jotted on a sheet of brittle onionskin wrapping the phials, that the nameless color had faded after a month, and the remnant compound was largely alkaline phosphates and carbonates. Well yes, the powder must have been somewhat "denatured," or it and the glass phials would have atomized each other.

Still, it was the only specimen available in 1982, and under the incongruous heading "A Modest Proposal," Thayer detailed a protocol to subject smidgens of the powder to x-rays, a major "reagent" undiscovered one hundred years earlier. It would be "instructive," he anticipated. And there the typescript ended. No findings, no discussion, no explanation for alluding to a Jonathan Swift satire endorsing cannibalism. Nor a References section, as I already knew.

Typically for me, the more I learned, the more it muddied the waters. My second and third digéstifs weren't helping. Something must have befallen Thayer or the university, which was on its last financial legs about then. Where could I look up whether 1982's *Faculty Annual* had even gone to press? The university and everything under its aegis were scattered, a dead issue. In the sober morning, would I see a way clear to plug Thayer into the next *OGAM Chronicles*? At the moment I couldn't get past his missing pages. To undertake the saga of the meteor and Thayer and his "instructive" experiment without knowing the outcome felt shoddy.

And more vexingly, why had I never heard of a meteor that had whipped up a "media frenzy" in newspapers from Occam to Boston, that according to Thayer had roused such "great excitement" in stolid professors? Pretty much a reflex for me to answer by positing a conspiracy that downplayed, trivialized common knowledge till it was forgotten, to cover alien tracks. But if I stepped into the more sensible shoes of those professors, their aerolite had dwindled into obscurity because it had physically dwindled into nothing. Its composition, its properties, made it *sui generis*, incompatible with anything else in science, and after it had vanished, what could pragmatic men do, where could they go, with mere scribbled notes on foolscap? Scholarly pursuit of the meteor had reached a dead end. Similarly, out in public, reporters and readers alike forgot the meteor when there was no more to write about it. Yes, that was the more level-headed take, which didn't, however, automatically make it correct.

Just before I eyed the bottom of my third glass and decided it was bedtime, I reflected further that Thayer might never even have read "A Modest Proposal." In the '80s, I'd swear it was, that tendency first surfaced among literary pretenders, from rock critics to infotainment hosts, to spice up headlines with quotes and allusions that sounded clever but made no sense in context. Thayer at the typewriter was simply behaving like a product of his times.

Fourteen

In the dead of night, woke up with urge to piss. Couldn't get back to sleep for two hours. Now, dammit, Atwood's blunt edict to stay out of his hair replayed and replayed at random junctures. And between times, the misgiving plagued me, Suppose I'm mistaken about the portal, and the meteor alone is behind whatever's emanating from the reservoir? Atwood might have listened if I'd had hazardous substances from space rubble to warn him about. No, that was bullshit. Atwood had been stringing me along from the beginning, till I gave him some excuse to read me the riot act. Very cunning, these fifth columnists.

My assignment at work next day led me to ponder if powers-that-be were cognizant of when the new *Chronicles* was due, and wanted to remind me of all the superiors I might offend. According to inviolable custom, hard copy of City Council agendas went to all managerial personnel, whether they wanted it or not, on the morning of a meeting, though e-mails would have saved trees and done the same job. The role of delivery boy fell to me, and my stops included Atwood's bewitching receptionist, whose smile was growing sphinxlike, and stern Ms. Lathrop, who made no eye contact while tapping mauve fingernail on the desk where Westcott's copy should go, and sepulchral Mr. Marsh, who seemed to stare right through me as he nodded passively, and the Recorder of Deeds, whose eyes narrowed testily at me and then at what I laid on his desk. Nobody said thanks or hello. Brusqueness as usual, or the slow burn of official rancor at my perceived insolence?

Afterward I labeled envelopes and stuffed them with overdue notices from the City Collector to delinquent homeowners. Pay your property tax or we auction the equity out from under you! Felt like a bastard putting the squeeze on the nouveau poor, even in such a peripheral role, but on the plus side, the monotony of the chore lent itself to contemplation, mostly of the potentially explosive new *Chronicles*. I had no material that would not be construed as thumbing my nose at the regime. A meteor crater radiating virulence from the bottom of the reservoir? Well over a century's history of madness, disease, and the occult surrounding that submerged site? Twitching roots and weeds that drank of the same water as Occam? Baneful dust from deep space whose sizeable beachhead by 1926 was a subject for Sunday painters, and which was spreading today via the water supply? I envisioned third-floor bureaucracy tuning in to any of this, and as their expressions curdled, I grimaced.

Presenting a confrontational half-hour would be inevitable, unless someone else did the presenting. That might mean a different figurehead hosting my content, ostensibly leaving me out of it. Or I could postpone riling up a hornets' nest altogether by extending my *OGAM* colleagues free rein over an episode, for once. A copout, yes, this desertion of a public trust, but didn't I deserve a little breathing room, to regroup, to lull opponents into thinking I'd desisted, to safeguard my income a while longer? As for OGAM, after a few months' hiatus, reconnecting and catching up with people was in order, and extra hands, if only with the camcorder and lighting, would be nice. A team effort, the way it used to be, before the personalities clashed and the fun wore off.

The team, as I should've predicted, had its own opinions. And possibly self-interest at heart. To save time, I grabbed a falafel at Abdul's, around the corner from City Hall, and kept it warm on the drive home by cranking the heat and venting it at the plastic carton on the passenger-side floor. On the floor of the backseat was a six-pack of Spaten Optimator from the liquor store next to Abdul's, to lighten the drag of dialing a dozen numbers. Dining was a futile race against rapidly cooling food, after which I poured a beer for dessert and phoned the Johnson twins. They'd moved here from Rhode Island five years ago, and had lapsed from active membership upon one too many rebuffs of their pro-demonology agenda. I could never distinguish Keith's voice from Carl's, so I was okay with Mrs. Johnson answering, though my long-term memory was unequal to naming which twin she had married. We put the bland salutations behind us, and I tried to crack the ice by asking, "Did you know a meteor came down around here in the nineteenth century? Kind of a big deal when it happened."

No, she didn't, and the ice was undamaged. I forged on, professed how that was a pity because I needed more info for a show about the meteor, but did she or Keith or Carl feel like pitching in with the production anyway?

A pause followed. I rashly hoped that fond remembrances were tilting her mental scales my way. "Pass," she finally resolved. "And I can speak for all of us. We don't hear from you for months and months, and now it's only because you want something. You can't expect a group effort out of us if you have to call all the shots."

"Well, maybe another time then." A dumb-ass thing to say, but better than a whole evening snarled up rehashing whose insistence on what priorities had planted the wedge between us.

"If you say so, but I don't know when." We went through the motions of civil good-byes, perhaps a concession for old times' sake. Well, I'd managed fine without them for ages. Would just have to go on doing so. In hindsight I might have melted some of the frost by asking after the Johnsons' health and job situations and news on other fronts. But I had a lot of calls to make. Unproductive chitchat, no less than psychodrama, would kill crucial minutes. Had to get through my Rolodex tonight and find out whether anyone was going to help me or not, so I could budget my time and submit the episode on deadline.

I disposed of one beer and opened a second. Wrote off that delay as an investment in firmer nerves. Punched in Lavinia's number. I'd sustained a crush on her for two naive weeks, till burgeoning high-and-mighty airs let slip that she was unequivocally smarter than everyone else, on the strength of an Associate's Degree from Kingsport Community College. That categorically quashed her sex appeal, along with my ambitions for an OGAM with officers and parliamentary procedure. Why give her such a handy outlet for throwing her weight around? But for now, she was welcome to throw her weight around in my humble home studio. Yeah, she might like that.

Wrong again. Told her who I was, and she needed several seconds to place me, or to debate hanging up. I skipped the come-on with the meteor, aimed for a casual tone. Did she have any ideas for a segment of *Chronicles*, or a hankering to direct?

She spurned the bait. "No, I sure don't. Sorry to be this blunt, but I haven't touched base with you guys in so long because you're not really a seri-ous organization, are you? I mean, you don't even have a chairperson or regular meetings. Please, do me a favor and don't pester me anymore. It's just not a good idea." She delivered that last sentence like a waitress refusing to date a customer, with implied threat that her boyfriend wouldn't like it.

"Okey-dokey then," I conceded and signed off. Took a liberal swig of Spaten to dull the accurate premonition of trending downhill from here. I ran into a streak of voicemails and old-fashioned answering machines. Spoke after the beep, but no one ever accorded me the respect of a callback. The next live one was nebbishy Ward, who wore black and lived with Mom, and was more partial to horror comics than to paranormal fact-finding. I hadn't finished my preamble when he cut in, "I can't be involved with this from now on."

"What? Why not?" Before the words were out, the reason why not re-verberated through me like a depth charge.

"I don't want to talk about it." What more to say? We took unceremo-nious leave of one another, and I realized that the end of each call marked a relationship severed forever. Drained the rest of my glass in a single me-chanical swallow, without tasting it.

As I had forecast, the following couple of conversations were basically a replay of Ward's. And at the rest of my numbers, machines picked up. I bleakly pictured ex-colleagues leaning over their telephone tables, screening the call, listening with relief at dodging a bullet while I recorded my mes-sage.

Naturally, this new wrinkle in my life resisted straightforward explana-tion. To infer that OGAM's membership had had it with me and my hot-and-cold leadership was perfectly credible. Alternately, I couldn't rule out someone either possessed or unethical, like Humphrey Westcott, enlisting third-floor cronies to research who else belonged in OGAM and harass them via phone at unseemly hours. Pressure to quit the group could have taken a slew of forms, from booting cars for unpaid parking tickets to eviction be-cause of a landlord's ongoing code violations. No great stretch to interpret Mrs. Johnson's and Lavinia's defections in the same light as Ward's. And what had Wil mumbled, off in the woods? "I shouldn't be talking to you?" I set my glass under the faucet in the sink and left it half full of water. In my present jitters, more beer would be a waste. Wouldn't have any flavor.

Coincidences stacked up on the side of a high-level campaign to dissolve my fickle troupe. The theory's only drawback was its innate paranoia. But as the saying went, that didn't prove "they" weren't out to get me. And for a delusion, it had left a lot of fingerprints in the real world. Official opinion had it, then, that I wouldn't cancel my "crusade" willingly, that I had to be isolated and deprived of collaborators and most probably worse, for the sake of neutralizing more potent gadfly capacity than I thought was in me. Not a species of flattery I could handle comfortably. In fact, that seed of defiance, dormant since Westcott's over-the-top rant, was sprouting and hungry for sunlight. Jesus, how much alcohol was in those beers? Would my overriding civic duty, personal risk be damned, beckon as vividly tomorrow? Lives and arguably the fate of the world would still be at stake, but sober city clerks tended to procrastinate.

Fortunately for humankind, my conscience had an ace up its sleeve. I had never flaked out on meeting cable company deadline, and this month it was full-blown exposé of the reservoir or nothing. Down to me for the honor of OGAM, as much as for anything else, no matter that it was currently a corps of one. Suppose this exercise in muckraking did get me fired, and achieved nothing else? If I were right, City Hall and everything else in Occam might soon be grey dust.

Fifteen

Thanks foremost to my faith in the dissolution of Occam and all my dealings there, I had the backbone to persevere in basement studio through Wednesday and Thursday evenings. I went for broke, and had to trim the fat relentlessly from my show-and-tell-all to fit within 30 minutes. Into the waters of the reservoir I mixed, as it were, the aerolite, the poor afflicted Gardners, subsequent events via my unnamed correspondents, the gilt-framed "Blasted Heath" of 1926, due credit to Francis Thayer, wherever he was, and signs of imminent crisis, entailing corpse lights, the exodus of dogs, bees, and geese, the upsurge of infant mortality, and its associated "crawling skin syndrome," with variants in parents and vegetation. Excerpts from last month's history of Gorman County were interspersed, a little recycling that went a long way toward finishing on schedule.

In proposing an exotic pathogen connected with the "Gorman taste," I carefully steered away from blaming an alien intelligence. Didn't wish to come across as crazy, which always happened upon introducing ETs, however logical they seemed in context.

Camcorder atop tripod was trained at me while I prefaced clips. My backdrop was that portion of cellar wall free of mold stains and white holes in the plaster's cyan paint. Beside me, and arching over me, was a dingy plastic ficus, with plastic ivy spilling over the rim of the orange pot and spiraling up wood-grained stem. A gift from the public-access staff, to add some color. I feigned relaxation in a yellow wicker chair, shaped like a punctured sphere, that I'd chucked into the car trunk from off a curb during college in Boston. I rationalized that my unmodish chair remained on the set for luck, despite a need to place conscientious hand just right and hide the missing rattan on one armrest. Seated there I wrapped up the program with an impassioned plea for viewers to write, phone, or e-mail with any suspicions, from the trivial to the incredible, about the city water or any problems remotely attributable to it. Could I mobilize enough respondents to impel a well-publicized investigation?

During this virtual declaration of war on my employers, at this one-way passage across the Rubicon, I discerned a quailing in my voice, and briefly regretted denying myself drink while I was in the studio. I had never dared undertake anything so stupendously and simultaneously right and wrong, depending on personal or professional angle. A craving had taken hold to learn how many townspeople had reported anomalies and met with stonewalling, as opposed to Atwood's more tractable good do-bees, whose docile silence forestalled riots and panic. Maybe I couldn't fight City Hall, but the aliens there had unwittingly goaded me into trying.

The episode's first broadcast was slated for Wednesday, and I was on tenterhooks at work through the intervening days, as if third-floor conspirators had flunkies at Pabodie Cable to check for seditious programming. When the new *Chronicles* began airing without sign of anything amiss, I was borderline surprised. I had also made ready to celebrate in case my pessimism proved unjustified. This special occasion required special measures to help me unwind. From my socks drawer I'd unearthed the baggie of pot that anonymous benefactor two years ago had mislaid on paper-towel dispenser in the men's room at the Aviator. I scraped together sufficient particles to fill a single-hit bowl. Couldn't recall how long since I'd last smoked.

To float tension-free through my best and final production felt wisest, detached from the fatalism that would've gnawed at me otherwise. In my cannabinol haze I sedately bowed to the inevitability of something somehow snuffing out my public-access career after this affront to authority. Whistle-blowers seldom found themselves bound for glory. I was drowsy from my one measly toke, and glad of it, before skimming the end credits that I tacked onto every show out of laziness, though they were now 95% incorrect in an OGAM consisting solely of me.

Aha! Occurred to me then how City Hall had acquired its list of members to hassle. Yeah, the damn outdated credits. Mea culpa, as usual. In my druggy fatigue, I could only shrug. The beauty of a tv in the bedroom was that I was already in bed. An hour before my standard lights-out, I simply switched off tv and lamp and drew up the covers, to begin girding myself with the extra rest I imagined was sorely needed before clocking into the lion's den tomorrow.

I was unaccountably wrong. The suspense that escalated at every ringing phone or approaching footstep grew intolerable till mid-afternoon, and as nothing kept happening, I became numb, desensitized, to the angst still ramping up my heart rate, my blood pressure. The day's peacefulness was in itself suspicious. No hectoring Post-its from lowbrow coworkers, no baleful summons from Ms. Lathrop, no hairy eyeball in passing from anyone on the third floor, and I was up there for hours in the City Planner's anteroom, processing requests for zoning variances. In fact, a studied disinterest toward me seemed to be the de facto policy. Not the cold shoulder as such, but a case of traveling on paths that never crossed. Come five o'clock, I was feeling less reassured by the lack of backlash than becalmed amidst the ebb and flow of routine activity, and Friday was the same. A foolish impatience began festering in me for my adversaries to deploy whatever was up their sleeves.

Even sillier, I kept expecting face-to-face reprisal. Some approximation of rough but fair play. The customary rebroadcast slot for *Chronicles* was Saturday at 7 PM. I tuned in to confirm I'd be equally proud of the show stoned or straight. Different nuances of my swan song, I speculated, would capture my drug-free attention. A minute early, I was sitting up in bed, back against the headboard, with the tv on. The standard between-show filler greeted me, of the station's programming lineup in 6-hour blocks, on screen for 10 seconds each, to tonight's soundtrack of the Turtles' greatest hits. I drifted along with the listings, through Thursday, Friday, and Saturday, till the title of my own show in the 6-to-midnight block jarred me into reading the time in a sidebar at lower right. Two minutes late! Someone was asleep at the switch, I kidded myself. At 7:05, reality broke past my flimsy defenses. While Howard Kaylan belted out how swell he thought Elenore G. was (or was that "Elenore, gee"?), I was muttering about "those underhanded sons of bitches, pulling strings, abusing privilege," indignant beyond the clarity to distinguish run-of-the-mill crooked pols from cosmic puppet masters. I've never been able to hear the Turtles again without gut-level cringing.

For the sake of racking up any sleep that night, tried cleaving to the less maladjusted notion that I was victim of the latest in Pabodie's tarnished annals of glitches. Resorted to that rationale whenever musings turned toward the long arm of shadowy persecution, which was pretty often. Spent three discontent hours flipping between a cheesy history of the Roman Empire and funny animal videos and a W.C. Fields movie I'd loved on four previous occasions. I sufficiently lulled myself into dozing off and awaking only twice, and quickly put myself back under by reciting the mantra, "A random screwup. They happen all the time."

I wore those blinkers of conventional wisdom during morning ablutions and my Sunday breakfast of Portuguese sweet bread and cream cheese, but when I carried a second cup of coffee into the bedroom, intending to watch some news, a blast of static and snow on the screen knocked the blinkers off. I surfed around. Nothing came in. I spared myself pointless inspection of wires and inputs. I knew my cable had been disconnected.

This was one earmark too many of systematic intimidation for me to blame chance, even though it was only the second in 12 hours. With as much anger as angst, I brooded on what a third might involve, to no profit, but spent the afternoon as a moving point, to elude whatever it might be. Groceries and gasoline were on the agenda in any case, and because erring on the side of pessimism seemed more prudent than ever, I was banking on a permanent shutdown of my cable. I couldn't even try getting to the bottom of this bullshit for at least 24 hours. The tech crew on weekends let voicemail field all incoming calls. What to do except buy a digital converter box and antenna, to thwart being divorced from the world altogether?

Down the street from Dyer Hall, a Radio Shack clung to solvency in the galleria filling the Greek Revival shell of the ex-university library. As I cruised along Ellery Avenue beneath the colossal gateway of the former campus, I remembered that the key to Wil's apartment was still in my left hip pocket. But I interpreted the lack of activity out front as bated quiet, sold myself the fib that I might brave a visit on the way home, and drove on.

The majority of shops in the galleria were defunct, and Radio Shack's relegation to the hinterlands of the top floor wasn't encouraging trade. In the archetypal scent of plastic bonding with metal, the guys by the counter may have been employees or their friends or customers. Or all of the above. Reluctant to puncture their social circle, I skulked around on my own till I had the goods to bring over. Of the five guys taking up space, one at the cash register and one idling next to me were creeping me out, through no fault of their own. Their cheeks and necks were puffy, the arm hairs below their button-down short sleeves sporadically stood at attention, independent of drafty air-conditioning, and their complexions under the stark fluorescents ranged from bluish to ashen, with appallingly deep acne pocks. The others paid these symptoms no mind. Were they polite or oblivious?

As the clerk with crawling skin rang me up, I set my sights on the countertop and reconstructed how he and his friend may have sought medical opinion and received a bogus or default diagnosis of some catch-all ailment like cyanosis, with scrips for antibiotics or diuretics or something else no better than a placebo. GPs with a conscience would have referred these patients to a specialist, though the typical weeks or months before an appointment might well prove fatal. Problem eliminated, and with Hippocratic ethics off the hook. The clerk manning the till seemed to have lapsed into a standing coma. The other clerk peeked over his shoulder and told me the total, and I placed exact change on the counter.

Black plastic bag rustled as my purchases went in, and the catatonic clerk shuddered, cleared his throat, and asked hoarsely for my zip code. Was Radio Shack still practicing that noxious marketing ploy? With reflex perjury I volunteered the code for Houghton. He then tried to enroll me in the Battery Club. Huh? Hadn't that gone belly-up in the 1990s, when this youngster would've been stashing baby teeth under his pillow? His peers ribbed him about yet another hilarious gaffe, and he loosed a few chuckles through his unblinking daze. My face must have telegraphed that I alone was blind to the humor here. "Just ignore him," someone advised me. "He's been under the weather lately. Huh, Dexter?" Dexter weakly nodded and smiled. I mirrored his nod, but failed to fake a smile. Were these guys making light of grave affliction because they were too shallow, or secretly too upset, in the absence of more productive options? How many victims and their families and friends were staving off despair with hollow laughter at the unknown?

Careful to retrieve my bag without touching the blue hand that offered it, I nodded again and hurried out. Hadn't breathed a word in there apart from phony zip code, had I? Odds were poor that I'd regain steady knees till I was out of the building, where three more casualties and their pokerfaced companions were in or around the Hallmark Store and Subway and an ear-piercing kiosk.

I put my imaginary blinkers back on at the A&P and the Citgo, confining my scope to merchandise and wallet and gas pump. Why oppress myself with more mental snapshots of suffering, or refine my estimates of how widespread it was, if I were helpless to alleviate it? My self-esteem for the day was based entirely on successful installation of converter box and antenna. At least I could have it out with the company tomorrow without pulling punches for fear it was cable tv or nothing.

Everyone at work resumed last week's routes of mute neutrality around me. This soon steeped me in a pent-up atmosphere where I was extra chary of committing the least infraction. Therefore I waited till midmorning break to call Pabodie from today's posting in the Office of Voter Registration. I pressed the extension for a service representative, and a gruff, froggy baritone, more in keeping with the foreman at a nail factory, startled me. In my shirt pocket was this month's cable bill, which I unfolded while recounting Sunday's media blackout. He pointedly asked if I'd double-checked the reception afterward, as something that might not have occurred to me. Why yes, I had, though I didn't mention it was during the course of digital conversion.

I recited the account number on my statement and he ran it down. Yep, terminated due to "delinquent bills" dating to June. I protested. Swore I'd paid off the new bill in my hand. And did I have the cancelled check to prove it? Well no, the bank hadn't returned it to me yet. Getting harder to restrain my annoyance, to regard this as anything but premeditated runaround, despite the wise misanthrope in me who'd seen it coming.

I struggled to slow my plunge down the rabbit hole. Could I talk to any higher-ups? No, they were at a meeting. Could I bring in the cancelled checks from June and July? No, don't bother wasting your time and ours, they might be falsified. So why hadn't the company sent any warnings in the mail? Allegedly it had, to no avail. "It's your word against our records, pal," the foreman summarized.

I wasn't quite resigned to bowing out gracefully. "I'd also like to ask about a show I produce for public access, *OGAM Chronicles*, that was supposed to air last Saturday night, but didn't. Any idea why not?"

"I don't know anything about that." No, of course not. "But you might want to ask yourself this: who'd you piss off?" He gave that a second to reverberate. "Now is there anything more I can do for you?"

For once, a riposte popped into my head as if by divine intercession. "No, you took back your cable and you took away my show. You want your plastic ficus back too?"

"Do I want what?"

"Oh, nothing. Good-bye." Might as well quit after spiking one over the net. Break was almost up, anyway. And I had time aplenty to weigh the implications of his blunt pronouncement that I was in the crosshairs, and to figure out whose. The second part was no mystery whatsoever. At issue was purely the percentage of City Hall personnel in cahoots, and I had to suspect everybody, to minimize the risk to myself. Where else in my life was persecution's long arm poised to reach? That was much more problematic. As was the question of how to advance my crusade from here, since push had egregiously come to shove, and my enemies were no longer satisfied with quietly keeping tabs on me.

Dreaded going home, and forbore picturing the aftermath of any retaliatory break-ins there. From the outside, all appeared well, and ditto the kitchen, aside from blinking red light on the answering machine. Gave it wide berth for a while, on grounds that it had to be bad news, harassment, trouble, till morbid curiosity lured me in and I steeled myself and jabbed the playback button. Then I had to listen twice to confirm what I thought I'd heard. The voice was neither deep nor feminine. Every so often it cracked, or squeaked, under the weight of age. "Hello, my factotum Castro tracked down your number. I want to discuss that program you broadcast last Wednesday. Can you come over here? The sooner the better. This is Francis Thayer." He entrusted his phone number to me before hanging up. I wrote it on scrap paper I habitually scavenged from work, and saved the message.

Made do with a can of B&M beans and a couple of tofu dogs for supper. Keyed Thayer's number with unsteady finger while my food simmered on the stove. After three rings, a wheezy voice answered, "Thayer residence." Castro, I presumed. I named myself and reciprocated Thayer's keenness to confer. I suggested tomorrow evening. Castro begged my pardon and muffled the receiver with what may have been a callused palm. His accent resisted pinning down. Hispanic without doubt, until French inflections cropped up, along with some diphthongs that nearly derailed comprehension. Catalan, or Louisianan? Castro removed his palm. "Yes, he says Tuesday is okay, at 7:30, please. And he says to tell you, you should eat first." All right, not that I had a free feed in mind. The address was on an unfamiliar street in Occam. He spelled it out slowly, with European enunciation of the letters that only added to the confusion. We thanked each other with comparable effusiveness, promoting an ambiguity about who was more grateful to whom.

Had to grab the spatula the instant I put down the phone, to scrape scorching beans off the bottom of the skillet. Generally an occasion for exasperated cussing, but I was too acutely giddy. Sleep was a lost cause for yet another night, but not, for once, due to resentments or anxiety.

Sixteen

Relations on the job persisted in their unsettling calm. But today I was less sensitive to it by grace of that fabulous rarity, something to look forward to. In a best-case scenario, conversing with Thayer would inspire my next move as heroic gadfly. Locked in the trunk of the Taurus were the lime-green folder, should he care to see it again, and a printout of Google directions. Akeley Street was squarely in the belly of moribund mill district, hemmed in by the river and the Commercial Street Bypass. To conserve time and gasoline, I lingered in town between clocking out and 7:30. The Aviator was en route, and recently I'd been staving off unwarranted cravings for microwave burritos. To be washed down with a draft IPA or two.

Happy-hour office and professional types were mobbing the bar, but most of the booths were open. I reserved one by hanging my sports jacket on a peg in the backrest of the seat, and pointed there while ordering two beers and two "deluxe" burritos from the stalwart barkeep. I watched him as I sat and waited. With scrunched-up features, he probed each customer's face, and though he didn't refuse anyone's patronage, he slid full glass at some with ill-concealed pity and distaste. Not the sort of reaction for which customers would be on the lookout, and these customers were way too self-involved to notice a mere bartender's expression. Was he searching for early signs of "crawling skin syndrome"? And finding them? In this low wattage, all yuppie complexions looked the same to me.

When he brought my drinks and dinner, he treated me to the same scrutiny, until his eyes lit up with recognition. "Weren't you and a friend in here before, having a chat about bad fish in the reservoir? You ain't drinking that water, are you?" I earnestly shook my head. "Good for you. How's your friend been?" Pretty sick, I reported. "Uh-huh." He'd only have been dumbfounded, I supposed, had I said Wil was fine. He leaned closer, and continued sotto voce. "I feel like I owe you one for tipping me off. I mean, about the situation with the water. You get a good look at some of these people? Something bad's in the pipes." He hurried off to his side of the bar and the rush-hour crush. Hadn't left me any hot sauce or napkins. That was okay. From sportsjacket pocket I retrieved a bottle of Tabasco from home and a wad of paper towels from the break room at work. Posted a mental note to pump him for more insights under less hectic circumstances.

Akeley Street lived up to my preconception. Industry had been extinct along its half a dozen blocks for 40 years, and what survived was a blue-collar counterpart of Ellery Avenue's salvaged campus. Some of the brick or older fieldstone structures had been repurposed as artists' studios or offices or discount outlets, and broad, overgrown lots with maple and locust trees on the rise implied the dimensions of buildings flattened in the likely wake of arson for insurance payouts. Thayer had his apartment in Danforth Manor, the furthest cry from "manor" in the dictionary sense, a former textiles operation of the same Danforths who'd bequeathed the Historic Society its hq, with factory floors now divvied up as subsidized housing, according to a graffiti-laden sign out front.

Between the sign at the edge of the sidewalk and the flaking white paint of the brick façade was a trashy moat, the vestige of a canal or millrace from the heyday of hydropower, now clogged with weeds, rocks, fast-food wrappers, Styrofoam cups, scrap wood. Spanning the moat was a faux drawbridge of weatherbeaten, splintery beams. Odds were good that it wouldn't have been able to complete an ascent to 90 degrees in one piece. Railings welded together from black iron pipes bordered it and the millrace as well. A floodlight over the frosted-glass double doors was out, but surplus illumination from the front hall helped me find Thayer's doorbell. Castro established who I was via the squawkbox, and buzzed me into a shabby, downscale variant of Dyer Hall. Hell of a retirement home for a tenured prof.

As I clambered toward the first landing on my journey to the fourth floor, my feet dragged with the ballast of the IPAs, and echoed languidly from the upper reaches. But no, those were someone else's footfalls, clumping nearer when I paused for breath. Strangers devoid of street smarts were liable to get mugged in here, weren't they? Would turning tail be smart or ignominious? With telepathic acuity, Castro shouted out for me to come on and spare him a trip down the damn stairs and up again.

I bellowed my okay and shambled ahead. He was standing on the bottom step above the third floor. The wall was supporting him. How could his slight and fragile husk marshal such a heavy tread? His burden of inordinate age was even more arresting. He was hairless and dark and wrinkled as walnut meat, and into his network of creases the years had rubbed a blackness like indelible ashes. Faded flannel shirt and khakis sagged loosely on him, to reinforce his look of desiccation. And in view of his own uncanny person, his next words, especially in that protean accent, were all the more extraordinary. "I had to warn you out of his hearing. Please be careful to control your response when you see him. He is always self-conscious about his appearance." I promised my utmost discretion, and Castro nodded as if that would simply have to do. He bade me follow, and stomped upstairs with his incongruously leaden feet.

Thayer's dull grey door was open a crack. Castro eased it wider with the flat of his hand and ushered me in with a cinematically curt bow. The congestively partitioned room was warm, dusky, and fragrant. Reminiscent of a greenhouse, or a funeral parlor? To left, right, and before me were bookshelves, packed from floor to ceiling, a mix of hardcovers and paperbacks, but no shiny new spines. Castro glided by. His oxfords' leather heels plunked along a central strip of hardwood floor between threadbare geometric hooked rugs.

He preceded me beyond the bookcases, where LPs and CDs in freestanding and wall units were even more densely stacked than the literary hoardings. In a nook among them was crammed a cushy La-Z-Boy facing an Eisenhower-era hi-fi console, into which a CD player had somehow been wired. Adjoining the recliner was what my grandpa would've dubbed a "radio table," on which headphones rested beside a German box set of Ernest Tubb CDs from the 1990s and a Charles Ives album from the '70s on Nonesuch. "Francis, we're coming in to visit now!" Castro chanted, as if averse to spooking a caged macaw. In an aside to me, with a gesture to encompass everything behind us, he murmured, "Sometimes I read to him, and sometimes I play music." He didn't seem to have laid eyes on the green folder under my arm.

"Whenever you're ready!" Elderly quaver resonated with offhand disdain for the kid-glove treatment. Castro, I gathered, had been factotum here a long time. His employer was in the alcove ahead, along with the single source of light, obstructed by a curio cabinet of 78s in plain brown sleeves. In the diffuse glow I managed to descry what accounted for the overpowering fragrance. In terracotta pots hanging from the ceiling, and crowding a plastic folding table, and crowning a podium shaped like an Ionic column were tropical plants run riot, among which the only familiar genera were orchids, hibiscus, camellias, and gardenias.

Castro stood by to let me through the gap between the cabinet and the hindside of an upright piano. I directed my attention toward the brightness of conical glass shade on a brass floor lamp, but nobody occupied the over-stuffed burgundy armchair beneath it. The quantity of flowering plants, in effect a library of perfumes to complement the books and music that gratified Thayer's sense of hearing, became apparent as I glanced left and right. Beyond open doors of dark bedroom, bathroom, kitchen, dominating random surfaces, on racks across windows, wanton greenery erupted. Watering must have been a full-time job. Pruning didn't visibly enter into it. During these seconds of cursory sweep around the room, no art, nothing of solely visual appeal, presented itself. The tv on a buffet table, flanked by exotic succulents, was smaller and crappier than mine. Thayer had not elected to speak again, and unbudging Castro made me think, not to my credit, of a cigar-store Indian.

At the piano, the bench was pushed under the keyboard, and the dust cover shielded the keys. On the shelf above the keyboard, a token exemplar of sheet music was propped, of my least favorite Hank Williams hit, "Kaw-Liga," the novelty ballad of a cigar-store Indian. This little arc of synchronicity from my head to the piano was disturbing enough, but as my survey of the room continued, it arrived at another armchair at the edge of the lamplight, and there sat Thayer. The weirdness over "Kaw-Liga" was suddenly trifling.

I shuddered, and my folder fell to the floor. "Did you drop something?" demanded Thayer, and I stammered a few words about no harm done. In most respects, he fit my image of decrepit gent, from plaid bathrobe over white undershirt that ill-disguised a sunken chest, to open-toe slippers over stocking feet, to white chevron mustache compensating for sparse, comb-over hair. But Thayer's face held the lamp's reflection as twin vertical streaks between his brows and cheekbones, and they twitched like flames when his head jiggled slightly on his stubbly neck. For a heartbeat or two I could cling to the illusion he was wearing goggles or coke-bottle glasses, except no strap or bows secured them. What once were corrective lenses, I inferred, had somehow melted, spread, and fused with eyes and flesh, blinding him and displacing the skin around their rims into permanent ripples.

"Why don't you sit down?" Thayer waved vaguely toward the well-lit armchair. "Castro may want to tarry on his feet for now." Castro raised no objections, so I retrieved my folder and complied, not without qualms, since the caregiver appeared markedly older and more infirm than his charge. I also had to overcome a vagrant, counterintuitive notion that he shared some quality of his stance with bodyguards and cutthroats.

Meanwhile, Thayer had fixed his glassed-in sockets upon me. Did he retain optic nerves to detect brightness, rudimentary shapes, motion? "Guess you could say we're fans of your program," he confessed. "We catch more of them than we miss. Castro gives me a running description of the visuals, as necessary."

I nodded, realized that was useless, and thanked him aloud.

"You were soliciting the public for information about what's in the water. What do you propose it is? What's your theory?"

Huh? Was he inflicting Socratic method on me? Why put me on the spot? "I don't know what I know. That's why I'm so happy to meet you, Dr. Thayer. To get the benefit of your experience."

His burst of laughter was abrasively strident. "I sure as hell didn't get any benefit out of it."

All right then, I did have a theory, and it had been perfectly viable until Thayer's typescript, whose green cover was growing damp in my clutches, started confusing me with its manifold facts. "Well, maybe you have a better handle than I do on one issue. Did the entity that's become more active lately originate entirely with the meteor from 1882, or did a portal at the underwater crash site open recently?"

He digested that, but not for long, and not with good graces. "A portal? How do you come up with a portal? For Chrissakes, you live in the town of Occam. Doesn't anyone here have any idea what Occam's razor is? When you have competing hypotheses, go with the least complicated! There never was a portal! There never had to be, to explain all the facts."

"My mistake." Saw no way out of adopting a conciliatory position. Good-bye, with regrets, to my own beloved paradigm. "But for the record, I am aware who William of Occam was."

Neither here nor there, said Thayer's lack of expression. He was on to other topics. "What were you planning to show me?" This, I took it, was an instance of blind man's irony at my expense.

"A copy of your article from 1982 about the meteor. Minus the Results and Discussion sections pertaining to your experiment. In case you wanted it back." The combined excess of heat and fragrance was almost stifling.

"Want it back? What for? If I had it in my hands, I'd shred it to confetti. Where'd you find it, anyway?"

"At a rummage sale. At the Historic Society. It was in a pile of sheet music. Was all of that yours too?"

He shrugged. "I donated a lot of junk to those people when I had to squeeze into tighter quarters here. My research must've gotten mixed in. Couldn't see what I was doing, could I?" He indulged a few dry chuckles. At least it didn't behoove me to smile politely at his forays into humor. "I sometimes wondered where that folder had gone. One haphazard sample of sheet music I saved, for decorative purposes. The instrument felt naked to me without it. I still play from memory when the spirit moves me." A discreet cough from behind impinged like a tap on the shoulder. "But I digress, don't I, Castro?" Thayer began lifting a hand toward his temples, as if obeying nervous habit to adjust his spectacles, then desisted with a quick scowl of self-reproach. "On the other hand, our guest might be grateful for a sketch in broad strokes of what brought me to this pass, though if he can add two and two, the essence of it should've occurred to him."

"Irradiating the grey powder?" What else?

He nodded. "I'd reserved the use of the Chemistry Department's fluorescence spectrometer for a Sunday evening. Downtime." Thayer's flat tone indicated that he'd honed his story, through chronic rumination, into its tersest, least emotive redaction. As if to guard against its potential to gall him, decades later. Exploiting scientific objectivity as a balm for the psyche. "I proceeded conservatively, since I had no guide for the behavior of the powder. I prepared a milligram of it in a suspension of purified water, placed it in the spectrometer's sample cell, and exposed it to a mere 30-microsievert dose of X-rays. At the low end of what the dentist aims at your jaw. Funny how you can believe yourself wholly innocent of hubris, and then the world tells you differently.

"For a fraction of a second, the buzz of the X-ray generator was unpleasantly loud, followed by a searing white flash in my face, as a shockwave pitched me across the room. I blacked out before landing.

"I woke up screaming deliriously in the dark, flat on my back, and an unbearable burning radiated like ringlets of white phosphorus from my eyes. I couldn't blink or produce any ocular movements, and a band of vise-like pressure tormented me at eye level. The darkness was unduly disorienting because of its suffusion with a marginal, faint light. My hands shook as I raised them to my brows, and instead of wire-rim glasses, I grazed a hard, smooth blindfold of some kind. The slightest touch of my fingertips compounded the throbbing agony in my head, and my consciousness gave way again. Several times I reawakened and passed out after an excruciating minute, with no idea where I was.

"Finally a state of happy disembodiment told me I must have been hospitalized. The beneficiary of a morphine drip. All too soon, though, the transition to less euphoric painkillers was underway, obliging me to listen and respond when visitors observed me tensing up and groaning as I reentered reality. Campus security, they said, had found me when they chanced to be in earshot during one of my howling fits. The damage around me didn't seem drastic at first. Most of the big machinery in the lab looked fine, even if the glassware had been reduced to shiny slag *in situ* or fused as sparkly bits on the walls and floor. And while nothing was superficially wrong with the spectrometer, its rivets and seams, at second glance, had burst loose, and a puff of breath would've collapsed it like a house of cards. Its glass parts had vaporized, of course.

"In lucid intervals between begging for intravenous relief and my next round of opiate dreams, I pieced together an understanding that my survival had been contingent on the rapid decay of the unknown force I had released. Had the pulse that melted my wire-rims been any less transient, the glass would've remained liquid long enough to flow down my optic canals and cook my brain." Grim demeanor may have implied lingering amazement at his close call, or lingering regrets about ever being born. "In a literal flash, I had destroyed my eyesight and my career, without a shred of data as compensation, since the spectrometer had been gutted. Moreover, thanks to funding cuts and mismanagement, the university couldn't afford to repair any of the damage, so if you were to believe certain deans, I single-handedly crippled the Department of Chemistry and presided over the beginning of the end for the whole school.

"After my discharge from the hospital, the university decided that early retirement suited a tenured professor better than outright pink slip. Mostly because it better suited the image of an august institution. And when that institution went under, my pension did likewise, which is why I'm living from disability check to disability check in subsidized housing. Well, that was Reagan's America for you. Not that we have it any nicer nowadays."

Castro expelled a more disruptive cough than earlier, indicating to me that his job included deflecting Thayer's reveries from treacherous downward spirals. For present purposes, he had pushed the reset button on our conversation, and I tried to make the most of it. "But Dr. Thayer, you proved that the grey powder is nowhere near inert. That has to mean something. And you proved radiation is one thing that can annihilate the alien contaminant. Maybe we could neutralize the problem at its source, in the reservoir, with some form of radioactive ammunition."

"No, no, forget it!" Just as well for my delicate ego that Thayer couldn't literally focus his scorn on me. "We're not up against an organism you can zap like the Beast from 20,000 Fathoms. Depending on how widely the alien presence has dispersed, and on how differently radiation affects it versus the residual grey powder, any attack at its so-called source might induce a chain reaction throughout its range of penetration. At worst, it'd be like nuking metropolitan Occam. And even if radioactivity in the drinking water didn't wreak immediate mass destruction or pandemic cancer in the long run, it might not accomplish anything. An alien sentience somehow arrived here in good working order after putative light-years and eons in the interstellar void. The glossy shell that harbored it while riding the meteor may have conferred protection from cosmic rays, or more tenably, the live entity, unlike its inanimate grey byproduct, may be endowed with some natural defense."

"Then what do we do about this?"

"We?" His nose crinkled as if at fishy change in the wind. "If anyone needs to do anything, you need to do some more thinking. Your broadcast was imprecise about a lot of details. On what dates were the corpse lights initially sighted? What were the numbers of stillbirths in June and July? How much postnatal mortality occurred in the same periods?" I enlightened him on these scores, but he was only getting started. When did the local news report on the exodus of bees? Of Canada geese? How many weeks postpartum had elapsed before my friend's wife had to be committed? How soon thereafter did my friend's mental impairment become manifest? How long ago had I filmed him in the woods? On that occasion, of what approximate width was the swath of dead vegetation by the reservoir? And how wide was the zone of rank, reactive growth? I did my conscientious best to answer, even as it sank in that as far as Thayer was concerned, I was here to be interrogated, that he'd never actually promised to educate me in the first place.

The humidity and the floral overkill and Thayer's acerbity had united to dull my wits, but his drift was explicit enough, and I felt he owed me, in the name of simple decency, the knowledge to sidestep oncoming peril. His inquisition had run out of steam and he was wistfully kneading his five o'clock shadow as if to coax forth any stray questions. "Dr. Thayer?"

"I can hear you."

"I can't help noticing you've organized a chronology. Would you mind telling me what the endpoint's going to be? Whatever has some bearing on your well-being probably has as much on mine." Castro cleared his throat like a bird of ill omen. I paid him no heed.

Thayer snorted through his nostrils as if dispelling fumes. "How many beers did you have, gearing up to face me? Christ, I can smell them from here." If I'd said only a couple, would he have trusted me or else his stereo-typically acute blind man's nose? "No, don't tell me. I ought to be insulted in any case. Listen, if I'm not casting pearls before swine, I'd advise you not to drink the water, to disabuse yourself of the idea you can do anything helpful, and to top off your gas tank and pack a suitcase for a quick getaway to the next county. You won't need me to say when." Pronouncements verging on the oracular! Castro cleared his throat again, with the same un-dertone of ill omen. I ignored him, a little annoyed at getting less than I'd given on the data front.

"Okay, professor, sorry to be overstaying my welcome, but I'd really appreciate a specific word or two about what this alien entity is like, what it wants, and what its ultimate effect around here is going to be. That is, if you're really better informed than I am." In my youth, I'd pretended that psychological manipulation was beneath me. Live and learn.

Thayer stretched his neck toward what would have been a sightline over my head. "Pray indulge us, Castro." He lowered his face toward mine again. "Castro can be zealous in enforcing my 8:30 bedtime, allegedly for my health, but I suspect he's in a hurry to tuck me in and enjoy several hours without me. His apartment is four doors down."

"You are wicked, Francis," Castro protested. "I am in no hurry for self-ish reasons."

"Then please, let me defend my scholarly honor from this little up-start." Fair enough. "Now, to assuage your curiosity, item by item, unless incipient dementia trips me up. What do earthly creatures want over the long run, as a rule? To complete their life cycles, and spawn more of them-selves. The thing in the reservoir is no different. Beyond that, it's parasitic, and everyone and everything that comes into contact with it is affected to an extent. But it's a finicky parasite, and has an arbitrary taste for some hosts more than others. Or if something particular does motivate its choices, we're unable to determine what. Moreover, on certain victims it simply feeds, whereas in others you can follow the stages of its life cycle. Or did you know all this already? Maybe, to paraphrase your earlier remark, know-ing it without knowing you knew it?

"As for what the entity is like, as opposed to what it is, it's been described as an indefinable color, a sensation of burning cold, a wave of hatred, a violation of the will. We have no scientific knowledge of what it is, and no standard of measurement to ascertain that knowledge. Hence your appeals to those in a position to deal with the danger will fare no better than if you were warning of an invasion by ghosts or elves.

"In regard to what's coming, well, don't quote me because I'm descending into guesswork. In Nahum Gardner's era, it couldn't exploit the pervasive liquid medium of a city water supply, so its future behavior may constitute a wild card. However, considering the theoretical upshot of its life cycle, it's 'here to go,' as one of your beat-generation auteurs put it, and when it does, whatever it's impregnated will go with it. On the matter of its lengthy gestation, I'm prone to speculate it left such a minuscule amount of itself behind in 1882 that only now has it matured into its migratory phase, or its homing phase perhaps. And if I were to anticipate when all hell should bust loose, my target date would coincide with the Piscids, or the Orionids at latest. Those are meteor showers, and I'll leave you to replicate my logic. Now is there anything else, before we make Castro cross? You don't want to do that."

"Francis, really, you are becoming too cranky. I am well aware you enjoy few chances to lecture any more. But you need your rest."

Could it be that Castro had taken umbrage at being treated like a cigar-store Indian? "All right, Dr. Thayer, one more thing. How did you meet Castro? Or would he care to fill me in a little about himself?"

Thayer abruptly sat back, unprepared for my change of subject. "My factotum had been on the payroll of the Anthropology Department till the university discorporated. He acted as a guide and an informant in various locales. Do you wish to add more, Castro?"

With a staccato of Oxford heels on hardwood to signal his approach, Thayer's factotum bent close and whispered in his ear. Trying too hard all the while not to eye me like a cutthroat.

Thayer nodded and summarily announced, "He says no."

I had scant cause to doubt Thayer about the foolishness of angering Castro. Stood up and said, "I hope you found out everything you were after."

"Likewise, I'm sure." Thayer then went blank and mute like a mechanical fortuneteller in want of nickels. Castro escorted me through the partitioned domains of music and literature, taciturn except at the door, where he bid me "Good luck." He sounded genuine but skeptical about my prospects and, if I weren't overinterpreting, about the likelihood we'd ever meet again. What a relief to exit Thayer's hothouse and shiver as my sweat beaded up in the drafty corridor.

Down the stairs, and across the drawbridge, I was in a buoyant mood at having navigated Akeley Street and Danforth Manor hassle-free, till I was unlocking the Taurus and saw how the driver's side from stem to stern had been keyed. A crude scar of grey undercoat, a crooked lance, to knock me off my cloud. The typical greeting for a stranger in the neighborhood, or to flout Occam's razor, was this a calculated display of official harassment that entailed trailing me, second-guessing my reasons for parking at that address, and choosing an especially petty means to dishearten me? Once City Hall was back on my mind, I regretted neglecting to ask Thayer if alien parasitism might include possessing bureaucrats without depriving them of their "normal" personalities. But had he considered that a stupid question, I'd only have earned more of his contempt to no good end.

I was home before realizing that I'd been separated from the green folder, and at an absolute loss to pinpoint when, and by what sleight of hand, Castro had snagged it. Who to blame but Castro, since I was never even within a handshake of Thayer? Had the odious typescript been shredded to confetti while I was still in the building?

Seventeen

I was probably wrong, reading a challenge into Thayer's low opinion of my competence in the teeth of disaster. On the other hand, I wasn't ready to write him off as one of those overbearing father figures who always brought out the unseemly teen rebel in me. One such dad, wherever he was now, should have served for a lifetime. No idea why I repeatedly evoked him in others.

Nor was Thayer an ally. Egregiously in it for himself, with indispensable Castro along for the ride. Thanks to me, two senior citizens, at any rate, were on the alert for portents of when to hit the road, the rest of us be damned. People were soon to die by the hundreds or thousands, and Occam might join Petra, Pompeii, and Babylon on the list of cities in perdition. Meanwhile, what was I doing to preempt mass suffering, or at least post the facts where the public could choose to accept them or not? What a paste pearl I'd have for a soul if I failed to muster even a token effort, now that Thayer had confirmed the scope of the crisis. Give him credit for that much.

So I wrote a letter to the editor. Basic exercise in free speech. With the stipulations that unblemished honesty was bound to backfire. That I had to withhold all except my most pedestrian talking points. And that the third floor would vent further underhanded spleen at my disgruntled activism. Unlike our elected leaders, I was, without reservations, only human, and in dread of ugly reprisals, but I was marginally more in dread of submitting to the bastards, alien or not, and wallowing in craven apathy.

Accordingly, to the tune of *North Star* by Philip Glass, and tapping into the creativity in a tumbler of merlot, I composed these paragraphs, and e-mailed them to the anonymous recipient at letters@occamadvert.com:

> To the Editor:
> As a longtime employee at City Hall, I have become increasingly aware for some months of unresolved concerns about water quality in the Gor-

man County Reservoir. Although each concern, taken individually, may seem minor or open to alternative explanation, the total picture presents a more serious argument for thorough investigation in the public interest. This picture includes diseased and inedible fish in the reservoir, a die-off of vegetation immediately around the reservoir and of various crops dependent on city water, the sudden disappearance of Canada geese from the reservoir, and tragically, a sharp rise in stillbirths and infant mortality. Because standard tests for harmful chemicals and bacteria detect nothing unusual, local government is understandably reluctant to exacerbate its budgetary shortfall by embarking on expensive analyses without knowing what to look for.

Therefore I am appealing to anyone with relevant observations, insights, resources, or expertise in scientific fields from epidemiology to chemistry. Please help identify and correct the problem in our water supply, before it proves unmanageable. I can furnish documentation and other supporting materials for every above-mentioned claim, and am reachable at City Hall during normal business hours.

If we do nothing, the impact on our lives, our community, and even the historic bricks and stones of Occam will be profound. The specter of Love Canal may be hovering closer than we care to think. This is, unfortunately, not just another idle gripe about the "Gorman taste."

I had so ruthlessly divested my plea of anything outré that it rang altogether false to me. All the same, I had to grit my teeth in advance of detractors who needed no affiliation with the third floor, or first-hand knowledge of my facts, to condemn them as fantastical, reckless. As hippie or eco-Nazi propaganda. That I would draw the ire of Occam's self-appointed white corpuscles, the lifeblood of any editorial page, was a given. But worth the aggravation if even one reader, in the course of debunking me, instead hit upon irrefutable signs of alien infringement. As anyone would, on dispassionately retracing my steps. Let me save but one life, with bonus points for more lives saved in turn, and my conscience might let me off the hook. That was its best offer.

The next few days at work persisted in their suspicious calm, as if I were skimming over still, dark waters while something big and hungry kept pace below. In that insular, deceptive tranquility, doing my job posed no hindrance to woolgathering, largely about my nascent plan for literally getting to the bottom of the reservoir's secrets, going explosively public with them, burning bridges between me and ever working in this town again, by pulling a stunt an order of magnitude ballsier than a basic-cable broadcast or a letter to the newspaper. I might wind up under arrest, though that was a badge of honor in the realm of civil disobedience.

The third floor's warped, cold-blooded attitude toward everyone's wellbeing, framed as fiscal responsibility, smacked of nonhuman values, even if my sidelong scrutiny of bureaucrats had yet to yield dead giveaways of extraterrestrial traits. Mr. Big Shot Recorder of Deeds, or Edward Orne in deference to the name on his frosted-glass door, was shaping up as my best study subject. When we passed on the stairs, his selective snottier-than-thou vision consigned me to the usual invisibility, and he still reminded me of a woodchuck. Otherwise he was becoming a different, lesser person. His pumpkin-colored suit fit him loosely, as if suspended on a wire hanger. Within flapping sleeves and trouser legs, his bearing was rheumatic, almost herky-jerky. Prematurely decrepit by a decade or two. His features were indrawn as with malnutrition, and his complexion bluish and grey and riddled with pockmarks, like the kid's at Radio Shack. But unlike that kid, he carried himself with no air of victimhood. Was he sustaining an iron sense of entitlement despite, or with the collusion of, arrogant cosmic parasite? In any case, he wasn't the kind of fond acquaintance whose health I, or anyone, would choose to ask after.

Wednesday evening, the one exception to spam in my e-mail was from an Alijah Hutchinson, so-called Content Editor at the *Advertiser*. Expressing perfunctory thanks for my submission. Without comment on what I had to say, but with instructions to say it in 37 fewer words, to accommodate their 200-word limit. And to tone down the sophisticated language, e.g., "exacerbated," "epidemiology," and "specter," for their average readership's eighth-grade education. None of this struck me like a bolt from the blue, though "specter" was too high-falutin'? Really? Was the *Advertiser* adapting to a decline in literacy, or contributing to it? I could argue, or I could dilute my message just enough to make the op-ed grade and stand some slim chance of helping people. I plugged away at an abridged version a couple of hours, and attached it as a Word document to a note thanking Hutchinson for his generous advice. A show of specious gratitude, operating on the premise that hypocrisy makes the world go 'round. And now I was good to go, right?

Even that cynically leavened optimism proved erroneous. I checked too soon for the letter Thursday and Friday in newspapers lying around City Hall. And then on Saturday and Sunday at gas station newsstands, buying a few gallons each time to excuse rifling through an *Advertiser*'s Editorial section. Forewarned was forearmed, I rationalized, and I didn't want to be the last man at City Hall to know when my screed had gone to press. But could I really brace myself for the third floor's reaction? Only now was it sinking in that the orchestrators of this cover-up might not rest content with firing me, that I was still playing a game where everyone else might be playing for keeps.

On Monday my rural gas stations were closed because it was Labor Day, and I had to shell out for a newspaper in town at the bus station. Waste of a half hour and a dollar. Good, I initially thought, I could clock in tomorrow without jitters in advance over what my employers had read today. Conversely, the delay in publishing me hadn't seemed excessive till I had this whole idle day to dwell on it. The tentacles of conniving authority had shut down my cable tv venue. As for an inside man at the *Advertiser*, hadn't some relative of the Deputy Mayor written that fluff piece about hive collapse and crop failure? Ephraim Atwood, wasn't it? Blindsiding City Hall from any direction was assuming the aura of a pipe dream. Official displeasure, though, had been slow to ignite if Ephraim had informed on me. With mixed success, I tried adhering to the wisdom that brooding on the unforeseeable would solve nothing.

In the morning, typical of Tuesdays after a long weekend, a collective laissez-faire prevailed. Hence nobody batted an eyelash when my personal call during 10 o'clock break went into extra minutes on hold, before a flesh-and-blood larynx at the *Advertiser* answered, "City Room." The voice sounded no more organic than the robot's that listed menu options, but now background bustle and chatter were audible. I gave my name and explained, with imperfect candor, that Alijah Hutchinson had okayed my letter to the editor for publication, and was it slated to run on any particular day?

"We have nothing from you." The City Room was somewhat too quick on the uptake with that. I'd seen this coming, but it still knocked the stuffing out of me.

"Are you positive? Alijah Hutchinson and I exchanged e-mails on Wednesday, and everything was on track at that point."

"Wednesday? Nope, I'm looking at what's supposed to go in for the next 10 days. Nothing by Joseph Slater."

"It's Jeffrey Slater."

"Still nothing. If you sent it last Wednesday and it's not going to press by next Wednesday, then it never will. No e-mails from you in the system either. Sorry."

I bet he was. "Well, is Alijah Hutchinson available, please?"

"He won't be in till tonight."

"I'm not speaking to Ephraim Atwood, am I?"

"Nope. Do you want me to transfer you?"

Oh hell no. Aloud, I demurred with hastily counterfeited tact. Proffered hollow thanks and got off the line. My ears were burning. What was that adage? Fool me twice, shame on me? Outflanked so handily again! Whether or not the cloud of intrigue in which I labored was halfway imaginary, I was priming myself to ignore snickering from behind coworkers' hands, mean-spirited Post-its cropping up everyplace like mildew. In fact, the impersonal hours plodded by the same as during the last two weeks. Which was cause for misgivings right there, in my overwound state of mind.

Back home, I put on the tv to dispel the ominous vibes that had dogged me from City Hall. Frying up hash browns and a cheddar omelet in cast-iron pans mercifully compounded the distracting noise. I sat at the foot of the bed and ate, spacing out to an episode of *It Takes a Thief* on some retro digital channel. The clatter of washing the dishes was another calming influence, and as I plunked the last utensil into the drying rack and turned off the tap, the rear doorbell rang. Who the hell? I debated that, unproductively. From here, the swinging '60's chase music in the bedroom had a funneled, tinny quality. The doorbell's subsequent silence began to convince me that the ringing was entirely in my ears, an aftereffect of running the faucet or banging cookware together. I toweled my hands dry and clutched the dishrag as if it might protect me. Peeked past the muslin curtain over the window beside the back door. Nobody. Neither on the stoop nor in the driveway. But someone had sprinkled glitter or sugar on and around my car.

I opened and closed the door behind me in slow motion, to deaden any creaks or clicks. My skittish survey hither and yon bore out gut feeling that the area was deserted. My field of vision narrowed to the car, and all the sparkles rudely shed their implicit magic. Nothing magical here, aside from my uninvited callers' disappearing act. Every unit of automotive glass, the windshield, the rear and side windows, even the mirror above the door handle, had been smashed into transparent imitations of baby teeth. Relatively few lay on the hood and trunk and pavement. Most were inside, on the dashboard, seats, and floor. My foolish, angry hands were striving to wring out damp dishrag, and I had to restrain them.

Just as well I hadn't gotten wind of vandalism and charged outside on the impulsive warpath. I couldn't have hindered the damage, but I would've become a part of it. The professionals behind this stealth destruction probably needed nothing beyond their little fingers to inflict grievous bodily harm. Furthermore, if they were setting an ambush after all, I might well loiter here stupidly till it was too late. Yikes! I spun around, probing the darkness left, right, fore, and aft. Nobody. The thugs' assignment must have been to leave a message, and they had.

Into my head popped the cable-company rep's needling question after Pabodie had disconnected me. Who'd I piss off? The answer was plain as ever, and brought to mind those City Hall goons moonlighting at the Historic Society yard sale. I pondered why they'd mobilized on an anticlimactic Tuesday rather than Monday night, which would've begun my workweek on a miserable note. But that would've meant working on Labor Day, and these were Yankees holding the purse strings, weren't they? Third-floor patricians may have been ruthless, but they were simply too cheap to splurge on holiday pay. Thereby adding to my injury the insult that I wasn't worth those extra dollars. With damp dishcloth I mechanically swabbed at fragments on the driver's seat. Not very efficient. I flung the cloth over the roof of the car and went back in the house.

Remarkably, I enjoyed a full, refreshing night's rest. The prospects of dealing with my busted-up car made for one stressor too many, and pushed my brain into shorting out and shutting down, till the 7 AM alarm went off.

Eighteen

I clocked in a minute early, despite fastidious purge of every window fragment in, around, and under the car after breakfast. I donned work gloves and
wielded whiskbroom, dustpan, and push broom against most of it, and sicced a
Dirt Devil on stubborn shiny grains and dust. Arrival at City Hall was further
delayed because I didn't want to hand any alien bureaucrats the satisfaction of
gloating at my incomplete Taurus, so it went into expensive seclusion in a parking garage, six blocks away. Where it was also less vulnerable to ticketing by
meter maids intolerant of missing windshields. Contemplated what to do about
replacement glass, while the morning trundled by as if nobody on the premises
had ever directed malice, or the least thought, at me. Leaving the car overnight
for repairs and walking home, and into town again tomorrow, was not an option. Especially when keys to another vehicle had been clogging my hip pocket
for weeks.

Up in oyster-like Mr. Marsh's musty vault of an office, I was filing 6
months of receipts for recycling and other city services doled out to private
contractors. Mr. Marsh was at a meeting till noon. I could use his phone
with impunity, and I had more than one reason to call Ranger Metcalfe at
Parks and Recreation.

Based now on two occasions in total, I decided that Ranger Metcalfe
always picked up the phone at the reservoir Control Center, and that he was
always chipper. Still, I erred on the side of caution and asked if I'd reached
whom I thought I had.

"Yes, this is he. Just call me Herb, okay? And you're Wil's friend,
right? We really need to talk."

"Why, what's up?" Suddenly the dynamic had flipped and it felt like
he'd rung me. Might as well play along with it.

"Wil hasn't come back to work yet. We're trying to get him on

128

Workmen's Comp because he's apparently suffering complications from his injury and he's run out of sick time, but we can't even persuade him to make a doctor's appointment. He let us in to drop off groceries a few times, but he stopped answering the phone and the doorbell several days ago. You have a house key, don't you?"

Jesus, what a sorry schmuck I'd become in the last 30 seconds. Herb referred to me as Wil's friend, a title he and his coworkers much more richly deserved than I ever would. All the same, how pleasing to hear him volunteer the info I'd been preparing to wheedle out of him. Wil's car was up for grabs. "Yeah, I've held on to his keys. Have 'em on me, actually."

Herb didn't want to trouble me, but could I possibly front some items at the market that Wil might be out of, and put them away in his kitchen?

I agreed without hesitation, though that made me twice as shameless a heel, since my own ulterior reasons to visit Wil were uppermost in mind. "And what about baby food or diapers for Morgan? How is he doing?"

"Morgan?" Herb was sounding flummoxed, and I kicked myself for complicating matters. "Nobody in there but Wil."

"Sorry, my mind was elsewhere a second. My mistake. Can you read me that grocery list?" I managed to scribble most of the order on a sheet of Xerox paper from a desk drawer, though between my ears, wheels within wheels were spinning. Herb was hoping I could let him know what shape Wil was in, and I suggested doing so at the Aviator tomorrow evening, where he could also relate that paranormal story he'd brought up at the reservoir last month. Who could say but that it mightn't give me a segue for inveigling him into my coalescing master plan?

My subpar ethics were turning into this Wednesday's leitmotif. Finished my filing a little shy of twelve o'clock, and snuck out early in case I needed a 70-minute lunch hour to get everything done. Hoofed it to the parking garage, and removed the car to an auto glass specialist without running afoul of traffic enforcement. A compact, toothy salesman in red jumpsuit promised, zealously and ambiguously, that in 24 hours I'd never be able to tell the car had been fixed. Had to hope his crew wouldn't include the two guys out front, on the precarious verge of sliding feebly off their bench. They could have been flimsy papier-mâché statues inside grimy

examples of company jumpsuit. Their complexions seemed uniformly suffused with faded blue ink, and a moment went by before one of them
yawned as proof of life.

Lunch hour was in peril of going into extra minutes after as well as before, with nothing in my stomach to show for it. But in for a penny, in for a
pound. Trotted over to Dyer Hall and found the signal on Wil's keychain to
raise the groaning portcullis of adjoining cinderblock garage. Time was at a
premium, and hunger was consuming my patience. Thus I excused my neg-
ligence in neither checking on Wil nor procuring his permission before bor-
rowing the Outback. Mockingly, a white paper bag from Subway was sitting
shotgun beside me, but its contents had festered so long in this stuffy, black-
upholstered oven that I loutishly poked it with an ice scraper out the passenger door. My appetite went with it. In the windshield was the ghastly
reflection of a dozen dead flies on top of the dashboard. Flicked them out
toward the bag with the brush end of the scraper. Driving with the windows
down should have done more to freshen the air, but plenty of stink lingered
to prevent my hunger from reviving, all the way to my expensive parking
space six blocks from City Hall. A blessing of sorts, since I didn't slip back
in till quarter past one, and eating something would've added at least 15
minutes to that.

Like most downtowns nowadays, Occam proper hosted no supermarkets, so Wil's groceries called for a round trip to suburbia during rush hour.
Preferable, still, to the exorbitance of renting a car. And didn't I owe Wil
whatever was requested of me? At the A&P, same as last market day, I
adopted tunnel vision, except to certify that strictly human clerks were on
duty at the meat counter and the checkout lane. In the Outback, the odor of
rotting grinder had subsided, and resurgent hunger nagged me into chomping down part of my putative supper, an A&P deli chopped liver on pump,
while on the road.

I pulled up in front of Dyer Hall. Rewrapped and rebagged the uneaten
portion of my chopped-liver pick-me-up, and laid it on the relatively un-
tainted driver's seat. Finessed my two paper sacks of foodstuffs into the
building. Lugging clumsy load upstairs engaged me, thank God, to the exclusion of dwelling on what waited inside the apartment.

I fumbled key into lock and elbowed in as if I lived there. Damn, but it was dark. Had I been the rightful, more knowledgeable occupant, I could have made straight for the wall switch instead of dallying while my sight adjusted, and the bags gained painful weight, and my nose wrinkled at worse spoilage than in the car. Definitely, leave the door open. Most unnerving, though, was the silence, deathly as the void, intimating that no one was alive here. Or at least that watchful eyes belonged to unnatural masters of concealment.

I strained to identify a potentially dangerous bulk, with several humps surmounting its outline, commanding the middle of the room like a Loch Ness monster. Okay, merely the brown leather sofa, of course, and at the nearer end, a squat lamp upon side table. Three steps forward, and the lamp's pull cord was practically in reach. But what the hell was that grit underfoot? Almost miraculously, I managed to bend at the waist and hug the groceries together and pincer the cord between two fingers. Didn't dare shut my eyes against the initial sting of illumination, nor relax just because nothing rushed at me or moved. Noted in passing, en route to the kitchen, that no light seeped from beneath the closed bedroom door, and that someone, presumably Herb or another ranger, had started tidying up. Dirty laundry, frozen-food trays, broken cups and dishes, dog toys, and mangled paperbacks and mail-order catalogues formed loose jumbles in neutral corners. And the grit? Had pulverized glass from the Taurus somehow preceded me here? If only! No, revulsive grey powder radiated in irregular crescents like multiple high-water lines across varnished hardwood and faux Persian rug, with unequivocal ground zero in the bedroom. Free of shoeprints or signs of sweeping. All of it must have emerged after the last Parks Department visit.

Dimmer switch for kitchen track lighting was right beside the doorway, where my elbow could nudge it. No dust on the green linoleum, and no presence waiting to pounce. However, even with back door in plain view, and black garbage bag in front of it posing no real obstacle, I felt trapped, anxious to brush crumpled soda cans from sticky counter into the sink, to set down and put away the provisions, and get going. Spotty cleanup by rangers must have predated the black marble island's open bag of Fritos and gutted package of hotdogs. Who but Wil would have clawed through the plastic and gouged the center from the two upper rows of franks? Mindfully held my breath in the vicinity of the island while emptying grocery bags into the refrigerator and cupboards that didn't really need restocking. Crammed everything in with escalating carelessness, and blamed my fluttering heart for leaving mauled frankfurters where they lay and racing from the kitchen.

Pressed the dimmer switch in passing, but was jumpy enough to dismiss turning off the table lamp as an idle gesture. The brightness of open doorway onto the corridor lured me like an unprincipled moth, until the mute bedroom door stopped me cold. Was Wil in there? Was he alive? All my noise in the kitchen would have given me away if he'd been eager and able to attack. And I'd be off on the wrong foot, to put it mildly, showing up at the Aviator minus a report for Herb on my friend's status. "Wil?" Thirty seconds ticked by on my wristwatch. Please don't make me try the door! "Wil?" Ten more seconds elapsed.

"Let me the fuck alone!" What stupendous relief to lower my hand from the doorknob, even as I recoiled from the gurgling, grating distortion that slurred his speech, as if bronchial passages were flooding and abrading at the same time.

Courage to broach the next logical question sprang from the predictability of his response. "Can I come in?"

"No! Go away!"

"I brought you some groceries and put them away for you."

"Don't want anybody here. Fuck off!"

"How's Morgan, Wil? Is he in there with you? Do you need me to get anything for him?"

"No! Nothing, nothing!"

"Okay then. But can I borrow your car overnight? Mine's at the shop right now." Permission may have been a moot point, but going through the motions at least paid my conscience some token respect.

The proposition seemed to stump him. Too much to process? In any case, his mind jumped the track. "Do you see Elsie around? Is she getting into the trash again?"

"No." Couldn't bring myself to say more. On the sudden verge of tears at hearing stray elkhound's name again, and gauging from its context the depth of Wil's derangement. On impulse, I grabbed and twisted the doorknob. Locked.

"Get out!" Wil screeched, with a jarring resonance, as if his voice box had mastered the overtones of a dog whistle. I got out. Wondering, since I'd never identified myself, had he ever realized or cared who I was?

I unlocked the Outback. Plucked the bag of my leftovers off the seat, sat down, and put the bag on my lap. Did I want to finish noshing this minute? A whiff of chopped liver stirred up newfound associations with rancid hotdogs and worst-case visions of Wil's physical breakdown, and would have made me vomit if not for my snap decision to dump the bag in the gutter.

Nineteen

O f all the things that might have scuttled sleep that night, it had to be the silliest. Too often to reckon, unrefreshing slumber gave way to remorse about the lamp I'd wastefully left burning beside Wil's sofa. But maybe fixating on worries less trivial would've broken the bank of my coping skills, particularly during the small hours. Told myself I'd make amends tomorrow, short of plotting how, exactly.

And I was good as my word, during a second protracted lunch hour that raised no eyebrows, fortifying my impression of employers feeding me enough rope and adding up infractions on a pink slip. Retrieved the Outback from outdoors municipal parking on Commercial Street, replaced it in Dyer Hall's garage, and before trotting to the repair shop and reclaiming the Taurus, let myself into Wil's condo for the express purpose of dousing the lamp, and as long as I was there, testing whether he felt more verbal, or (at the apex of my wishful thinking) more social, not as far gone as I visualized.

He was dramatically worse. Neither grey dust nor living-room middens betrayed activity since yesterday, and bedroom door, impassive and impassable, still rebuffed me. I didn't reenter the kitchen. To prevent the same oversight two afternoons running, I immediately tended to the lamp. The room fell into oppressive darkness, despite open doorway onto the corridor. Drapes had sealed out noon sunshine, and sealed in the squalor of sick, unwashed flesh and ripening garbage. Softly, then personably, then sternly calling Wil from the prudent distance of the sofa accomplished nothing. Each rank intake of breath boosted my heart nearer my throat as I stole up to the bedroom door. I rapped timidly, and after a pregnant moment, more smartly.

The door never opened, but something lashed out at me from the other side, like a choppy wave knocking me off-balance, backward into the sofa.

Earsplitting, ongoing scream restated, less articulately but more forcibly, Wil's hateful warning yesterday to get out. It was harsher as if saturated with bloodlust, as if he meant to hurt me with it, or murder me if only that were possible. Adding to its nastiness, that overtone of dog whistle, without words or any human inflection to mask it, came through louder and clearer today, inflicting vertigo. And something else in the discord brought back to mind an August evening in front of this building, when someone whom I'd prayed was not Lucinda screamed with equally inexhaustible lungs and almost subliminal shifts and gaps between pitches and vowels, as if code were embedded in the hysteria.

To stay and listen was intolerable, but some new texture in the sonic assault made me pause. God, yes, two voices, and not one, were targeting me, and the second was thinner and trebly, like a sickly infant's. No match for Wil's lung capacity, but piercing all the same. Morgan resurrected, or simply the vessel of his corpse recycled, as by a hermit crab? I beat a panicky retreat.

Nobody was up in arms, or even spying through cracks in doorways, at the vocal torrent spilling into the corridor. An assortment of neighbors too inured, too spooked, or too ill themselves, after a summer of officially debunked tribulations? Locking up the apartment did, by way of small mercy, lock in most of the decibels. Thankfully, I didn't see or hear anything else in the building to alter my perception of hurrying from a deserted mausoleum.

Though I knew the outcome all along, I wrestled till five o'clock with the quandary of what to do about Wil and Morgan. I was too remorseful to admit outright that I wouldn't lift a finger for them simply because they'd been parasitized beyond anyone's power to help them. No personality or soul to salvage. Even less defensibly, I couldn't afford to let Herb, my lone ally, deal with anything except executing my plan, with its potential to achieve the much greater good. Suppose we did break down Wil's bedroom door? What then but to phone the ambulance and consign the godforsaken bodies within to oblivion in a hospital instead of their home? No good would come of it, not to Wil or to us. More rational for Herb and me to operate below the radar, and keep our names out of hospital and police logs.

Whittled away an hour at the residually Deco, dirt-cheap Koerner's A Lunch. That was the name on the flaking sign dangling over the sidewalk. Another ornery holdout of the "Old Occam," off Commercial Street, between the padlocked former addresses of a credit union and a law firm. Took a gamble on the corned beef hash, though it didn't always sit peaceably. While I was dining, an ancient drunk wobbled up to the chrome counter, and the owner, a stout, balding Greek, slid him a doughnut and coffee, surreptitiously, as if reluctant to come across as a softie and encourage more moochers. The owner also wiped down all the white enamel tabletops with industrial-strength bleach before I was finished eating, as if to handicap my appetite. He locked the door after me. After the citywide scourge, this would be one place I'd wish I had patronized more often, despite the first flutters of indigestion in five minutes.

Be that as it may, selfish of me to fend for myself and condemn Herb to the Aviator's bill of fare, but I just couldn't hack a microwave burrito tonight. Hell, between manipulating and deceiving him, our relationship was already on a rocky course. Parked right about where Recorder of Deeds Edward Orne would have landed upon ejection those many weeks ago, at the corner, within spitting distance of the Aviator's door. Such a prime spot seemed a stroke of luck till I went in. Business over at Koerner's was always so sluggish that its year-to-year survival was mystifying, but for the Aviator to be comparably spacious during happy hour? That was eerie.

Projecting an air of absurd ease in his starchy uniform, Ranger Metcalfe had beaten me here by a good while, based on Styrofoam plate before him with its remnant grains of rice and greasy streaks. Great! Any awkwardness about dinner arrangements was water under the bridge. Right off the bat, unfortunately, Herb had me up to my neck in discomfort again. He bypassed any niceties and wanted the latest about Wil. Bought myself a moment by hopping up to the bar and ordering a round. Our intrepid host, in standard striped shirt and bandana, carried on apparently unfazed by the dwindling commerce. I belabored the obvious for the sake of friendly small talk. "Slow night tonight."

"They're all slow." He pushed two IPAs across the bar at me. "They will be from now on. Till that last call one of these days when that'll be that, once and for all." He moseyed off and swabbed peanut shells from the bar into a tin pail as if we'd been discussing nice weather. But as he'd said, that was that for now.

Plunked Herb's glass in front of him, raised mine slightly in the universal gesture for "Cheers" while I sat down, and commenced evasive verbal maneuvers. "I never literally saw Wil. I don't have to tell you how antisocial he's been lately. He was holed up in his bedroom. Locked in, to be more precise. He didn't want company, and he didn't want to talk past the point of convincing me he was okay and didn't need anything. Foodwise, I'd say he doesn't. His kitchen is pretty well stocked now." All true, in essence.

"But he's not flourishing by a long shot. Did you see what a mess his place is? He can't really look after himself, can he? I think calling him severely depressed is putting it mildly. What should we do?"

Herb's tenacious concern was beginning to make me peevish. I took a big gulp of ale. This wasn't what I came to discuss at all. However, my brain was adequately limbered up with alcohol to plot a devious route toward my goal. "What can we do, Herb? I've never met any of his relatives. No idea how to contact them. And we don't have power of attorney over him. The burden to prove he's a danger to himself or others would be on us, and those legal wheels turn pretty damn slowly in any case. There is a more indirect way to help him, though, that might help a lot of other people in the same boat. If you're game." Swallowed more ale, peeked over my glass at his reaction. He was waiting on my next words. Reserving judgment. Not balking yet, anyway.

"Since you don't work in town, and maybe you don't live or hang out here either, you might not be in a position to appreciate that more and more people have been coming down with his symptoms. Some unfamiliar pollutant or microorganism must be the culprit, and based partly on things both you and I have observed at the reservoir, I believe the disease is spreading via the city water system."

Bone tired as I was of making my case in purely environmental terms, it had become a reflex, and to be realistic, when was the right time to start blabbing about alien invasions? I plowed through well-worn routine, touching on stillbirths, stunted crops, fugitive wildlife, and, on Herb's own stomping grounds, the shoreside flora that grew rank and then self-destructed into dust. I did venture to invoke the Gorman County meteor of 1882, citing some byproduct of its slow dissolution in the depths as a credible source of the contamination. And why shouldn't I? The meteor, esoteric or not, was writ indelibly in the historic record. And what harm in stream-lining my presentation by tinkering with the fact that the meteor had actually dissolved after a few days in earthly air and rain?

Scanned Ranger Metcalfe's body language for preparations to bolt. Instead, he pensively sipped his ale, and caught me profoundly off-guard by musing, "The one explanation, then, for all these miseries occurring together boils down to some malignity dormant in the submerged meteor till this summer. Something of extraterrestrial origin. Animate, though not necessarily conscious as we define it. That scenario would even accommodate the corpse lights you and Wil were chasing."

Wow. This seeming epitome of level-headedness had followed my drift further than I'd dared escort him. Of his own volition, and without humoring me. Boldly delving into the actuality of nefarious aliens. Funny, but listening to my own premise in someone else's voice, it started sounding dodgy. "Well, I wouldn't jump to any conclusions." Rhetorically incumbent on me to say so, even if it ran counter to my higher purpose. Or was Herb playing coy about admitting he'd already learned what I had, if not more? Easier for my battered ego to believe that than in anyone intelligent accepting my story at face value.

All for the well, though. Recruiting Herb might not be the uphill battle I'd been dreading. "Wherever the problem comes from, it's getting critical. I hate to picture what'll happen in the span of days if we don't start coping with it. Wil might have told you I work at City Hall. For Mr. Marsh, in the office of the City Clerk. Every fact about what's happening is on file there, but the administration's been stonewalling any move to investigate and isolate what's responsible. It's simply the economy. A request for extra spending is always controversial." Between what I wasn't saying, and what I was distorting, and the unvarnished truth, this was shaping up as a pretty seamless fabrication. My pride at newfound expertise in spinning a web of deceit had to be wrong, but I didn't care at the moment. "By going over municipal heads, we can produce some answers and win the public support to overcome bureaucratic inertia. And God willing, save lives and avert catastrophe. But we'll be shut down if word of this gets beyond my department. Therefore I'm meeting with you on the q.t., if you're cool with that."

Herb's turn now for a leisurely swig of ale, and for stalling till the right words occurred to him. Pray continue, his arching eyebrows signaled.

"Those alleged corpse lights are extremely relevant. They mark the site of the meteor crash." Did they, like X on a treasure map? Why not? "Any environmental watchdogs you can wrangle on a state or federal level, we need to send down there in the very near future with camcorders and sampling equipment and their most sophisticated testing kits. And I'm afraid it has to be a night dive, because corpse lights don't show up during the day, and we have no other means to nail the location. At the risk of jinxing myself, I guarantee the results will be compelling, and with political pressure from above, the city will have to launch a cleanup, or a ban on tap water, or an application for Superfund status." Too little, too late for rescuing Occam altogether, but coming across as reasonable was becoming an idée fixe with me. A neurotic bid at proving I was rational despite my irrational statements.

"This fucking city. Good luck, boys." The bartender slammed a fresh glass upon the table for each of us. Christ! How long had he been listening at our elbows? How had he crept up on us? A technique he'd picked up in Nam? "Here's a round on the house. In case I don't see you again." He leaned in to remove Herb's Styrofoam plate and counseled, "Don't set your hopes too high on City Hall. Those horse's asses won't ever wake up. Waste of energy, if you ask me."

He straightened up, turned to go. I had to talk fast. "Please, hold on a second. Thanks very much for these." I gestured toward our freebies. "But don't you think we're obliged to do what we can to try saving people?"

He didn't spend any time deliberating. "You can lead a horse to water, right? The facts about the reservoir have been around since day one for anyone who cared to ask. The signs right now couldn't be clearer. At some stage, people have to take charge of their own skins. Every man for himself, in the long run."

"Okay, granted, but there's something else I should've asked you a long time ago. I still don't know what your name is."

"I never said. I'd rather not have anyone looking me up. Especially not these days."

"Sure. But one last question. Can I just ask you point-blank, what's going to happen in this town, ultimately?"

He didn't pretend to mull that over. "If you have the brains to ask, I don't need to tell you." He vamoosed, and to my horror, Ms. Lathrop, formidable henchwoman of that City Collector asshole Humphrey Westcott, was occupying the barstool directly behind him. She was facing us, cocking her head attentively in the fashion of a mantis. Was she spying on me for her boss?

Steady now! Herb was saying, "Free beer. That's always nice." Doom-laden pronouncements from our nameless barkeep seemed to have slid inscrutably off his back. How much of a regular was Herb here? Or how accustomed to "old Occam" ways at a place like this?

"One point we ought to address before going any further." With some effort I turned from bug-eyed Ms. Lathrop to laidback Herb. "What kind of hot water are you in for at work, if you lend me a hand?" Give me credit for some functioning conscience in spite of my machinations.

"No hot water. I'm vested, I'm union. A lifer. Too much trouble throwing me out for it be worth their while. And why should they? I'm only passing along a request for service from a city office, and acting in good faith that everything's on the up and up. What about you, though?"

"I'll be fine," I lied for simplicity's sake. "I'm vested and union too, you know." More to the heart of it, the workplace shouldn't long outlast my severance from it.

Meanwhile, Ms. Lathrop had been staring at me nonstop, and Herb's lack of comment on the barkeeper's fatalism was feeling curiouser and curiouser, unless he held the same opinions, derived from his sub rosa well-springs of knowledge. Would've been a shame had I ruminated on these issues to the exclusion of what Herb was saying. "I'm friendly with the folks at the Water Resources Authority in Boston. They've always been prompt and reliable, and they have a dive team on call. Referring to a hazmat complaint about the reservoir ought to light a fire under 'em, but with a caveat to be discreet and set off no premature alarms. You'll have answers after the weekend."

Oh God! That rarest joy, of hearing a wish fulfilled to the letter, had lasted scant seconds when Ms. Lathrop lumbered from her barstool and toward us like an icebreaker through frozen seas. Hairline cracks of worry finally showed in Herb's sangfroid. As she bent oppressively close, much closer than the barkeep had, her abdominal flesh in sleek paisley blouse sank into the edge of our table, and rebounded. She swayed in a brief quest for equilibrium, lacing the air with her usual lilac, mixed with the distinctive reek of multiple B and Bs. News to me that anyone still drank those. Her magnified eyes bore into me through thick lenses as she professed, "You're the biggest fool in this goddamn town, and about the best person."

She said no more, but goggled on and on at me, with an occasional corrective sway. I was at a speechless loss. Was she coming on to me? She'd unerringly chucked a monkey wrench into my inner gears. Couldn't wrest my gaze away from hers. Were both our expressions equally inscrutable? In the fullness of the moment, I noticed some skin-tone plastic attachment curving around and into her left ear. A simple hearing aid, or one of those sleazy surveillance doohickeys, as hawked on late-night cable? At least she presented none of the stupor or discoloration that came of too much acquaintance with the Gorman taste. At length, without a parting word, she disengaged and plodded back to her barstool.

"I think she likes you." Herb smiled in assurance he spoke in jest, but I must have blanched fearsomely at the idea, for he swiftly added, "On the bright side, I should be able to charge the expenses from the dive to Parks and Recreation. Much less of a paper trail leading to you. It also means we and not you will get all the glory for saving the town, though I don't see why you couldn't incorporate what we find into a future *OGAM Chronicles*."

"Thanks, except the program seems to have been cancelled," I hedged. No desire to enlighten him in any detail. Better to return the ball to his court. "All the same, whatever paranormal story you wanted to tell me last month at the reservoir, if you want to run it by me now, I'm all ears." And in no case repeat the blunder of letting line of vision stray into Ms. Lathrop's territory.

"All right, but then I have to get going." Reddening complexion testified that his day had mostly run its course. He stretched, spreading his arms apart into the semblance of a crucifixion or a scarecrow, and his uniform went taut against his bulky torso. In a more abstracted demeanor, he seemed to be addressing his empty glass. "Near the reservoir shore, there's a house that may be occupied or it may be haunted, where there isn't supposed to be any house at all. I've never seen the alleged squatter, ghostly or otherwise, and neither have the rest of us at the Control Center, though we've all heard it tromping around, day and night, including Wil. In fact, I'm surprised he never mentioned it to you."

So was I, but good luck calling him out on that now.

"In any event, it's a thing that shouldn't, in any respect, be where it is, and it kind of induces the creeps, and that's why I was somewhat, say, evasive when you questioned me about a bear or something big in the woods. I didn't want to risk freaking you out in earnest."

I was hankering for another ale, but didn't dare pull the brakes on Metcalfe's train of narration.

"The house is old, possibly hundreds of years old. Between its disrepair and piecemeal renovations over time, hard to tell its age at a glance. But it gives off an aura of being too old, which accounts in part for the gut feeling that it shouldn't still be standing there."

"You're saying it escaped the deluge somehow when the rest of Gorman County was submerged?"

"No, no, when the properties surrounding the reservoir fell into state hands and all the buildings were demolished to let second-growth forest take root, that house was exempted for Parks Department headquarters. Afterwards, the Control Center went up where it is today because the old place was too far from where they laid out the ring road, but no one ever got around to knocking it down. It's just off that cove where you and the apparent bear almost met up, set into the slope above a former road. My own hunch is that a homeless person, in the depths of despair or derangement, is living there. Primarily because we noticed neither hide nor hair of anyone till a couple of years ago, whereas a haunting should've made itself manifest long beforehand in a house from the eighteenth or seventeenth century. And until we're under orders, we've been disinclined to evict someone in such dire straits as to call that shack home. Whoever it is has been so good at covering tracks and avoiding us that it might as well be a ghost. Zero environmental impact that we can find. But I'd be glad to show you the house sometime. Next week, if that works for you."

While I agreed unreservedly that it would, he laid his hands palms-down on the table as prelude to standing. Out of the blue, the bartender swooped in with another pair of IPAs. "Looks like your lucky night!" he professed. "Your lady friend sprang for these and then took off." Lucky inasmuch as the ales were here and she wasn't? That was the meaning I chose. Yes, I confirmed at a glimpse, her barstool was vacant. Herb's eyes, in the meantime, were bulging dubiously. One good thing too many was no longer a good thing, they fairly lectured. My thanks to the barkeep were effusive enough for both of us, and I hastened to ask, "Is she here often?"

He shrugged. "I seen her before." Away he strode, as if no words more portentous had passed between us tonight.

To Herb I remarked, "Don't sweat it. I'll dispose of these. They're only 10 ounces each." His frown raised graphic doubts about my competence in traffic if I did so. "I'll be fine," I pledged, and pledged moreover to phone him Monday at the Control Center for a progress report on the dive, and to firm up a day for trekking to the house in the woods. As a failsafe, jotted down my phone and e-mail info on a paper towel wadded in jacket pocket since my last burrito here.

In his absence, I lingered over our complimentary drinks and meditated on the stunning development of Ms. Lathrop's entry into the ranks of "old Occam." One more soul who'd never volunteered the time of day, and at the drop of a hat became chummy, conversational, demonstrative. Furthermore, my chronic ignorance of the "real" Ms. Lathrop, political spy or not, rendered extra proof, as if I needed it, of how I didn't really know my own hometown at all.

Twenty

Between me and Monday sprawled a pointedly uneventful interval. Had a feeling I should savor final workdays and weekend of lovely boring tranquility. Yet I greeted the workweek raring to go, itching to find a secluded phone during midmorning break for an update from Herb. Had been clockwatching circa 30 minutes in Permits and Licenses at the same window where the grumpy coot had railed about rotten fish in the reservoir, when Ms. Lathrop, among the missing since her disappearance from the Aviator, materialized wraithlike in my personal space, with only a whiff of lilac as last-instant calling card.

"You're wanted in the City Collector's office." Her ordinary frosty, sober City Hall monotone. Inappropriate for me to do more than nod and tag behind. Do not, especially, thank her for those farewell IPAs. An interaction from a grossly incompatible other world. As would be any species of small talk now. Smiled mirthlessly at the arrant image of Ms. Lathrop as a valkyrie, devoid of affect after eons on the job, sent to fetch me upstairs. I was stricken numb, and couldn't bring myself to care who, if anyone, was going to sub at my deserted post. Hell, I wasn't coming back. Fight-or-flight reactions were underway, but that tingling might as well have been in someone else's throat, that turmoil in someone else's stomach.

On the third floor, Ms. Lathrop did an about-face and raised a puffy-sleeved arm toward her open anteroom door. "Go right in." My mood must have contributed to finding her diction sepulchral. She then proceeded down the corridor to parts unknown, out of earshot, I gathered, of what was pending, which could only have one foregone outcome.

As I trudged ahead to the inner sanctum door, also gaping open like the jaws of malice, I might have wrung some cheer from the insight that the dive must have yielded valuable results. And jangled a few autocratic and/or extraterrestrial nerves. But I didn't. Too numb even for that.

This self-detachment helped me plant one foot in front of the other till brazenly illicit cigar smoke beclouded me. Or was shock taking premature hold to cushion me from the moment of reckoning? Westcott was seething speechless from across the glossy flatland of his mahogany desk, and the multi-paned windows were down, as if to make this preserve of Victorian elegance as stuffy and inhospitable as possible.

To spare my eyes the glare of his, I averted them to the leather-and-walnut ladderback chair on my side of the desk. With an inward shrug, I presumed to sit. No use at this stage in standing on ceremony, was there? Anyway, that gesture broke the ice. "Go right ahead," Westcott bristled, "but don't plan on getting comfortable."

When it sank in that no smartmouth reply was forthcoming, he blustered, "You were warned!"

"Yes, three or four times." Was that correct? Keying my car, pulverizing its glass, censoring my letter to the editor, canceling my cable tv, busting up OGAM? Five, for starters. No matter. Westcott was off and haranguing on his long-stoked head of steam.

"Have you the faintest clue about the amount of damage control we're going through to stop that report from leaking out? To clean up your shit? The kinds of promises and deals it takes to hush something up at a state level?" He may not have trusted himself to rise and pace around with a deserving target like myself at hand. Maybe on his lawyer's advice. But his cheeks were burning, his basset hound nostrils flared, his jowls were trembling, and so was his desk, whose edge he gripped with ivory knuckles.

"But what the fuck do you care? You're only technically a town resident. You're not affected by it out in the woods, so what's it to you if everyone else's property turns to worthless shit? Just because of your crazy speculations? You're a reckless idiot like the rest of those radical environmentalist bastards. Do you remember what happened to the price of land around Love Canal?" Couldn't tell if he was pausing for rhetorical impact or awaiting a repentant answer.

"I remember what happened to the people around Love Canal."

"Well this isn't Love Canal!" His spray hung sparkling between us in the

shafts of sunshine from behind. "We could sue you for fraud, for malfea-
sance, for misuse of your nonexistent authority by recruiting those divers.
We won't, because this mess has to die quickly and quietly. But that's as far
as the good news goes for you." His present gloating pause was definitely
aiming for dramatic effect. With it came my one likely opportunity to steal
some of the s.o.b.'s thunder.

"Strictly speaking, I work for Mr. Marsh. Shouldn't he be firing me? Is
he aware I'm here?"

"You don't think I have the power to bounce your ass to the curb?" he
thundered. "When you get the boot I don't want it to be a senile asthmatic
whisper. You're hearing it loud and clear." He found himself halfway out of
his chair, reconsidered, and plopped back down. "I bet you think I'm an asshole, don't you? You want to know why I'm an asshole? Because I can be.
Because everyone is, to the extent the market can bear. Including you, if
you were in my shoes. Look at the way you tried dragging Water Resources
into this. Except you're not and never will be an asshole in my exalted position. So here are your options. Exit the building immediately, without talking to anybody or doing anything on your way, and never set foot in here
again. Or security can throw you out."

I nodded and the chair scraped crassly on the hardwood as I got up. "Before I go, though, would you mind telling me if you even glanced at that
water quality report?"

He reached for his shiny black phone.

"Okay, forget it, I'm going." He stayed his hand, but not his acid glare
at me. "You're only human." I swiveled about and never looked back. If
Westcott was wondering what the hell I meant, he kept it to himself.

Just as well. I'd have been hard-pressed to disguise what I was actually
saying, that he was completely, merely human. Occam's razor had cut to
the marrow once more. No need to posit alien influence on third-floor
mentality, when disordered Yankee priorities, shortsightedness, and narrow
minds covered all the bases. Another cherished paradigm lost. City Hall was
not a beachhead for cosmic trespassers. This late in the game, infusion with
the "color," as Professor Thayer coined it, would've left its telltale stain. As
it had on poor unlovable Edward Orne, whom I always seemed to pass on

the stairs, and who today was rooted to the second-floor landing, clutching the rail, too dazed or fatigued to climb farther. Blind to me, but not due to reflex arrogance. His grey lips were busily contorting into shapes that wouldn't have produced syllables in English, had he been vocalizing them. These mouthings might have been the visible spillover of soundless communication with fellow vectors of the "color." Or they might have reflected his semi-human exertions to process whatever unearthly vista his infested vision was showing him in lieu of a staircase. His fixated pupils reminded me of gaping black pits, manifesting his entrapment in a torturous, profane variety of out-of-body experience.

No problem in this case complying with Westcott's demand to broach no conversations. On ground level, I clocked out, violating Westcott's injunction to do nothing, but met with no opposition from uniformed goons.

Brilliant sunlight beating down on glazed brick plaza out front presented too drastic a contrast with my wretched morning. Sent me into emotional tailspin. Manfully sought to regain control of the figurative joystick. Monetarily, the forecast wasn't dire yet. Like anybody else in my straits, I'd be putting in a claim to collect. Had a hunch it wouldn't be contested, lest I wind up in court, where the facts of municipal cover-up would hemorrhage gruesomely into the public record. On another bright note, I never had to wait for coffee break again to skulk off and make personal calls. And I also had a blank slate on which to pencil in that hike to the haunted shack by the reservoir.

Twenty-one

With nothing but freedom on my horizon, I had no heart to go anywhere except home. Warmed up my eMac, which knocked phoning Herb off the top of my to-do list. His e-mail had arrived at 9:40. Pretty much the moment I was getting canned.

He engaged in minimal preamble. Hoped I was well, the Aviator sure was a trip, trusting I wasn't pulled over for DWI. Attached please find a précis of the dive-team leader's report. Kudos for persistence in shedding light on this situation, and prepare yourself, it reads like an episode of *X-Files*. That's how it felt to Herb, and he had stayed aboard the launch, fathoms above the action:

By approx. 8:30 PM (at least 2 hr. after dark) the boat was offloaded from the trailer into the water. Herbert Metcalfe of the Parks Department accompanied us as guide. Another hour elapsed in finding the general "ballpark" and cruising back and forth to locate purported "hotspots" of hazardous material(s).

When a luminous streak or patch shone several yards off the starboard bow, we could not resolve whether or not we had previously traversed that area and seen nothing. The flashes were concordant with the low-temperature combustion of methane and phosphine gas released by the decay of organic matter, alias a "will-o'-the-wisp." In keeping with folklore, the luminosity seemed to behave capriciously, i.e., repeatedly vanished and reappeared at random places around the boat. In addition, it initially floated on the surface like a chemical slick, but on sustained viewing shifted to various depths, as if daring or enticing us to give chase. It was reasonable to conclude that we were anthropomorphizing the visual effects of chemiluminescence refracted through cross-ripples from the wake of our zigzagging boat.

The dive went ahead, if only to verify the source of the methane. The four of us who participated can all vouch for the accuracy of my sometimes outlandish-sounding disclosures. For brevity, I will i.d. individuals, when necessary, by their initials. We learned right away that the antics of our "will-o-the-wisp" must have been an optical trick, because as long as we regarded the phenomenon through our scuba masks, it nestled immobile in a circular structure that proved to be a well. However, becoming stationary made this "will-o-the-wisp" no less off-putting and no less illusively alive. It was already a given that we were contending with more than swamp gas. Based on the agitated probings of our flashlights here and there, safe to conjecture we labored under a common anxiety in our descent toward the glow. (I say "conjecture" because we restricted ourselves to communicating information rather than emotional states on our person-to-person radios.)

We had our first material indication of "troubled waters" when our roving LEDs found a fish. Rather than darting away, it swam along listlessly in the beam from D.R., with a diseased, inefficient kind of shimmying. This was attributable to ping-pong ball-sized lumps on its side and at the base of a pectoral fin, and to the crippling 45° bend in its spine. Because of these deformities and the unhealthy, uniform grey of its skin, classifying this specimen as a bass must remain an educated guess. The fish maintained its lethargic course, even as D.R. approached it, holding out her flashlight. It made no effort to elude being nudged by the flashlight, but on contact, a good part of its flank broke loose and sank, presenting a homogenous consistency as of plaster or compressed ash. The main portion of the bass proceeded as if insensible of what had happened, though it was unable to continue in a straight line and also sank from sight, casting off a trail of grey flakes, unfortunately before any of us could regain the composure to try containing the specimen. A.G., however, did shoot confirmatory video, as he attempted to do from then on (*vide infra*). We noted more fish in the distance, but voted to concentrate on the putative cause of their condition, several fathoms below.

Comparing our impressions later, we all felt more unwelcome, and more disliked, the closer we dove to the bottom. At the same time, we experienced an involuntary, almost hypnotic pull toward the glow, which on nearer view resembled smoke of indeterminate color that cohered unnaturally, as if heavier than the water on top of it. Our subjective conflict of attraction and repulsion persisted for the duration of the dive. On the other hand, before we ventured any farther, the Geiger counter provided reassurance on one front, i.e., the site was not radioactive.

We attained a depth where careless overuse of our flippers should have raised too much sediment off the lake floor to see through, which might have been a happy accident, in retrospect. Technically, our environment was safe. Spot tests for pH, bacteria, and medical and industrial waste produced results within normal range, consistent with routine state and local analyses. Contrarily, everything preying on our nerves had us bracing for serious danger. Our "will-o'-the-wisp" never budged from its shallow cylinder of the fieldstone well, peeking over its lip like a cork plugging a bottle, but none of us trusted it to stay put. Nor were we in any hurry to come within arm's length, even if it was our logical focus.

Between our LEDs and the twilight surrounding the well, we were able to distinguish a nearby house foundation, rectangular, and scarcely exceeding the dimensions of a cottage, and at the edge of visibility, the much bigger square foundation of a barn. As a rule, our actions would have produced some turbidity, but the silt in a wide swath around the well was sticky as tar, porous like French bread, and oily black, releasing only an iridescent bubble from time to time.

A white, haphazardly woven texture in the black made for a grisly contrast, upon our realization that it was a multitude of bones, similar to a fossil record of disaster, and though distorted and fragmented as if by geologic processes, these were recent, and mostly no problem to classify. Many were of geese, and of mammals ranging in size from deer and coyote down to possum, raccoon, cat and squirrel. Smaller rodents, birds and fish were also plentiful, without being recognizable in terms of species. Immediately beside the well lay a human skeleton that must have predated much of the deposition, because most of it had sunk into the muck, except for the crown of the skull, a few tubercular-looking ribs, and a badly worn pelvic bone. Adhering to the letter of the law, we did not disturb these human remains, insofar as they might constitute a crime scene, regardless of their number of decades here. In collecting samples of the black silt, some small bones were necessarily admixed; otherwise we declined to acquire larger bones, in order to avoid gratuitous contact with the noxious sediment.

Regrettably, no video exists of the "mass grave" or of the well and its contents. Fluctuating, amorphous areas of "dropout" marred all such footage on playback, and for these I have to blame the luminosity, though no difficulties were apparent to A.G. while shooting. Then as now, we had no idea what we were facing, and only a few as to what we weren't. Nothing radioactive (as the Geiger counter revealed) and no manufactured compound (to our knowledge) would be acting as a fatal attractant upon wildlife and human alike. Our one brittle, tumescent fish, however, had demonstrated a toxicity as potentially severe as that of radium or dioxin.

The embedded human ribs we treated as extempore cordon between ourselves and the well, and even that much proximity may have been reckless. Hopefully, no physical repercussions will come of short-term exposure to the anomaly. Its effects on our mood, in the meantime, were becoming more pronounced, as if it could emit negativity, and its properties were proving more enigmatic and, in direct proportion, more disturbing.

A.G., who had the phenomenon under the most intensive observation via his camcorder, had become motionless at some indeterminate point, as if catatonic or mesmerized. D.R. shook his shoulder, and A.G. showed brief signs of disorientation, after which his behavior gave us no cause for concern; he denied knowledge of going into any kind of trance or altered state.

During visual appraisal, the color of the phenomenon switched arbitrarily from blue to beige to pink to grey, or approximations of these, rather, as if our eyes were repeatedly failing to register some wavelength for which they were not equipped. However, the interplay of the light sticks in our belts, our LEDs, and the tint of our masks may have been at fault.

There was less room for ambiguity in our finding that nothing in the well was casting the glow, that the well held nothing but the glow, which within its circumference flexed, and winked, and churned so as to suggest prismatic planes as much as vapor or smoke. On the premise that the glow might consist of particles, C.W. briefly experimented with trapping some of it in a sample vial. Pinching the plastic base between thumb and fingertip, he scooped gingerly into the edge of the brightness. He pulled away an empty vial, and while the rest of us can vouch for his care in avoiding fleshly contact, he complained of a concurrent acute sensation sliding across the heel of his hand; whether it was freezing or burning he could not say, but it inflicted an ugly red soreness in an unusual stippled pattern (he is under medical surveillance for additional pathologic changes).

We were also aware of a worrisome new development, or perhaps we had slowly become sensitized to something present all along but verging on subliminal. Previously we had thought in terms of a discrete phenomenon with a definite boundary and generating some modest candlepower, whereas now we perceived that the luminosity was not confined to the well but only most condensed within it, and gradually diffusing beyond it, such that we were floating in its attenuated but implicitly harmful range.

I doubt that I alone was guilty of anthropomorphizing again, in crediting a luminous force with "tricking" and "catching" us. To the degree my comrades' expressions were readable behind tinted plastic, I would say we were united in dismay. We had foremost to resist any urge to decamp prematurely. I promptly ran through our checklist of tests and procedures, and only after confirmation of mission accomplished did we resurface. Everyone later confessed to some relief at escaping the expansive luminous zone unscathed by another mysterious discharge like the one that had stung C.W. Moreover, the dive team will undergo medical follow-up for the next 6 months, to ascertain any sequelae after being enveloped in the inexplicable glow. At least no early-onset symptoms have been reported.

Results of sample analyses and tests are still several days away, and need to be collated with our anecdotal and preliminary findings; interpretations and conclusions will come still later, before state government can mandate a plan of action. These several preparatory steps, while scientifically compulsory, may prove too time-consuming in terms of the public interest. Given our fundamental ignorance of the luminous agency, its documented mutagenic and irritant effects, and our present inability to measure its dispersal beyond the reservoir, I would advocate a ban on human and agricultural consumption of the Gorman County water, until sufficient understanding of the problem allows us to neutralize or remove it.

> Randolph Angell
> Dive-Team Coordinator
> For the Mass. Water Resources Authority

X-Files indeed. Vindication was mine. To bask in it for a long-deferred respite wasn't asking too much, aside from pyrrhic upshot of livelihood down the drain, everything else in my life laid waste. Nope, my affect was flatter than morning-after beer. Herb had appended a few chatty lines more before signing off. He hoped none of this would get back to my bosses. Could only grimace sportingly at that. In case he hadn't passed it along yet, here was his home phone so I could call this evening after business hours. And don't forget, he'd gladly guide me to that "haunted hovel" in the forest, at my convenience, even if it didn't clinch his 15 minutes of local-access fame. His closing exhortation of "Stick to Your Guns, It's Paying Off" smacked of Boy Scouts more than park rangers, but maybe I wasn't being fair. He hadn't had the rug pulled out from under him yet. Why spoil his sunny illusion? Official channels would do that for him all too soon. No need for him to associate me with that lesson in realpolitik.

Instead, I dialed up the Department of Labor to apply for Unemployment, banking on Westcott and company to pay me off, in effect, rather than risk answering questions about my dismissal. Or else they might choose to kill me as the lesser evil. Barring all that, funny if workmen's comp proved the vehicle to drag everything out into the open.

But these were the possibilities of a hazy future, sometime after the ages I squandered trying to file. For the balance of the morning, was shunted to and fro among flacks who uniformly insisted it was someone else's job to help me, and more than once I was put on hold till the third full replay of "Daniel" by Elton John obliged me to slam down the phone, only to punch redial after a momentary cooldown and submit to the same rigmarole all over again.

At noon I desisted. Idiotic to believe I'd make it beyond canned oldies during lunch hour, or to torture myself with canned oldies till 1 o'clock. And then I had to jump through the same infuriating hoops of misdirection for another everlasting stretch, till at a whim, some world-weary civil servant saw fit to transcribe the sordid facts re me and my former livelihood. Tempting to fib and paint my departure as a layoff, just to see if City Hall would go along with it in following the safest, quietest course of least resistance. But by the same token, I probably didn't have to lie, so why bother? Hell, did Mr. Marsh even know I'd been axed? Inevitably, the nasal drone hovering between me and my benefits harped on the problems posed by getting fired, but would look into the matter, and set up an appointment for Tuesday when I'd come in for "adjudication," whatever that meant under the circumstances.

The clock on the wall read half past three as I hung up. Debated kicking myself for neglecting to brave the Department of Labor while I was still downtown this morning. Might've wrapped up this business before noon, or I might have butchered the same precious time in dismal offices as opposed to the comforts of home. Case in point, at work or in the dole queue, I couldn't have responded to sudden fatigue by bedding down for a nap. A paltry ten minutes to relax was all I asked.

My little lie-down ended in the dark, and it took me a while to place where I was. Today had exacted a dearer toll than expected. At least I'd skipped over those hours of twiddling my thumbs before Herb was back home. Slapped together a grilled cheese, the kind of supper I'd better get used to as a man of leisure, and plunked it in the ticking toaster oven while I tried the Metcalfe residence. Herb answered on the second ring. I forwent the niceties, loath to discuss how my day had gone. That could only be counterproductive. Let's aim for the bull's eye. Had he received any updates about closing the reservoir since this morning?

Well, he hated being the bearer of disappointment, but the Resources Authority was holding off on a water ban or any official announcements. Only temporarily! Some test results hadn't come back yet, and the Directors were ordering more research with the aim of understanding the first thing about whatever the hell was going on down there. Made sense to him, and these guys must have been cognizant of the urgency involved, so don't fret, it's not like they were stalling or giving us the runaround.

To burst his bubble of childlike faith would've been cruel. Still and all, his egregious blindness to the neon script on the wall began pissing me off. Westcott hadn't spelled it out for him as he had for me, granted. Not that anyone should have to spoon-feed a grown man the subtext of "ordering more research" or of waiting on test results, not when the initial findings were so scary. Nor was it incumbent on me, or pragmatic, to cuff the scales from his eyes.

"Okay, sit tight you say, then we sit tight. Nothing to stop us from sizing up that derelict shack in the woods, is there?" Meeting him on any workday afternoon or morning would be fine, I volunteered. Babbled some malarkey about sitting on a lot of vacation days.

A tropical system was due to move in tonight, he informed me, but was supposed to be out at sea as of Thursday morning. By 1 PM, definitely.

Great! See you at the Control Center at 1 on Thursday, then. Pretended I had to get going, to forestall Herb asking how I'd been. Sooner or later I'd have to admit how I'd joined the unemployed and what that boded for our "crusade." Forty-eight hours to tinker with my phrasing couldn't hurt.

What the hell, meanwhile, was burning? I had studiously ignored everything during my chat with Herb, but now the odor pushed past my peripheral awareness. Had thugs from City Hall torched the house? From eye level to ceiling, the kitchen air was grey with stinging smoke. Plumes of it were streaming from the loose door of the toaster oven. Shit! My grilled cheese! I yanked the plug, threw open the windows, and climbed on a chair to silence the smoke alarm on the third obnoxious beep. Speared my blackened supper with a butter knife and dragged it to the counter. Scraped some of the charcoal off and ate the charred remainder over the sink, palatability be damned. Most people might have written it off as a total loss. I, however, had to get used to living under reduced means.

Herb was right about that tropical system. And now that I'd been canned, at least I didn't have to commute in a deluge. Or go anywhere. Plenty of time to brood in a conducive atmosphere. There lingered the riddle of what more I could do as a whistleblower. Especially after my last best shot at going over municipal heads had misfired so abjectly. But honestly, these ruminations had become a parlor game for my conscience. Rainy-day busywork of the soul. Let's see, I hadn't explored talk radio. For the life of me, though, couldn't tease out how to describe the looming tribulations without sounding like a "homegrown terrorist." And no worse place to end up than jail under the Patriot Act as zero hour ticked down. Much as my ex-bosses would love the excuse to put me away. Nope, might as well roam the streets of Occam in a sandwich sign proclaiming The End Is Near!

Tuesday's lashing downpour carried on through Wednesday. Drove me deeper into my hapless funk till the mailman delivered a soggy bill from Pabodie Cable. For the last four weeks' basic service. As if those bastards had never fraudulently cut me off for nonpayment. Grabbed the phone to give them an earful, then let it ride. What the hell, the cable company would likely be a bad memory before those charges went to collection. The upside of unspeakable disaster! In fact, guess I owed Pabodie one for goading me out of my brown study.

Twenty-two

Midmorning on Thursday, dismal overcast was still shedding mist and showers. A broken promise of clearing. I warmed up the computer. Herb had sent an e-mail late last night, and as breakfast reading went, it was no aid to digestion:

> Jeff,
>
> Hope you're still up for that excursion tomorrow. I think you would have spotted the house yourself last time if so much else hadn't been going on. In winter when the trees are bare it's visible from the reservoir shore, only a couple of hundred feet west of the yellow trail after it makes that steep descent and crosses a rocky glade of black birches.
>
> Also I had another thought about our hazmat site. Because of those human bones down there, which seem to have slipped the Water Authority's attention, we're dealing with a crime scene, which is something the State Police and/or FBI have to analyze. And bingo, we have our publicity after all. Will start making calls early in the morning, once I touch base with the guys in Boston to make sure they haven't brought in law enforcement themselves. Kind of hard to imagine they wouldn't have, and leave themselves open to allegations of criminal negligence. I'll definitely be in by 1 anyway, so don't worry about that. See you then!

Good grief! Stupid of me not to have raised a stink about those human bones myself. Pestering the Water Authority again, though? Didn't sit well with me. Any intention of his to enlist the Staties or the Feds might travel the grapevine back to City Hall, from whose thuggery Herb misconceived himself immune. Tried Herb's home number. Got his voice mail. Left no message. Let's not leap at too extreme a conclusion yet. One o'clock would roll around soon enough.

Pulled up punctually at the Control Center. The drizzle had been less punctual about letting up. And Herb, according to his two colleagues, had never shown at all. Called in sick at 10. That sat worse with me than his e-mail, and so did the rangers' signs of galloping decline since the summer. Maybe they'd aged 20 years in a season too incrementally for Herb to have noticed. Or else I was uniquely sensitized to how the freckly, beefier man had deflated, his arms dangling flaccidly when not in creaky operation, and to how his lanky, well-tanned comrade had parched into a caricature of brittle planes and sharp angles, like a mummy or a mangled catalpa pod. That "pollen" harassing them during path maintenance had plainly set up permanent occupation. It had recruited two more passive receptacles like the kid at Radio Shack or the benchwarmers at the auto glass joint, imbued with enough inertia, enough force of habit, just that much of their "old selves," for guiding them to workplace and home again. To go through the motions till anatomy failed them. "I'll be off on a little hike now." I had refrained from stepping in past the threshold. "How're you guys doing?"

They favored me with a couple of bobble nods. As firmly planted behind their desks as dashboard ornaments. I hastened into the much less oppressive damp and gloom.

I had my rough directions, my camcorder in a watertight case, and a plastic satchel of tawdry faux calfskin for any papers or artifacts worth looting. No trouble to follow the yellow trail's dots, but grass and weeds and debris hadn't endured a tidying hand for weeks, had they? A moot point where substandard labor ended, and overstimulation by reservoir water began.

Similar lapses in upkeep must have been creeping inexorably across Occam, in broadcast studios, supermarkets, public transportation, banks, with a semblance of business-as-usual tottering along where employees were a mix of townies and the non-residents who could take up the slack for those who were "down with something." Special sympathies went out in advance to those intrepid out-of-towners whose reward for holding down the fort might be their ill-timed presence in the fort when it went to hell.

And how would the aftermath look? The yellow dots led to a possible preview. The path became almost impassably unkempt, and the off-trail vegetation more matted and intertwined, as if stalemated in one mass deathgrip. The taller oak and maple foliage that should have lent this dismal afternoon some red and yellow respite was already mottled brown. The cluttered path conducted me round the bend where I'd first stumbled upon Wil's sweating, bedraggled coworkers, but now I met with before-and-after views of impending devastation. The forest and its understory still stood to my left. Straight on and to the right, however, the grey dust clung to the lifeless ground, and only trunks of mature trees languished upright, though leafless, mostly branchless, and of a necrotic black. August's initial consumption of greenery around the cove had become voracious. The trail itself was free of dust, like some dubious demilitarized zone. The drizzle and humidity seemed to weigh down the powder. With less than sturdy confidence, I stole onward.

On the verge of the steep incline, I had to reappraise the terrain and my nerve. Had never laid eyes on this panorama before, but it wasn't exactly new to me. Then a flash of pattern recognition made my breath catch and rattle in my throat. I owned this view. It was leaning against my laundry hamper. Scarcely earned a passing glance anymore. The Blasted Heath! A nightmare scape whose essence had been captured as expertly as anyone had to, by a Sunday primitivist of 1926. I committed myself to the descending path as to a dire prophecy. No more clumps of grass for footholds.

Accelerated to the bottom without tripping onto my face, incredibly enough. Scanned past the boulders and birch trunks projecting from the dust, and a few hundred feet away, as described, was the house, its weatherbeaten, sun-bleached clapboard walls an arrestingly colorful brown amidst the ashen land and charcoal trees. With shallow breaths and a handkerchief pressed to nose and mouth, I emulated a weightless moonwalk into the realm of desolation.

Halfway there, a barbwire fence delayed me. It ran to the vanishing point to either side of me, but hung slack like a detuned fretboard, and the highest wire drooped at hip level. Dereliction of upkeep these days must have included straightening posts and tightening boundaries. A steel sign adorned with a few rusty bullet holes was clamped to the nearest iron stake, and it warned, "Posted! State Property. Unlawful to Trespass Beyond This Point." Didn't think they'd mind making an exception for me at the Control Center. Pushed down on the wire midway between barbs and lifted one leg over, and then the other, in even more exaggerated slow motion. Thank Christ the grey dust wasn't slippery when wet!

I soldiered on. Extraordinary how a ruin that would've huddled sinister and forbidding in the healthy forest of past months had become a haven, a godsend today. And extraordinary how the gambrel roof, for all its absent shingles and swayback beams, hadn't caved, and how the door at the center of the squat, bulging façade was attached by even one hinge, and how several courses of brickwork remained to indicate the dimensions of stout central chimney. Window frames, less remarkably, were altogether vacant, and to one side, the solid rust door for a fieldstone bulkhead was stuck straight up, generously admitting the elements and anything else into the cellar. The granite stoop was so worn that rain had pooled in the middle. I vigorously scuffed off vile dust to left and right of the puddle. Grasped the door by a hand on each side and eased it around to let myself in. Couldn't help sighing with relief, prematurely or not, at being out of the dust, and out of the resurgent rain.

Tensed up again at the patently obvious, that I had barged into the den of someone or something feral that might spring from any direction. Damn my eyes for not adjusting more quickly to the gloom. They probed back and forth, bored into shadowy recesses, finally gave me leave to breathe easier. I had the place to myself.

Either the vandalism of natural processes or aborted efforts to refurbish this as Parks Service hq had reduced the interior to one big room. The ponderous chimneystack alone bridged the space between floor and ceiling, and in cavernous Colonial-era fireplace, raindrops pattered into residual soot. The floor was an uneven wasteland of fragmented, rotten plaster and lathing and horsehair fill that had crumbled off the four walls around me or mapped the downfall of dividing walls. Whatever wallpaper and plaster clung to vertical surfaces was overwhelmingly black with water stains, and scraps of plaster between the ceiling's naked beams were likewise darkened. Toward the rear, at the end of a hypothetical front hall, a cupboard-like enclosure must have supported stairs to an upper half-story, but only a few splintered bottom steps survived. A marvel, and a testimony to the strength of a simple box frame, that this shell had survived at all.

That same solidity, to its discredit, had trapped the stink of mildew, of a pervasive, nameless putrescence, and of a lifetime's piss. Which in its sordid way bespoke inhabitation, along with the straightback chair at a humble oaken table with hand-turned, bulbous legs, and beside it, a Victorian trunk with convex lid and brass ribs green with tarnish. Thankfully, the furniture was a mere pace or two across the squalid, perilously sagging floor.

A viscous film of plaster dust and grime overlay the table and every-thing on it. Black-and-white photos of quaintly clothed people, letter-size envelopes and their scribbled contents, postcards of beaches and main streets, and newspaper clippings were barely readable and nothing I cared to touch. Had to transcend my aversion, though, in light of something por-tentous about a sheaf of various papers, veterinary bills, feed store receipts, Grange announcements, splayed out like a poker hand but fastened at one corner by a twisted loop of baling wire threaded through ragged slits inflict-ed by a knife or screwdriver.

My skin couldn't help but crawl as thumb and forefinger hoisted the bundle by its wire loop. Turned it tentatively to and fro in midair. Aha! A positive development, for once. Blank backsides had functioned as station-ery. An elderly hand had mostly won the struggle for legibility, and blue ink hadn't faded too badly. Best of all, for however long these sheets had been lying facedown, they were largely free of the disgusting film. I carefully lowered the pages to the table and perused them from a standing position, bending the minimal distance to bring penmanship into clarity, refusing to acknowledge the ache that soon radiated from between shoulder blades. The manuscript seemed to commence *in medias res*, or else some of it had come detached:

> What it left behind was like a mustard seed, weak and tiny yet des-tined to blossom into something a millionfold more powerful. I told that surveyor in '26 I'd be glad when the valley flooded, but it didn't help. The thing was never going to drown, though I prayed the water might slow it down or confuse it. Then I find that Nahum Gardner's and the Blasted Heath aren't even the first places to go under. Now the blight has that much more time to spread toward me inch by inch, and the color those extra months to cross the heath and bedevil my dreams and my will as it pleases. I am fearful about it, but I can't hold anything against the state engineers, who have their obligation to the reservoir's best interests and not mine.

Up until the U.S. entered the Great War, Canucks, Poles and Italians tried tilling the abandoned farms between my land and the Gardner well. The thing haunted them and sought me out less often in those years. In hindsight I should have moved away then, but I couldn't raise the gumption to do so when the problem belonged to other people and mostly left me alone. Afterward, as soon as the foreigners fled, it was too late, and the color came prowling every week or two. I was glad to be a widower without issue, lest what had happened to Nahum's family would have happened here as well. This was still by and large how matters stood in '26, when I had tricked myself, or the fiend had tricked me, into thinking I had the situation in hand, and that I was holding off the hateful thing on my own.

These days, I wish more than anything for the wits of a younger man, to help me separate the signs of getting older from what the color is doing to me. I have found myself sitting in the parlor, or lying in bed, or staring out a window, always in a daze and slow to regain my faculties. I never recollect what I had been doing beforehand or even why I am in one room as opposed to another. The daylight or the dark around me may seem wrong, giving me to suspect I was out of the world for a fair spell. It is always possible I am going senile, except sometimes I return to myself with chills and with a hot, chafing sensation, as if I have had too much sun, and for a good while I am sickly. On those occasions I am reminded, though for my peace of mind I wish I weren't, of what Nahum had said about the living smoke that was "cold but burns." Heavens, that was over 50 years ago, but still feels like yesterday!

There are worse moments, too, when my senses come back and I hear myself blurting out the last of some syllables that stay in my mind for only a few seconds. They are nonsense, to put it mildly, or like nothing in a language of men, and my throat is always sore, which leads me to wonder if anyone listening would say I was screaming pure and simple. There are also sights that are quick to fade, like afterimages from harsh light, and mercifully they fade from memory at the same rate. The words to express any details, or anything definite, about these glimpses are beyond me, but an impression lingers of the room and its contents making up only a small part of what is around me, and merely the foreground of a vision on a scale I instinctively shrink from, and of forms and events my mind cannot abide without shutting down. I have spent earnest thought on how to put all this more plainly, but sorry to say, I cannot do better.

For more years than I am competent to add up, the Chief Engineer, a nice man called Williamson, has been paying me visits. He sees to it I have provisions and warm clothing, on top of what the delivery truck brings from town every two weeks. With him I always rally to put on my best face and keep my mind sharp and mention none of the unbelievable happenings, so that he will think the better of me and keep returning. He seems to feel a particular sympathy toward me in my isolation, which I gather is based on understanding and not pity. Piecing together some items from my stock of old newspapers, Williamson, it turns out, had a cousin who went on a disastrous Antarctic expedition in 1930 and retreated into his own solitary world ever since, quite possibly in an asylum. Williamson may be taking an interest in me because he considers both his cousin and me as kindred lost souls, and forgotten on the outskirts. Williamson does not bring his cousin up, and far be it from me to pry and discourage our friendship. Unspoken bonds of sympathy can be the most genuine kind.

Now Mr. Williamson has come with an offer of stupendously more money than the pittance of relief I've been getting in the mail once a month, since sometime after F.D.R. took office. The state wants to buy all my land along with all the land that will be on the shores of the reservoir when it is full, and save it as forest. I should jump at the chance to get away from here, but am so rooted on this property where I have lived for 80-some years, and which has been in my family since before the Revolution. I ought to start packing today, but am too muddled now to stand up and know the first thing to do. Mr. Williamson never ceases to be patient with me, though in light of how the state has been operating around here, I will be forcibly removed sooner or later. For God's sake, let it be sooner, before the color takes too much of me!

The Gardner place and part of the Blasted Heath have been under the restless water for several months already, but that has been of no help. I am being hounded with what feels like renewed purpose, as if I cannot be allowed to escape and reveal what I have learned. The thing had been planted like a mustard seed in my mind for ages, and at leisure has been coming into its own. If the pressure of fathoms does deter the awful smoke from exiting the well, it can, to as good effect, draw me to it, the way an angler plays out more or less line as he sees fit after hooking his dinner. Williamson informs me with some concern that when he has knocked on my door recently, I have not been home. He does not look reassured as I shrug off his worry and invent excuses about picking apples in my back lot or riding into town with the postman.

The truth is, I have been finding myself out of doors, a fair distance from home, with no inkling of how I came to be there. It is like a gross worsening of those spells from which I would revive somewhere in the house, and the chills and that chafing, sunburnt sensation also occur every time, along with a sickening notion that a great bite has been snapped out of me, although I can discover no bodily wounds. Sometimes I end up in the woods, or else in the middle of the Blasted Heath, where I have to fight off my panic, not least because I have been breathing in that damned unholy dust. Without fail, I am led during these episodes toward the reservoir.

I was faring poorly when Mr. Williamson was here this morning, or was it yesterday morning? He got around to the usual topic of selling out to the government before push came to shove, and my feeble nod when I gave my assent left him tongue-tied a second, and he blanched at how I nodded and shook my head and whispered yes or no in reply to his next questions. Shaken as he appeared at my sudden frailty, he said nothing more about it after he asked if I was well and remarked on my grey complexion, and I groaned and had to hide my face in my hands. Once I took charge of myself again, he said he was sorry that preparing the paperwork for the transfer would take a few days, and wanted to know if there was anything he could do for me in the meantime. I did not have it in me to express any sensible wishes, either in my mind or with my voice.

We shook hands, and I watched his black Packard raise dust down the Main Road. Next thing I knew, I was standing at the edge of the reservoir, and what restored my faculties might have been the cold water sloshing over my shoes and soaking my feet. The crust of grey powder and the dead mud underneath it were sliding into the water and bearing me with them, and I had a scant instant to right my balance and twist out of the muck. Sluggish as I was, I made tracks homeward as if death almighty was nipping at my heels, which it truly was, and I was ready to drop from exhaustion when at long last I hobbled onto my doorstep.

I pray to God I will still be here when Williamson comes back with the sales papers, though I cannot credit that the thing with its hook in me comes from a place where God exerts any influence.

That was the last line. Academic whether he had written no more, or sheets were missing. I blinked and stretched the kink out of my upper spine, which transported me from ancestral cozy farmhouse to modern wreckage, where rain cascaded down the flue and pattered across the roof. Through the distorting lens of meandering, repetitive prose by an unschooled rustic, out of his depth and going to pieces under stress, I could still vividly appreciate the stoicism, the self-reliance, the blend of stolidity and resilience in this extinct Yankee archetype. Making me all the sadder to conclude that his must have been the bones mired beside the well, among the geese and deer.

This journal of decline was even more poignant for lacking a signature. Foregoing text may have introduced his name, or subsequent text may have entreated Mr. Williamson or posterity in general to remember it. And a heedless squatter may have consigned that name to the ashes in the hearth, or let it fuse with the sodden, moldy mess on the floor. I tightly rolled the manuscript and tried flipping over some of the crusty postcards and monthly statements with it, to ferret out any legible reference to the addressee, but in my hands was the one item that wasn't glued to the festering tabletop.

Frustrating, yes. Was I stymied? Not quite. Planted one tentative foot in front of the other, and dared take one more pace, and the trunk was in reach. I heard no groan or split of floorboards. Held my breath and swung wide the creaking lid by its sprung lock plate, which protruded like a dislocated arm. A more distilled whiff of corruption made my eyes water, and when I squeezed the tears away, I was peering down at tintype portraits of a bearded man and chinless woman under cracked glass in gilt oval frames, and a photo album in leatherbound cardboard cover warped into drastic corrugations, and jumbled Sunday garments with streaks of black mold on white fabric, and white mildew on black fabric. Callous trespassers, perhaps over decades, had rifled through these keepsakes and must have scattered much else, for the trunk was half empty. Was I gawking at the face of the anonymous author, at his wife, at his one decent suit?

With a fingertip I flipped back the cover of the photo album, in last-ditch search for captions and inscriptions. My retinas had absorbed nothing beyond the palsied, violet "To A.P." across an invitation-size envelope on top of the first black page of bleached-out pictures, when a prolonged scream from somewhere almost sent me scrambling. The prospect of ambush at the door cowed me into an indecisive crouch, in semi-pirouette. Impossible to localize the outcry because of a bewildering muffled or stifled quality, for which mucus or confinement or infirmity were as likely responsible as distance. Couldn't even gauge if it expressed anger, fear, or pain, none of it necessarily directed at me, but the implicit message about my wellbeing was unmistakable. The squatter, or whatever had clumsily stalked me down by the cove in August, was coming home, and I didn't want to be intercepted out on the Blasted Heath, let alone trapped in here. Did I have minutes or seconds? Enough, anyway, for more than a craven retreat? Camcorder and plastic satchel were hanging idle off my shoulder. Bluntly testifying to my limited presence of mind. To live with myself, I had to decide, on the spur of the instant, did I dare whip out camcorder for a token sweep of the premises, or go straight to stuffing the satchel with A.P.'s relics?

Even that choice died in the making. The thump of some soft, wet mass against squeaky metal arrested everything in me apart from my loud, racing heart. Whatever was out there had already erased the buffer zone between us, and the yielding sound of its flesh connoted nothing so straightforward as a homeless person. Not anymore, at least. And where was it? Not at door or windows, though I should've reckoned with a back entrance hidden by the remnant stairwell. Devoted my attention to catching telltale shadows and rustlings from that direction, till the detail recurred to me of squelching body's impact upon metal. What could that involve except the bulkhead? And while I'd been all eyes and ears, a foul scent had blossomed around me as if a coffin had popped open. I drew convulsive breath and gagged at lungs full of putrescence as another inhumanly prolonged, inhumanly expressive scream assaulted me from underfoot. Did the source of the stench prefer dwelling in the cellar, or was it hatching some stratagem against me? Was it screaming to rout me, or to summon help?

The table and chair had blocked the rubbish from accumulating in several spots, where loose floorboards still showed. Through the gap between them erupted a pallid bluish glow, like that of Lucinda's water when it broke or the meteor samples in 1882 or the anomaly in the submerged well. And something must have been feeling its way along the basement ceiling because particles of plaster were coming loose beneath the floor, and clattering like sleet.

The screaming ceased, and something metal thrust up amidst the glow between the floorboards, inches from my shoes. Before it slowly sank from view, a sunburst-shaped stain halfway along its shaft jogged my memory. Here was the saw with which Wil had mangled himself on the path to the reservoir, and which had vanished before I'd fled from the reservoir shore. That was when my self-control collapsed. Minus souvenirs or footage, I careened out of the house, into the drizzle, toward the barbwire fence.

With more haste than care, and without stopping first, I pushed down on the top wire, but misgauged the midway point between knots, one of which punctured skin at the base of my thumb. Shit! After hopping over, I paused to squeeze out blood, and swaddled handkerchief around the gash, and whenever tetanus crossed my mind, or worse, the grey powder, I stumbled to another halt and expelled more dollops of potentially tainted blood.

Despite so much going wrong, luck hadn't entirely deserted me. My footprints in the Blasted Heath had held their shape and led me to the yellow trail. If the thing in the cellar had been signaling for an ally, I staggered and loped from grey wasteland to matted wilderness to the parking lot without any signs of it. I headed straight for the car. No profit in chatting with the rangers again. And even if I hadn't seen it face to face, I'd been confronted all too vividly with the long-term effect of drinking from the reservoir.

Twenty-three

Scrounged my inelegant excuse for supper from the freezer. Veggie burgers, sweet potato French fries. To get eating out of the way a.s.a.p. before I set about blurring today's additions to my list of shame via single-malt and basic rocking out. Blasting the Who and Bevis Frond and the Stooges instead of brooding over failures to shoot video, and fill my satchel, and observe what had actually happened to the squatter, and jump a fence without jabbing ghastly infection into my bloodstream. On top of bungling every opportunity in the last three months to avert the looming crisis. Toyed with smoothing rough mental edges in earnest by scraping together another toke from my vestigial stash. Was moseying toward the baggie in my socks drawer when the blinking red of answering machine snagged me in passing. Stop the music! Jesus, I couldn't pull one right move, could I? Innocent bid to sooth my psyche with drink and decibels had blotted out what might have been Herb reporting in, maybe with City Hall thugs at his heels. I fought to overrule my McClelland's buzz and the ringing in my ears and hit playback, and then the world turned upside-down. It was Wil.

"Jeff, were you here today? Or when?" Each gurgling, raspy word seemed to struggle laboriously past his lips. "Where are you? Can't talk anymore after this. Bones all coming loose. It made me accept Morgan, you know. And then it got me. Dissolving from inside. Not myself anymore. Can see someplace all flux and ripples and folding. No eyes to see with here. Nothing with eyes here, ever. Lucinda, don't do that! Stop it! Won't work!" End of final message.

In my subpar condition, had to sit down before the emotional crosscurrents floored me. Lucinda was home? Applying Occam's razor for want of better tools, much more sensible to lump her among Wil's patently hallucinatory experiences of "flux and ripples," et cetera. But wherever his wife was, Wil had been relatively lucid, and had been reaching through his torment toward me while I'd been selfishly immersed in Iggy belting out "Raw Power." Another wretched fumble I'd never live down! And my levy of guilt burst under pressure from the related question, How many days since my best and only friend had even rated a thought? Worse, I'd written him off as deceased, and here he was valiantly clinging to sentient life, without an ounce of help from me.

No, get a grip, letting the tears flow while under Scotch influence would sideline me for the evening. Had to rally, and I cross-examined myself, So why was the onus for Wil's slow, lonely expiration wholly on me? Began seeing red on considering the thousandfold victims like Wil who might've been shepherded out of harm's way if city priorities had ever transcended property values and "budgetary responsibility." My every stab at "working within the system?" Deflected and belittled, or outright sabotaged. With the opaque threat of violence hanging over me for the duration.

Damned if I wasn't going to lurch off the sofa and phone Wil and start making amends right this second. While dialing, I gave short shrift to my inner reprobate crossing his fingers that Wil wouldn't pick up. For better or worse, the reprobate won. After four rings, voicemail activated. I refrained from saying anything. What could I tell Wil that I'd want the entity infesting him to hear?

Call me feckless, but I wasn't up for driving to Dyer Hall in my present state. Hitting the road now and then with a blood-alcohol handicap courtesy of the Aviator? A calculated risk, yes, but I had to get home, didn't I? On the other hand, to quit that comfy home and embark logy on a grueling, probably futile errand in the dead of night? Especially when town was a hundred subjective miles away? Blatantly foolish. Enervated me to contemplate it, and besides, the room had commenced spinning at 16 rpm, and could only accelerate from there.

Tomorrow morning, refreshed and sober, I vowed, that's when I'd exploit Wil's house keys again. But bed was where I belonged, with the tv to divert me from bedspin, at this ripe hour of 10 PM when one channel broadcast local news. Ages since I'd sampled what passed for current events in Occam. Foresaw shallower banalities than ever, thanks largely to city government's informal chokehold on meaningful reportage. Good for a sardonic laugh, I wagered.

No familiar faces on camera. Even the weathergirl was a sub, new hire, or intern. Merciless ailment had purged the ranks of everyone handsome, buff, slim, perky, cute, or sexy. After ads for a Connecticut casino and online dating, a portly matron who could've been Ms. Lathrop's older sister recapped a developing story that must have aired initially when I was in the bathroom. A good thing I was lying down. In a trice I was stunned and faint, with bulging eyes and a profound tingle in my throat. This in spite of blatant amateur's fractured reading off the teleprompter.

"Lethal force rings out in a house of healing! In the third such incident this week, police responded to a 911 call from the Osborn Clinic in Armitage, where several women, apparently without warning, simultaneously displayed erratic and destructive behavior." The station had tastefully pixelized the faces of patients and orderlies alike in jumpy CCTV clips. Spastic women in hospital gowns were screaming, running wild, and throwing furniture and potted palms around a solarium. Staff were out of their depth, and doing their utmost to avoid collisions and flying objects, accomplishing nothing, but standing their ground, maybe out of professional pride.

Cops blipped from out of nowhere into the next excerpt, and their dark uniforms added salt-and-pepper contrast, and sardine-tin overcrowding, to the white-coat disarray. Then healthcare personnel disappeared, and cops were roaring at inpatients to disperse, and just as vainly clutching at elbows and hems that jerked away. One strapping lawman tried restraining someone half his size, who yanked him off his feet. He weathered a few hysterical kicks and slams in his scramble to rejoin his squad at the dumbstruck periphery.

Crazy or not, these rioters had felled a peacekeeper, justifying escalation to tasers. Or, as the newscaster yammered, "When the mob ignored verbal commands, stronger measures to restore calm became necessary. In surveillance video released exclusively to News Tracker Team at 10, you can see how some of the patients continued to act up after one, two, and three attempts to pacify them. One officer sustained minor injuries and was transported to Houghton General. Participants in the disturbance were remanded to the custody of the clinic, with a single exception. Tragically, patrolmen were unable to subdue one patient, who was fatally shot, according to a public liaison officer, in self-defense. She's seen here charging at police with what appears to be a fire extinguisher." The image froze as cops drew and aimed sidearms at their attacker, who had fuzzy cubes for a face and electrode wires sprouting like lionfish spines. Had to be grateful for the station's policy of freezing footage before bullets found their mark. Wondered how long broadcasters could resist airing snuff films in the name of "people's right to know."

The clarification I'd been dreading, and hoping against, and never in any doubt about, followed. "Pronounced dead on the scene was Lucinda Rice, age 37, of Occam. The Osborn Clinic has been unable to reach her husband, Wilbur Rice, for the past month. Anyone with information on his whereabouts is asked to contact the clinic or the Armitage Police. The Osborn Clinic specializes in holistic group therapy for postpartum depression, and to quote a spokesperson, has never had to deal with security problems, least of all on account of their clientele. The same spokesperson speculated that a rare drug interaction or virus may have given rise to the irrational behavior, but in the wake of tonight's third such outbreak, the state licensing board is launching a review of the facility's standard of care and practices." While the story wrapped up, and used car salesmen and mattress outlets pitched their wares, and callow weathergirl muddled through the seven-day forecast, my fizzling mind could only entertain the sentiment, "Boy, Lucinda really hated people blabbing about her age."

I struggled out of neutral and clicked off the set at the anchorman's advice to "Stay tuned for *Seinfeld*!" Had seen 'em all three times, safe to say. Also a solid bet that Lucinda had died as Wil was entreating her, and watching her via the "color" in his eyes. Meanwhile, what a convenience for City Hall that the Armitage cops, knowingly or not, had expunged this most dramatic case of a *de novo* syndrome that would have cast publicity sooner or later on the Gorman County Reservoir. The News Tracker Team had mentioned nothing, and may have been privy to nothing, about Lucinda's physical symptoms, which surely would have hoisted red flags anywhere outside the Osborn Clinic's circle of quacks and Occam's muzzled brotherhood of physicians. As for an autopsy? Cause of death was no puzzle, Lucinda's next of kin was unavailable to sign consent, and once the corpse was back in town, it might be misplaced or cremated, but dissected, never.

Without the tv blathering, the ruckus of fugitive dog pack carried to me from deep in the woods behind my yard. I found it contrarily soothing, in part because it was too far off for me to worry about paws toppling my garbage cans tonight. And in part because the dogs were sounding endowed with way more life than townsfolk I'd met recently. If Elsie was in the chorus, she was in tremendously better shape than the rest of the Rice household. Occurred to me, might be nice to get up and holler for Elsie, and short of coaxing her in, be able to assure Wil I'd seen her anyway and she was okay. However, mulling all this over used up my last ounce of energy, and I capsized into sleep till 9 AM.

Twenty-four

Yes, I was bound for Dyer Hall, in spite of my serial procrastination, both conscious and unconscious, commencing with my late tumble out of bed. I deserved a hangover, but in its absence, had to endorse that myth of clear-headed mornings-after thanks to single-malt purity. Already on the cusp of lunchtime as I jiggled the key into the ignition. How prudent, really, was dropping by Wil's without some fortification first? By the time I finished debating that, I was parked in front of the Aviator. Intrepid barkeep might have some pithy counsel for me on this mission. Or so I told myself. However, windows and door were boarded up, with massive plywood sections, as before a hurricane. In disarmingly fancy cursive was a ballpoint inscription, directly on the plywood over the door, "On Vacation. Watch for Reopening." The mordant humor of a Nam-era fighter pilot?

Next stop, Koerner's. Convinced I had hunger to assuage, even if washing down food with a pint of courage wasn't an option. But a napkin taped to the inside of the glass door announced, "Closed for Illness." I grimaced to picture the softhearted old gent laid low, in bluish, brittle collapse, palsied, deranged in mind and senses. Scant days ago, he'd acted hardy as ever. Had cosmic infection slipped from soapy water into some little cut while he was scrubbing knives? Unhelpful, morbid thoughts ensued about my own barb-wire laceration beneath a Band-Aid, and to leave those ruminations behind, I had to hop in the car and peel out.

On to Abdul's, striving not to dwell on its proximity to City Hall. Fewer drivers and pedestrians were out than on a Sunday morning; I also strove not to study any of them in passing. Plenty of parking, too, and when I stepped out on the sidewalk, I was in sniffing range of grilled onions and chickpeas. Ah, this one restaurant was surviving, or more precisely, some townies were letting no tap water cross their lips. Westcott's dictum to consort with nobody from former worksite had no expiration date, I reckoned, making this noon hour the riskiest to hang around here. And speak of the devil, Mr. Big Shot Recorder of Deeds himself burst, as if shoved, out the wildly swinging door of the neighboring Fleur de Lys Spirits.

I didn't have to worry about Edward Orne reporting this encounter, even though we were face to face with the length of a pool cue between us. He may well have been summarily ejected from the liquor store. He bore no likeness to the image of a preferred customer. One hand was throttling a fifth of Smirnoff by the neck. No nicety of a paper sack for his merchandise. And he may well have slept a week in his standard pumpkin-colored work attire, baggy on him now like folds of liposuctioned skin, and rife with accordion creases, and various shades dingier in places. In complexion and posture he was a sagging column of ashes, and he swayed transfixed, enthralled, apparently by vistas filling his bug eyes through no intermediary of smudgy tortoiseshell lenses. Twitching jowls and cadaverously prominent overbite still gave him the air of a tame woodchuck, but with an expression that no one, I'd daresay, had ever seen on a woodchuck before. Not in me to dawdle there and clock how long until he moved again or else crystallized like Lot's wife.

The headier aroma inside the shop had me salivating. Guess I had scared up an appetite for real. One customer was at the counter, murmuring his order to a gangly Syrian youth practically begging him for the third time to "repeat louder, please!" My worst misgivings proved legit when the whisperer shuffled aside to wait for his shawarma, and I pushed forward and beheld in profile my soft-spoken ex-boss Mr. Marsh.

Told the Syrian teen I'd like a falafel in whole-wheat pocket, heavy on the hot sauce if he could, and a medium Mountain Dew. I was the end of the line, but shuffled aside out of habit, and found Mr. Marsh fixing his wan blue eyes on me. Dammit to hell!

He smiled cordially, and I really expected it to sound like paper crinkling. "Why, Jeffrey! You haven't been in for a while. Are you on vacation, or were you sick?"

I was so nonplussed that they'd kept him in the dark, and that he'd gone along with it in such naive complacency, that I stupidly jabbered, "I was fired on Monday!"

The news palpably shook and bewildered him. "I was never informed." Here was his golden chance to pump me for details, but he only took a mental note. "I'll have to look into this." And then his sandwich was ready. His incuriosity toward me was both off-putting and a big relief. His intention to dig for answers at City Hall, on the other hand, was alarming, but what could I say to dissuade him? Oh don't bother, Mr. Marsh, I don't care, it's fine? I'm counting on a tacit deal with the Third Floor to score Unemployment, but if you start snooping around, they'll kill me? How about a change of subject in hopes it'd sidetrack him into forgetting this inquiry on my behalf? Quick, the cashier was doling out his change.

"I see you're drinking bottled water. A lot healthier than my beverage of choice. Wish I had your strength of character."

"Oh, I don't know." His smile had grown more wry than congenial. "A lot of our blueblood Mayflower types won't touch the city water. Including the Westcotts and the Lathrops and the Pabodies. Too common for them, I suppose, or otherwise not to their taste. By the way, my own vacation starts next week. Peak season for foliage in the White Mountains." I watched him turn and go, then blinked in surprise to see he was gone. With 20/20 hindsight, it was dawning on me that Mr. Marsh was one more example of the "old Occam" I didn't understand at all.

For dining in, a silver Formica shelf ran the width of plate-glass frontage and the wall to either side of it. I took the corner stool, with my back to the indoors and my nose to the dull brown paint. I ate in blissful ignorance of anyone else coming in. No one violated my space. No goons on my tail yet!

After my last bite, jitters set in again. But the better part of valor couldn't be simpler: flee with my unfinished Mountain Dew from City Hall environs, and to where except Dyer Hall? Well, there was Danforth Manor, to collar Professor Thayer off-guard and solicit a scrap or two of the grudging wisdom I'd sought at the Aviator. Yes, okay, that was arguably to good purpose, I conceded, but no further detours would be tolerated.

Akeley Street afforded ideal parking spots, like everywhere else today. Better yet, as I observed from halfway across the Manor's gangway of decaying railroad ties, a cinderblock was propping ajar one of the frosted-glass double doors. In my climb up the four starkly echoing flights, I was impressed that someone was still clearing away litter, all but the apparently freshest burger wrappers and paper cups and wet condoms. I also braced for exchanges of screaming between apartments, and when none had overtaken me on the uppermost landing, envisioned tenants too far gone, mute and hollow, spellbound by nonhuman perspectives in their parasitized retinas. How many caregivers had been made to "accept" their unliving dependents, as Wil had "accepted" Morgan, and were now corrupt vessels themselves? And why were some victims simple fodder, like the kid at Radio Shack, while others like Lucinda became conduits for unearthly temperament?

Spacing out on rhetorical issues was not a smart option at the mouth of dismal corridor leading to Thayer's door, which hung open a few inches, disgorging a glow of more UV tinge than the sallow output of humming overhead fluorescents. Knocked twice, grasping the doorknob lest door creak shut and lock me out. No answer. Tried again. Still nothing. I was batting zero everywhere today, but if Thayer wasn't home, then neither was his sinister factotum Castro. That was some consolation.

They didn't seem the type to take off and leave the lights on, and as I stole in and confirmed, they weren't. The bluish glow hindered instead of promoting clarity, and was it really bluish, or grayish, or that unreadable, baneful color hovering in my periphery ever since that midnight on the reservoir? Moreover, it had become the apartment's dominant note. Gone were the bookcases, record shelves, CD units, all their contents, the stereo, the La-Z-Boy, the piano, the armchairs, and the rest of what had parceled one big main room into sections.

Numerous black scuffmarks had the pine floorboards to themselves, almost to the far wall. Over where television and Ionic podium and tables used to be, there were only the plants that had crowded them. And thanks to them, it felt like I was inhaling from a vase in which a bouquet had been wilting for days. Splotchy black and brown, carbonized, exuding ugly stink despite chilly draft from fully open windows, they were also the source of unclean radiance. More of the murky glow was manifest through kitchen and bedroom doorways. The soil in terracotta pots, though, was still dark from recent watering.

Occurred to me that after my visit, Thayer may have switched from bottled to tap water for his houseplants. Using them as coal mine canaries. With everything disassembled or in crates for the moving van as soon as the "color" in foliage reached lethal proportions. And had blind, feeble Thayer lifted a finger? All that hard prep work must have devolved upon antique Castro's uncanny reserves of strength.

Decided I might as well make the most of illegal entry, and stepped over limp fronds and stalks sprawling from their crockery like limbs of squashed crabs, and checked out the kitchen. In tighter quarters, the smell of floral rot was worse, emanating from hothouse exotics distorted beyond recognition on countertops and floor. Evacuation had excluded stove, dishwasher, and fridge, and magnets in the shape and size of carpenter ants fixed an 8 × 11 piece of paper to the fridge door.

Castro, presumably, had done his arthritic best, in a compact, spiky cursive redolent of the Belle Époque, to transcribe Thayer's message: "Piscids arrive Tuesday after next. Help yourself to whatever's in the fridge." I had a powerful hunch this note was meant for me. Pulled it loose, and sent a shower of black iron ants to the linoleum. Wasn't about to humor any invitation to open that fridge, though. Sounded too much like the setup for an unsavory prank. Before folding up the paper and sticking it in my denim jacket's inside pocket, I had a look at its backside. Huh? God damn their bastard idea of a joke! It was a page from Thayer's 1982 typescript about the meteor, out of the folder from which I'd somehow been divested when last at this address.

Maybe the folder was in the fridge. Getting damp in the vegetable crisper. Or nestling amidst gruesomely expired meat and produce. No, on reflection, the message seemed ever more like a leering come-on. Incumbent on me to resist temptation.

So how did I know some or all of the missing pages weren't strewn around the bedroom? Worth a peek. The rotten miasma was at its most stifling in there, with one narrow ineffectual window toward the northeast corner. Had to count my blessings on thinking that some rooms in these Section 8 apartments might have no windows at all. Bed and other furnishings were removed, and the closet with partly retracted sliding door was vacant. The pots of ruined herbage had sole occupancy, but on one moss-green wall, above a dark oval where the back of Thayer's head must have rested on his pillow, was a design indecipherable across a room of livid haze. Had to commit myself to point-blank range before it would resolve, and then I was impossibly torn between flinching in disgust and ogling till I gleaned some meaning from what was in front of me.

In Castro's anachronistic hand was a circle of Latin text, wide enough to crawl through, indelible in black Sharpie, within a square of Arabic jotted down, I guessed, by a quill pen loaded with indigo dye, within a triangle of Punic or Egyptian hieratic, maybe, or something even more arcane, daubed by thin brushstrokes in the brownish red of blood. Outside the triangle were white chalk symbols that coincided with the four compass points, and that seemed equally animal or vegetable, and most reminiscent of Mayan glyphs to my amateur eye. The southern emblem overlapped the grease from Thayer's scalp.

At the core of this elaborate framework, carpet tacks impaled a used condom, the easiest fetish object to find in this building. No mean skill had stretched the latex taut like a cowhide, and the placement of tacks echoed the four compass points. In the center of the condom, a sewing needle skewered the thumb-sized molt of a wolf spider. This sordid display didn't feel directed at me, especially if it were intended to deliver a curse. Where was Castro's motivation? What had I done to him? Or was this an unusually literal treatment of prophylactic magic, and to what end? Of all my fellow townsmen whose depths I'd belatedly come to acknowledge, Castro was in a class by himself.

I wrenched myself away from his handiwork and hurried, queasy and unclean in more a spiritual than bodily sense, out of the apartment. Derived some consolation from finding the Taurus hadn't been further vandalized, and from telling myself that whatever else the day had in store, it couldn't get any weirder from here. When would I learn?

No more excuses blocked the road to Dyer Hall. Akeley Street and Ellery Avenue had effectively become one community joined in desolation. Any demographic gulf between them had imploded. Cosmetically different at most. Not a soul hither or yon in front of Wil's building, or traversing its stairs and corridors. None of the encoded screaming, no mania like Lucinda's, penetrated the insulating doors. The similarity to a mausoleum was more convincing than ever. More than at Danforth Manor. Not even a spent condom on the burgundy carpet as a sign of life.

In deference to formality, I knocked before using Wil's key. That served only to make me skittish at defiling the grave-like silence. Had this corridor always acted like an amplifier? Spurred purely by worst-case conjecture that something fiendish in neighboring apartment might be on to me, I ducked inside, encouraged by the normal level of daylight through parted drapes.

Then I inhaled, and that sunny first impression fell to pieces. No layer of smoke dimmed the air, though my sinuses clogged and stung with its rarefied acrid traces. A roast in the oven, a shirt on the ironing board, dust and mold in a heating vent, all had seemingly scorched in tandem, along with some ingredient more foreign that conjured up the ruin in the woods. Walls and ceilings, open doorways into bedroom and kitchen, and the clustered rubbish on the floor had withstood no blackening by fire. The floor, meanwhile, was somehow cleansed of the grey powder's snaking tidelines. And where was Wil? The funereal hush out front and on the way up persisted in here, but some subliminal input warned I wasn't alone.

My eyes were studiously avoiding the bulky furniture straight ahead. Accidentally on purpose, I guessed. Easy enough to rationalize that I had no reason to look because nothing was moving. The side table of bamboo and rattan had a blue porcelain lamp on it and partly screened the gap between brown leather sofa and glass-top coffee table. A much broader gap separated the coffee table and the jumbo tv in profile on its squat modernist stand. None of these had been singed, either. I had yet to account for the reek in my nostrils. The toes of scruffy black slippers poked past the side table's bamboo legs, and blended in well with the red and black faux Persian rug. Between bamboo leg and the edge of the sofa I spied a sliver of khaki trouser. All right then, whether quiescent or lurking or napping, Wil had to be slouched on the sofa.

I prowled up to him, and my mental gears jammed harshly at efforts to process that he was, and he wasn't. He was present only up to his shins. His former position was demarcated by a charred half-moon on leather sofa cushion and a cutout of roughly head-and-shoulder outline in the glass tabletop. Where Wil's legs ended, flesh and fabric alike had cauterized into surreally smooth, glazed cross-sections the color of caramel.

Grief and shock at my friend's freakish death collided helter-skelter with my struggle to reconstruct what had happened. The tableau evoked some association buried deep in my brain full of esoteric rubbish. Spontaneous human combustion! Lurid docutainment on the Discovery Channel had lingered upon photos of victims annihilated except for undamaged stumps below the knees. Unlike historic examples, though, the cause here posed no riddle after brief reflection. Thayer's précis of the incidents in 1882 referred to "mutual assured destruction" when meteoric samples came into contact with glass. For whatever reason that occurred, it was manifestly also the upshot after too much "color" and its byproducts had accumulated in human cells. At and around their intersection, Wil and the coffee table had simply cancelled each other out, in compliance with some rule of chemistry beyond human supposition.

Had Wil passed out or dozed off and unwittingly slumped face-first against the table, or had he observed or guessed or learned through osmosis of sorts from the "color" itself what the glass would do, and drugged or steeled himself into self-immolation? Perhaps in throes of emotional overload after empathic linkage with Lucinda as she died? Could I have prevented this by picking up the phone last night instead of deafening myself with Iggy and the Stooges? But given the option, should I have? By design or not, he may have been better off, compared with more ravaged casualty in A.P.'s cellar.

A chill lifted the hairs above my denim collar and skittered down my back. At first I credited my body with its own autonomous reaction to this macabre tragedy. When a stiffer breeze ran through my thin graying hair, it broke my horrorstruck fixation on the Ozymandias-like remnants on the rug, just when I had devolved into mouthing inappropriately, "Look on my works, ye Mighty, and despair."

The drapes were drawn apart, but the windows were down. I'd neglected to shut the apartment door, and now I faced a draft that flowed into the hall from window frames completely devoid of glass. Eradicated, I reckoned, the same millisecond as the stripes of grey powder on the floor. Nor did any glass shine in the heaps of trash or in the chassis of the tv, which had only been nudged a few inches backward and a few degrees off a head-on view from the sofa. A uniquely selective shock wave that belonged in no rational physics had consumed all glass and tinges of "color" before it, while exerting scarce impact otherwise. Akin to how that more propulsive backlash had behaved after Thayer exposed grey powder to X-rays.

Taking a breath, I was grateful to the draft for blunting the sting of caustic smoke a little. At my next breath, my knees almost buckled out from under me and I fought to keep from retching. Some new, much worse odor, as of death in swampy fermentation, reminded me of the presence in A.P.'s cellar, but this was tenfold more potent. Behind me, on the hardwood floor at the edge of the rug where nothing had been before, was a sebaceous, mealy puddle that seemed foremost like vomit, maybe because I was too racked with nausea for likening it to anything else. What was it? Not the first time today I compulsively studied something from which I dearly wanted to flinch away.

Contours gradually suggested anatomy, despite my difficulty reading their incomplete, disorderly pattern within mottled, gangrenous grey and olive and ochre. Tiny vertebrae were aligned diagonally and off-center, like the minute hand of a clock. Limbs and extremities were discontinuous ridges, with lengths of disarticulated bone leaching through, and disjointed fingers fanned out between webbed tissue, as in the wingspans of bats. And again like the minute hand of a clock, this corporeal slag appeared motionless, but had imperceptibly advanced. Most of its amoebic outline was on top of the rug, and that much closer to me, where I apprehended how much less inert this thing was than I'd thought. Spells of fine, gelatinous quivering possessed it, and tumescent red and blue veins throbbed sluggishly, in the service of brackish vasculature.

Only now did I have to concede that something animate was inching toward me. Not alive, but imbued with life. And though face and skull had totally subsided into the morass of viscous tissue, two filmy nodules toward its leading edge jolted me when I realized they were eyes, and they were locked on mine. Sprouting from the bodily debris, they upheld their basic structures like stubborn islands after the sea had reclaimed everything around them. Dead eyes, askew and adjacent like those of flounders, but not sightless. Without the faintest gleam of curiosity or emotion, they were cognizant of me, and judging by their soulless fixation, their owner was creeping toward me simply because I was there. It wanted nothing of me, or to do anything to me. I picked up no sense that it knew why it was doing what it was doing, as if the blank slate of infantile perception still somehow informed an utterly alien mentality.

Corpus and mind of baby Morgan had been fodder for something that battened on the material and immaterial as if they were no different, and Wil had been forced to "accept" this ghoulish residue, potentially forever because the permeating "color" functioned as both solvent and adhesive, binding together the corruption it expedited, and to what opaque, inhuman purpose? Wil may have needed no further incentive to lay his head on the coffee table as on the chopping block.

While I pondered all this, the sickening detritus of Morgan had shifted most of itself onto the rug, almost within stomping range. Not about to find out what effect that would have! Nor could I abide this mockery of life and do nothing. It made too apt a scapegoat as months of belated anger welled up at fumbling along helpless, semi-hysterical, laboring under a craven shellshock that was bound to be my behavioral norm till further notice. Should I heave some crushing weight at it? The shell of the big-screen tv? No, the risk of splattering was more than I dared imagine, even if a Sorcerer's Apprentice scenario didn't result, with some dozen sentient gouts of rancid blood and flesh surrounding me. By the same logic, using the lamp or anything else as a club was out.

What more did I have to work with? Piles of trash. Keeping Morgan in peripheral view, for he didn't seem to move so long as I did, I scanned the wrappers, cartons, junk mail, cans, dishes, cups within the rubbish. No, an unqualified bust as far as fashioning impromptu harpoon went.

But a lot of it was flammable. One eye still on Morgan, I sidled to the nearest midden. Extracted a 24-ounce Styrofoam tumbler that may have contained gravy or lo mein or a slushie or coffee. The stickiness inside no longer allowed for identification. Plunked a shard of ceramic mug to the bottom for ballast. Added a loose fill of crumpled, shredded newsprint, catalogues, paperback, Yellow Pages. And what luck! On a crust of fossilizing toast perched a dab of translucent butter, which I smeared around the inner rim of the tumbler. Poor man's accelerant. Yanked my lighter from denim jacket pocket. Nasty as the blend of flaming butter and Styrofoam would be, they hadn't a prayer of cutting through the fug of unburied death.

Oh shit! While I was cadging together my incendiary device, Morgan, in stealthy minute-hand manner, had slid past the side table and tv, and was slowly stretching a tubular outgrowth of grayish skin and blood vessels toward my left shoe. I skipped back a pace. A cold surge of panic compromised my righteous anger. After a couple of vehement tries that nearly sprained my thumb, I got the lighter going. Dipped it into crinkles of paper above the buttered Styrofoam rim till each ignited, one, two, three, four in rapid succession. The cup was blazing up fast, and fearful now of burnt fingertips as well as this abomination pawing at me, I fitfully chucked my lowly weapon, which landed upright and dead-center on target.

A spasm throughout the organism, in response, perhaps, to no more than the novelty of being touched, shook the sizzling container onto its side, and scorching contents spilled out. I suppressed a desire to bolt, to give Morgan wide berth without a backward glimpse. I had to see what would happen. The greasy, porous hide around the de facto kindling immediately gave off thin, black smoke, and tiny combustions like candle or pilot lights rapidly multiplied and joined together into a broad-based pyramid of fire, with plastic cup melting at its heart.

Independent of each other, Morgan's lidless eyes rolled lazily away from me and toward the conflagration on his midsection. They watched passively, without signs of concern. Amorphous flesh didn't buck or writhe. Pain receptors must have rotted clean out. I stood spellbound, staring at Morgan staring at himself on fire, until a hot updraft of cremation, suffusing the already insufferable stench of oily, spoiled meat, smacked into me. At that instant the smoke alarm, wherever it was, began assaulting me with earsplitting pulses. For all that compunction about holding my ground till I was good and ready to exit calmly, sensory overkill propelled me out the door, which I slammed behind me if only to seal off sights, sound, and smell. Very little of the bedlam leaked into the corridor, and deathly peace reigned absolute once I was on the stairs.

Blinking in the sunshine on the steps of Dyer Hall, I had to disengage a while from dwelling on those images of Wil obliterated above the shins, of his baby converted into animate slag and disinterested in his own incineration. I could steep myself in this tranquil moment on unpeopled Ellery Avenue, or I could start gibbering, and I'd never make it home that way. But I couldn't rid my head of the unconstructive notion that Wil had never really wanted to be a parent in the first place.

Twenty-five

Home again. Jacket I hung up, for once, by the back door, a couple of pegs from the nearest garment, instead of flinging it over one piece of furniture or another, in impromptu quarantine because of the tainted places it had been today. Shoes I exiled to the doormat. Trousers came off and went directly into the washing machine. Washed my hands on the wrong side of neurotically. Crashed for the remainder of the afternoon. Needed to go blank, let my brain cool down. But unfinished business, loose ends had followed me from town and barred me from relaxing. Didn't have to dwell on their specifics. Enough to know they were there.

Threw in the towel at 5:30 and turned on the news. Ms. Lathrop's putative older sister was at the helm, with no word of Dyer Hall going up in smoke. Great. Cross off one loose end. Maybe the fire on Morgan's back had burnt itself out, or had consumed him without spreading. Such was now an example of situations working out for the best.

Had no appetite, so the hell with supper. Something more important nagged at me, something I had come away with and forgotten about. Had to peel down today's journey like layers of onion, reconstruct my actions everywhere. The Aviator, Koerner's, Abdul's? Yes, I had decamped with an unfinished Mountain Dew after lunch, non-potable by now in the car's cup holder, but that wasn't it. Next stop had been Thayer's vacant quarters, through which I retraced my queasy steps. Into the unwholesome blue glow, the funk of dead houseplants, the stifling kitchen, and bingo! That message waiting for me on the fridge was still wadded in my jacket pocket.

High time I quit my bed anyhow. I half expected Thayer's note to have spirited itself away, like my green folder the previous time, but no, there it was. I unfolded it and read aloud, "Piscids arrive Tuesday after next. Help yourself to whatever's in the fridge."

Might have turned on the computer and googled the Piscids, but Thayer had said they were meteors, and I had it on his good authority when they were due, so what extra research was needed? The professor had hinted at a life cycle of the "color," which had traveled earthward in a meteor, and become more active during the Perseids, and must have been preparing for climactic exertions the "Tuesday after next," or else why single out that date in writing?

So in essence, Occam had a week to live. Followed by ill-defined but total devastation. And could I name a local who'd greet my warning without skepticism or hostility? Who except Ranger Metcalfe, and he'd been M.I.A. since sending an e-mail Wednesday night. Yeah, right, another loose end to tie up. Check in at Herb's home number, make sure he was okay. That need to remember was finally easing up.

A woman answered his phone.

"Hi, I was wondering if I could speak with Herb, please?"

"No. You can't." She sounded profoundly grim.

Holy cow, did Herb have a wife? Kids? I really knew as little of him as I did of Castro. What's more, based on the tone of those three words, I'd blown any chance of finding out. "Is this Mrs. Metcalfe?"

"No. I'm a friend of the family. Eliza's in no condition to talk. Who is this, please?"

"Jeff. A friend of his."

"Jeff? Never heard of you."

"We met not too long ago."

"Uh-huh." Great. Whatever the hell had happened, I had blithely strolled into the circle of suspects.

"Look, I have no idea what's going on. Could you at least please give me a broad outline?"

"If you insist. Do you mind if I have this call traced?"

"If you insist."

Somehow that prompted her to grant me the benefit of the doubt, though hopefully she was bluffing. "Hold on, I'm taking the phone in the other room. No point repeating this in front of her."

"Thank you. I've been concerned about him." At any rate, a slew of butterflies had been beating wings against my stomach wall for a minute or so.

"He didn't come home from work yesterday." The voice had dropped into a lower, more guarded register. "When he was four hours late, Eliza called the police, but they put her off with the usual crap about waiting 12 hours to declare him missing. She tried the hospitals and even the city morgue, three times, but no one of his description ever turned up."

I dreaded the direction this was heading, and wished I hadn't asked, but the figurative horses were out the gate and galloping. As if this recital may have had some therapeutic value. "This morning the police got off their duff, and when Eliza said his last known whereabouts had been the Parks Department by the reservoir, they sent one measly car out there. She went on her own. The cops started by interviewing Herb's coworkers, but they were useless. Down with that bug that makes people dopey and out of it. The police are apparently shorthanded from guys calling in sick with the same thing."

"I'm glad you and Mrs. Metcalfe aren't affected."

"Well, we live a few houses over the line in Hoyle. It hasn't spread here yet, as far as I can tell. But as it turned out, the men didn't have to widen their search off the hiker trails. He was in plain sight, face down, feet still on the path in the middle of some boulders and dead trees. The one who found him shouted for his partner, and Eliza happened to be in earshot. There was a lot of blood. She went kind of crazy. He'd been stabbed and pretty badly hacked up. And not only had the killer made no effort to hide the body, he'd also dropped the murder weapon right next to it. A rusty old saw, the type with a pointy tip."

I went cold, and was thankful I'd had no supper to risk retching up. Couldn't say how many seconds passed before I realized my informant was waiting for me to express my feelings. "I'm sorry, that's beyond horrible. I'm beyond shocked." That amount of babble seemed to satisfy her.

"After they got her calmed down, Eliza called me on her cell. When I arrived, the place was lousy with uniforms and forensics and a photographer and the coroner, which I was already expecting from all the official vehicles clogging up the parking lot. I took her home, and then prevailed on a neighbor to drive me out again to fetch Eliza's car. Funny, but Herb's car was nowhere to be seen. Not by the Visitors' Center, and not in the driveway at the house."

I grunted to acknowledge it was funny, and she resumed.

"As long as I was in the vicinity, I hiked back to the crime scene, in case anyone had further information I could pass on to Eliza. Well, I stepped into a disaster area. You know, a homeless person's been holing up for years in some ancient cabin, on land off limits to the public. Herb told us after a few drinks at dinner once. It's one of those public secrets. The homeless person was the prime suspect right off the bat. Especially as you could see the shack from where Herb was lying. Except now it was completely engulfed in flames. Nobody would give me a straight answer about what had gone wrong. The chief and a lot of backup had surrounded the cabin to make an arrest if the squatter was inside, and suddenly it was an inferno. One medic told me he thought he'd heard screaming from in there, but nobody else would even talk to me about it. So if the homeless man was the murderer, that's all the justice he'd ever suffer in this world. Nothing left of him to bury."

Just as well that no pregnant pause here obliged me to act shocked, because I wasn't. Destruction of evidence with implications for much more than one nasty homicide? The liquidation of a "homeless person" whose capture would have opened a gigantic drum of uncontrollable questions? Occam's "top cop" on site although the deceased was nobody of so-called consequence, and in charge of operations when the proverbial shit hit the fan? Moreover, where were the Staties or the Parks Department in country technically outside Occam's jurisdiction? All these mysteries swirling around, in fact, merely beclouded the core issue of who had actually killed Herb Metcalfe and dumped him beside an implement that pointed, as it were, to the wrong perp. As if I had to narrow down the parties who'd overplayed their hand before Herb's ingenuous delvings could tarnish civic order and those sacrosanct property values!

"Everyone was more focused at that stage on how they'd bring in fire equipment, and I was less welcome underfoot every time someone blinked. When those same police wanted statements from me late this afternoon, though, I couldn't grace their presence fast enough."

I liked this friend of the Metcalfes, whether or not it was reciprocated. "I hope they treated you right. What did you do that wasn't unselfish and supportive?"

"They're not paid to see it like that, are they? Eliza got grilled too, and she's the bereaved widow, for Chrissakes. We compared notes after, and for what it's worth, we were each under some pressure to divulge any information on someone named Wilbur Rice."

"On Wil?" Oh shit, that was stupid. Boost my "index of suspicion" a notch or two, why don't I?

"Friend of yours?" Words, as I pictured it, to accompany her antennae bending toward me.

"To the extent I knew how much he hated that 'Wilbur' on his birth certificate. It's weeks since we've been face to face." As evasions went, too clever for my own good? Or simply transparent? Not too late to shift the subject. "Why the interest in Wil? Though I don't suppose they let you in on that."

"Not apart from the fact that nobody can find him. Eliza did relate for posterity how upset Herb was last summer when your friend Wil hurt himself with a saw and the saw disappeared the next day, and we decided it must have been the same saw that the murderer used. Could the cops want Wil as an alternative suspect for some reason? Seems so open and shut to blame the homeless person."

"Unless they're hoping to pin a second murder on the homeless man, which they could never prove without a *corpus delicti*, and if Wil's body was in that burning shack, they may be permanently up the creek. Whether he was in there as a victim or as the killer."

"But you don't believe he's either, do you? Listen, you'll have to do better than that to throw me off track. I used to make a living at shell games. You know damn well he was nowhere near that shack. I don't care about this Wilbur one way or another, but if he's someone who can clear up what happened to Herb, you owe it to his family to contact the police. What'd you say your name was?"

"Jeff." That was indeed the sum total of what I'd said. And woe to me if the Metcalfes' phone had caller ID. The chain of inevitabilities flashed ahead of me. Police haul me in for interrogation. I lie badly, or dole out the truth selectively, and then I put my foot in it, strain credulity once too often, and slam! I'm in a cell, padded or not, a captive audience with courtside seat for impending catastrophe. "Whatever your name is, I promise you, my conscience is my guide. Has a date been set for the funeral?"

"Immediate family only."

"Okay. But does it trouble you that you were the one civilian witness at the crime scene and the fire?"

"Please don't start dragging me into cover-ups and conspiracies. You sound like one of those geeks who used to do that amateur ghost-hunting show on cable. On the trail going out, I met camera crews going in. The story should've been on the 6 o'clock news, but the local stations are having the same staffing problems as the police, so they couldn't get it together on 2 hours' notice. All the gluttons for tragedy will have to tune in at 11." She paused for breath and emphasized each forthcoming syllable. "There was no cover-up."

"If you say so." I was still smarting from that dig about OGAM. "And would you please convey my absolutely sincere condolences to Mrs. Metcalfe?"

She said yes, in a noncommittal tone that guaranteed nothing. What a relief to hang up. I did like her, though it felt like I'd been sparring ten rounds with an opponent out for blood. Typical. She impressed me as someone I'd like to have dated, except we'd never have run into each other outside of circumstances that made her thoroughly distrust me. Plus she wouldn't give me her name.

Meanwhile, had "Occam's finest," in the context of solving a homicide, really been content to knock on Wil's door, shrug after a minute, and call it quits without obtaining a search warrant? Or did they have nowhere to search because Dyer Hall had gone up in smoke, without benefit of reportage at 6:00 thanks to the same staffing shortfall that relegated Herb's murder to the 11 PM news?

Foolishly or not, I broke out the Spaten Optimator. A strong, malty ale on an empty stomach. It wouldn't lighten my psychic burden, but maybe I wanted it to make me miserable. As I richly deserved. I'd cultivated a new friend, and mixed him up in my harebrained "crusade," and now he was dead. I didn't kill him, and the cause was noble, but had he never met me, he'd be alive today. Anger at myself, and at those who'd more directly done him in, was as overwhelming as it was useless.

Two bottles along, and that anger softened up, and at the realization that the shack's previous owner, gentle old A.P., belonged entirely to the ages henceforth, or to oblivion really, with the journal and photos and house that preserved memories of him gone forever, I became weepy. The man had not been completely eradicated until this afternoon, and it felt like I'd killed him too.

The devaluation of my own life hadn't begun to sink in, and couldn't penetrate the atmosphere of emotion blanketing my mind, but I was cognizant that the reality of it would be ready to pounce, as inevitable as hangover, in the morning. Three-beer binge did confer one fortuitous blessing. I didn't have to subject myself to whatever spin the 11 PM news attached to misfortunes in the woods and maybe on Ellery Avenue. I was dead to the world by 8:30 or 9.

Twenty-six

I'm fucked. A deceptively simple thought upon awakening. Equally germane to my headache, and the dire outlook of cops at the door, and the pittance my life was worth, given Herb's cavalier execution. A moot detail, whether his death had occurred according to plan or in an overheated moment. Attempted to bolster my slumping psyche and flesh with black coffee, a four-egg cheddar omelet, and the proposition that I'd be home free if I could tread like a ghost, assuming that was softly enough, till the Tuesday after next. It might not be, based on my notoriety as a loose cannon, predisposing me to make noise about the Third Floor's resort to mob-style assassination. All I could do was blow smoke, but with perseverance, people might start believing that where they smelled smoke, there had to be fire. Did I entail less risk at large or in a secret grave?

I could neither second-guess nor change City Hall's choice of response. A prime example of mental fodder that would drive me berserk in a week unless I studiously avoided it. Had never really acquired the habit of accepting what I couldn't alter. Ditto for taking one day at a time, but sanity hinged on not getting too far ahead of myself.

One day at a time was plenty to contend with, for the shape I was in. To start, had to make this a lost weekend from the outside world's perspective. A policy predicated on going nowhere. Didn't even unlock the front door or raise the front window shades. Switched off the answering machine, to preempt any messages meant to jar my equilibrium. If enmity wanted to send out feelers before it struck, let it have that much less to work with. The phone did ring on several occasions when I was indoors. Mostly a half-hearted three or four times, and rarely a dozen or more. Always a sinister air about it, arresting me in midstride as if echolocation through the wires might detect brash movement. But I'd be the last to vouch for my own extrasensory accuracy. In my wound-up mood, no differentiating between stress-enhanced clairvoyance and paranoia.

Someone may have leaned on the doorbell while I was out back, out of earshot. Another case of ignorance as bliss. Periodically roved into the woods behind my yard from morning till dusk every day, beyond sight of the house. Carried minced-up hot dogs and cold cuts in a Ziploc baggie that I crammed into jacket pocket. On the lookout for Occam's pack of strays, in hopes of befriending them with meat, conquering any shyness they might've developed since previous association with humans. I whistled and shook a can of pebbles that maybe passed for kibbles, but the only word I called was "Elsie." Wishing foremost to lure her home and redomesticate her, in memory of the Rices. And before some bastard neighbor could coax ex-family pets into eating poison treats. Couldn't name anyone particular who'd do such a thing, in fact was ignorant of my neighbors' names or faces, but I automatically refused to put it past them.

All my strivings were futile, as usual. Wherever the pack went during sunlit hours, it was audible only after bedtime. Still, those hours were better spent than indoors lying low, stewing in my insecurity, ears peeled in vain for footfalls beneath the windows or in the next room, muting the tv or stereo for cadences originating without exception in the soundtrack or my imagination.

Such spikes in anxiety goaded me mercilessly, especially Monday night, into agonizing over Tuesday's appointment. Should I or shouldn't I blow my cover and go downtown to Unemployment for "adjudication"? Brave a run-in with City Hall sons of bitches down the block? I'd be a sitting duck for harassment or worse. But whatever befell Occam, I'd have to eat, gas up the Taurus, eke out some trickle of cash flow afterward. And insofar as I was qualified to collect, my checks would be issued through a state data-bank, unaffected by one town's disruption. To be honest, I lost sleep en route to a decision etched in stone all along, but pushing myself out the door Tuesday morning was much easier in a dull, punchy mood.

Twenty-seven

By midmorning, post-rush hour traffic was nonexistent on the inbound side of the Occam Pike. That didn't ring any ominous bells. It had to happen every so often. Also shrugged off several outbound cars speeding fit to go airborne. They conformed all too well to our famously oblivious style behind the wheel, and I was deep in my own fretful brown study. Also seemed reasonable at first to blame scofflaw drivers for the blockage on Ellery Avenue, between double-parking and idling in midlane, until the number of immobile vehicles, with engines running or not, disabused me of supposing they were the sum of isolated incidents. Too many cars lay ahead for me to suppose I could steer around them, or if I did, that I could turn around and get out. Bottleneck was becoming a cul de sac. I put the Taurus into reverse and maneuvered a dozen car lengths backward, and with growing trepidation, pulled up to the curb.

An explanation for this auto graveyard dawned on me, and squinting into cars only helped confirm it. Every single passenger and operator sat with upraised face and arms, craning their necks, forearms pushing against vinyl ceilings, jaws hanging slack. If my eyes could have penetrated blue sky and cumulus clouds, would they have fastened on the vanguard of meteors swarming earthward, as the eyes of these hosts full of "color" seemed to be doing? The note on Thayer's fridge had forecast this for the "Tuesday after next," but how long ago had he posted it? Dammit, I might've been ready for this had I mustered the willpower to open the fridge and gauge how long the food had been rotting. No use denying it. The "Tuesday after next" was today.

Finding Dyer Hall intact as I trod by was some small consolation. At windows there and elsewhere on the avenue stood abundant proof that occupants had held the fort, and now they pressed against the glass and strained arms toward their ceilings, as if playing at synchronized statues or

194

pillars of salt. And from here, each figure seemed to be reaching for a light bulb or candle, practically cupping it in their palms. Too distant for exact determination.

No joy came of marking how life didn't languish universally in suspension. In yards and hedges and weedy strips alongside the curb, squirrels and pigeons and sparrows, infrequent consumers of the tap water at best, hopped around and scavenged as on any normal day. Temporary though it was, this confluence of separate worlds felt more and more grating and pathetic, to an excruciating degree at the intersection with Commercial Street, where subsidized apartments for the elderly, dating to 1960s urban renewal, towered on city land. Underground irrigation, on the taxpayer's dime, piped reservoir water to the grubby lawns out front and the gingko trees lining the sidewalks.

Pedestrians, the first to emerge from the woodwork since my arrival, indiscriminately dotted the sidewalks and street like mushrooms, amidst the cars as if overtaken by stasis while trying to learn why traffic was stalled. Through common taint in blood and sap, people and trees shared a fleeting parity, in which the vertical arms of octogenarians with walkers, and of healthcare professionals in suits or uniforms, and of more nondescript passersby mirrored the vertical branches that had formerly projected every which way from ginkgo trunks. Limbs human and vegetable, whether in sleeves or decked in yellow, fan-shaped leaves, were reaching so hard that wood as well as muscle succumbed to faint trembling.

The ginkgos' fleshtone, globular berries littered the pavement and exuded a profanely suitable odor of vomit. A pungent trope for the direction in which all life here was headed. Even as bluish-grey, pitted, sunken faces gazed up in submission to the "color," so now the trees that had been sturdy enough to retain their leaves submitted, from their roots up, to splitting bark and grey, granulating rot to the pith. And unless my imagination was overreacting, the progress of disease was visible to the patient, naked eye.

Doomsday couldn't have come on a nicer mid-October morning, for all the difference earthly climate must have made to alien mood. I paused in my ill-considered errand to the Department of Labor and admired the sunshine on the lustrous red hair and turquoise smock of a willowy nurse, who wore the ravages of gauntness and discoloration remarkably well, as if she might've ingested Gorman County toxicity only through occasional resort to a coffee machine. Sadly, she'd swallowed at least the modicum for damning her to a part in the spectacle. And did I have a worthier subject for an impromptu experiment in saving somebody, even if I turned out to be someone she wouldn't touch if I were the last man in Occam?

I clenched her wrist and tugged, and after overcoming resistance like that of a thick, rugged bough, was briefly thankful to see her supple again, gasping, staggering to rebalance herself, and clear-eyed. But eyes glazed almost instantly as she bared her teeth and snarled and yanked her wrist free, and in one torpid gesture regained her footing and uplifted her arms and face, as involuntarily as a bough unbending after being released. Very much like the foreign will in Lucinda, lashing out angrily when Wil dared apply a steadying hand to her shoulder. Okay then. What more to do here, short of dragging one uncooperative victim inch by inch toward an extremely nebulous goal of liberation? What made her more deserving of rescue than the thousands around us, beyond my attraction to how she probably used to look?

Before I could bring myself to move on and leave her to her fate, a titanic stack of clouds obscured the sun and cast a pall upon her, in which was revealed the flickering of transparent, bluish flames above each hand, camouflaged by full daylight, barely discernible in the reduced sunshine not only in her case, but atop every uplifted arm and branch in the landscape. Seek no farther to explain the glow whose source was hidden by lintels in every tenanted window. Nor could those mock St. Elmo's fires in dusky rooms be anything but that elusive, living color, not exactly blue or grey or violet, ultimately nothing with a human name, and primed like pilot lights for God knew what?

Forging onward toward less populated sidewalk, I wondered if this bumper crop of medical personnel signified an awareness of the crisis flaring up throughout town, perhaps one of many calls to action on the strategic level of ants storming out to defend their hill. Too little too late!

The breeze shifted like a pat on the cheek, cool but tasting contrarily of burning oil and paint and barbecue and rubber and less explicit fuels. It constituted one more imperative reason to reverse course, clear out of a place where my stated purpose had become invalid, where I was about to witness something I really didn't want to. No matter. My feet would only work in one direction, past the dollar stores and donut shops and display windows with "For Rent" signs, beside the glacial floe of bumper-to-bumper traffic that restricted my view to a few car lengths.

I must have flustered myself into short-term myopia, or I'd much sooner have noticed the smudgy, sheer veils of black smoke that came and went within a distorting shimmer of heat from the next intersection. Into the fraught silence crept a low crackle of flames, and into the autumn chill, an ongoing ebb and surge of warmth, and as the acrid fumes strengthened into choking intensity, I reeled to a standstill. The accident was suddenly too close for comfort.

Judging by the extant wreckage, two SUVs had smashed together at a right angle and at similar speeds, and had melded into an untidy circumflex. No telling any longer what models they'd been, but both had been on the macho scale of Escalades or Suburbans. The inferno sparked by their collision had peaked a while ago, for their steel carcasses now fed an unflagging but sedate fire. I vanquished a perverse urge to see what was left of anyone inside. Enough for me to realize where the scent of barbecue had come from. Averted my sight to twisted shrapnel on the pavement. Here was a type of carnage that hadn't needed the catalyst of alien trance to happen year in and year out, and maybe it hadn't today.

And though it was no solace to the casualties, their immolation had acted as a stroke of mercy, obliging drivers to stamp on their brakes in a chain reaction that overspread all downtown, before the "color" took over. At worst, I observed a few fender benders as I skirted the radius of serious heat and smoke. The nearest vehicles had suffered some bubbling paint, and the nearest motorists, a touch of facial redness and blistering, but nothing to wince at. Damn lucky, apart from the doom about to engulf them.

Some other cars had been deserted, their doors wide open, hinting at the panic of nonresidents as unearthly stillness set in. They may have been scrambling around trying to understand the situation, or may have made an intelligent beeline for the border. In any event, I had yet to see an ambulatory soul, and didn't necessarily expect to, any more than I expected that rescue wagon, fire engine, or police were en route to the intersection. Meanwhile, the excuse of distancing myself from this grisly scene lent new momentum to my fool's errand at city center.

Fewer vacancies and a higher class of chain eateries and clothiers and druggists distinguished the environs of municipal offices, with tenacious mom-and-pop holdouts like Koerners, at least till recently, on side streets. And though City Hall's main entrance was also on a side street, my knees felt rubbery at the thought of being targeted from the many windows in the wall of former workplace overlooking the main drag. But what made me believe sentient humans were still in the building? Any more than I should believe the Department of Labor was open, two blocks beyond?

In my scatterbrained state, the simplest evasive maneuver burst into my head like an epiphany. Why not turn left at the next corner, and parallel Commercial till my hypothetical enemies were behind me? Then repeat the detour on the rebound after tugging on the locked door at Unemployment and confirming I'd come here for nothing, on the worst possible day to loiter in Occam?

The only address to merit a farewell glance on my alternate route was Abdul's. Better feast my eyes now, since I'd never see it again. Hadn't sunk in on a gut level yet that all this would shortly be gone. But what was going on in there? The lights were on, and people were moving about. Christ, what did it take to close that place down, if our local apocalypse couldn't?

I zigzagged past the several idling cars between me and a clearer view of who was minding the store today. The several guys on both sides of the counter were preposterously overdressed for kitchen work. In three-piece suits, no less, restricted to a tedious Waspy palette of opal-blue, charcoal-grey, black. Whatever these rash folk were up to, I had to prevail on them to bail right now, even if I wasn't exactly practicing what I preached. Meanwhile, something familiar about their wardrobe's range of tones was bothering me, and before I'd set foot on that side of the road, the charcoal-grey clotheshorse had spotted me and was barging outside, and all became too lucid.

Deputy Mayor Nathan Atwood stopped short halfway across the sidewalk and ogled me incredulously. I did pretty much likewise, minus his posture of entitlement. Then his eyes narrowed as if studying me through crosshairs. He'd deceived and betrayed me time and again, yes, but I saw some portion of myself in him just the same, and couldn't hate him quite yet. And if our alleged kinship made me a passable judge of what he was thinking, its gist must have been, "Why the hell, of 90,000 people in this town who might not be a zombie, did it have to be him?"

A quick survey over Atwood's shoulder established that everyone else inside also belonged at City Hall, that Abdul's sensible employees had indeed lit out, and that self-serving high officials were helping themselves to a free lunch. Not that minor pilfering under the circumstances rated any moral indignation, but it still made for a telling mark of character. I suppose in self-defense they'd say they couldn't deal incisively with a dire situation on an empty stomach.

Our standoff dragged on for a restive while, I with one foot on the curb, he with greasy fingers clutching leaky pita crammed with inexpertly chopped lamb. I toyed with gesturing broadly to encompass greater Occam and greeting him, "Now are you convinced?"

A smoldering that started in his eyes and inexorably reddened his whole face dissuaded me. His empty hand rose laboriously to point at me in accusation, and as if connections inside him were burning and circuits were shorting out, his brow and cheeks empurpled before he could spew out, "None of this came as news to you! Not at any stage. You had to be in on it. You engineered it somehow. Nobody else saw it on the horizon. Your fault!" He brandished his sandwich toward me. "I'll see you hacked up in this for what you've done, you fucking bastard!" Killing the messenger still counted among the sports of the elite, didn't it?

Atwood's tirade had drawn the attention of his cronies, but they weren't on the move yet, maybe waiting for him to stop blocking their view of me before they decided how to proceed. He, however, had seized up with misguided wrath, powerless to pull loose from the immobilizing sight of me. Every bird of ill-omen on my watchlist, despite Atwood's efforts to ignore them, had come home to roost this morning, and by all indications, his sanity couldn't contain them. Or was the guilt too much? For a few tol-

erable seconds I peered into his bulging, untethered eyes and grimly marveled, Between the two of us, who'd ever have suspected that successful,
straight-arrow Atwood would go off the deep end first?

As if these stinging sentiments were audible, he spat out a garbled ex-
clamation, flailed unseen chains away, and stormed back into Abdul's, wav-
ing his arms and denouncing me at a volume that bounced off the walls on
both sides of the street, lunch still clenched in viselike fist. His audience included Humphrey Westcott in the opal-blue linen, and burly associates in
black sharkskin or woolens, with buzz cuts or ponytails, hatchet features or
deceptively baby-faced.

My first face-to-face scrutiny of City Hall's plainclothes goons was cold-
ly reciprocated as Atwood berated and gestured, one arm and then the other swinging vaguely backward at me, raving at the least, presumably, that
I'd been banned from showing myself around here, and at worst, that I had
masterminded Occam's catalepsy. His words came muffled through the
plate-glass storefront, as did Westcott's afterward, though the city collector's murderous glare while jabbing forefinger at me and then contemptu-
ously flinging a balled-up paper napkin left little to speculation.

Rationally, he'd have ordered I be captured in fit shape for them to in-
terrogate me on what I'd done and how to undo it. But did anyone in there
currently qualify as rational? And even if they did, nobody seemed inclined
to ply me with gentle persuasion, and by the time they concluded their en-
hanced techniques were ineffective, I'd be much less of an irritant dead.

My tingling throat and weak limbs underscored the shifting feel of this
day from bad dream to full-fledged nightmare, as municipal henchmen, with
rancor plainly stoked at having to ditch lunches half-eaten, lumbered for the
door. In my last glimpse of Atwood, as I began to swivel about, the well-
modulated spokesman for fiscal responsibility, for calm and restraint, for
preserving normality at any cost was staring holes into me and gleefully
cramming messy sandwich into his leering mouth as if already chomping on
my flesh inside pocket bread. Now I could say without reservation that I
hated him.

And as I dashed for my life, my uppermost thought was, Christ, what
an imbecile I'd been! No one else to blame for persisting in the folly of my

march to Unemployment. Despised myself as well for hatching no better
exit plan than reaching the car with time to start it and step on the gas before pursuit caught up, pulled handguns from holsters, and blew out my
tires. I wasn't trapped in this nightmare to the extent of fleeing in slow motion, but didn't need, and couldn't bear, a glance behind to verify that ath-
letic goons were going to outpace me blocks away from setting eyes on the
Taurus.

Think! At the corner, I'd be turning onto Commercial in the direction
of my car, right? In my frantic state, that seemed to be the move anyone
would expect, never mind that nobody actually knew where I'd parked. So
instead, I charged into the intersection, crouched down, and crept hidden
amidst the permanent gridlock. Knew I was continuing up the side street
when my crablike scuttling met autos head-on rather than broadside.

Paused after half a dozen car lengths to hazard a peek over my shoulder.
No heavy footfalls or breathing, no verbal exchanges beset my ears. Too
good to be true, this childishly facile escape from professional bruisers. And
so it was.

With fists on his hips, Westcott, from atop the roof of a minivan in the
intersection, had me squarely in his baleful sights. He comported himself
like an overseer of a chain gang, and may have been tracking me for a minute or two, content to let me fumble on in false hope till I beheld him and
spoiled the game. He let loose an extraordinarily shrill whistle, then affected a broad gesture like an overhand pitch that ended with a finger stabbing
at me. I read impatience in his eyes as they followed one and then another of
his attack dogs, who weren't closing in on me soon enough to satisfy him,
but who were hurrying with irreproachable stealth, especially for big guys. I
ducked low and scurried onward as an aimless end in itself, with even less of
a future than racing headlong for the safety of my car.

Twenty-eight

Was starting to fixate on the yellow centerline between my feet when a displaced manhole cover eclipsed it and tripped me. I nearly toppled into my salvation, and doltishly shrank away before seeing it for what it was. One of two white-and-orange striped traffic cones had been squashed under the chrome bumper of a barge-like Buick partly blocking an open manhole. One tire balanced on the precarious brink of rolling in. Below was my only port in this storm, the only hideout where I couldn't be cornered. Refused to lift my eyes from headlight level as I twisted about and plunged in feet first. If goons were going to grab me, what good would it do to watch them lunge?

The overhanging bumper made for a tight fit, but stress inspired once-in-a-lifetime agility. Clamber recklessly, and I might sprain an ankle. Clamber timidly, I'd be dead for sure. The instant my head sank beneath the pavement, two goons were converging on me from around the nearest vehicle. At first I climbed down several iron rungs in a concrete cylinder like a well, and from there, a metal ladder propped above the lip of the concrete descended to the floor of the sewer.

The base of the ladder sat in the muck, braced against the edge of a fieldstone shelf that must have dated back to the original construction. I hopped backward off a low rung and onto the shelf, and kicked over the ladder to lie flat in the sewage, where it all but submerged.

Nobody was coming after me yet. From the most vehement snatches of conflict sifting down, I gathered that Westcott wanted me "flushed out" immediately, but his hirelings were balking because he didn't appreciate "how much these suits cost."

Criminal of me not to make the best of this head start. Invested precious seconds squinting left and right, not trusting in my sense of direction to guide me toward the channel underlying Commercial Street. Grimaced sympathetically as I hustled by four waxen sewer workers whose hardhats, filter masks, overalls, and rubber boots were uniformly tinted by the pervasive "color." Plastic lantern flashlights had landed at their feet, beams of yellow light crisscrossing randomly and diluted by the sickly ambient glow that rendered them extraneous. Above the fingertips of upheld arms and the naked portion of upturned faces between mask and helmet flickered that combustion of unreadable tone, in sharper outline than back on the gingko-lined avenue.

Maybe the DPW had sent down crews after receiving too many reports of luminous storm drains across Occam, or maybe these men had been performing routine maintenance till the first ubiquitous pulsations of "color" had spooked them toward the ladder. In either case, they'd been enveloped as implacably as citizens of Pompeii.

The bickering from above grew more heated, the farther I receded from it. My progress, meanwhile, was hindered by some unnatural slickness on the damp glowing stones, as if they themselves were writhing under my shoes, pushing up against them, slowing me to a squeamish shuffle. I also had to steady my legs when the ripe, obnoxious funk that went with this territory proved much more rancid, charnel, dizzying away from the manhole. Compelling me to pull handkerchief from back pocket and press it to my nose and mouth for the duration.

The raging debate around the manhole had escalated into three or four voices versus Westcott, and one shouted down the rest. "He took away the fucking ladder, but here's what I'll do for you!" I instinctively flattened against the curving wall, and it too was damp and oily, seeping right through my jacket, and more palpably motile, as if a sheet of moss were exerting itself. Spaced with cold deliberation a heartbeat apart, six deafening gunshots, at the shallowest angle through the half-blocked opening, tore into the muck or ricocheted off my ledge or the ledge opposite. A frustrated henchman, I gathered, was telling Westcott with ammo that he was fed up and really didn't care if he missed me or killed me, only get off his case.

Couldn't decide whether shrieking like a victim was a good idea or not. A moot point, since I could do no more than tremble. As dumb luck had it, I was unscathed, but one of the DPW workers had quaked as a bullet slammed into him. He neither collapsed nor even stumbled from where he stood rooted. No blood oozed out of the exit wound in his lower back. Instead, a pencil-thin beam of bluish light sprang from his apparently hollow shell, and dissipated with a weaker and weaker outline into the general glow of nameless color, brazenly violating earthly laws of physiology, optics, physics. I could only hope that he was too far gone to know he'd been punctured clean through.

My feet began working again as I came to believe the shooting was over. Then a resurgent squabble, trickling through my slowly fading tinnitus from a figurative mile away, showed that Westcott still wasn't satisfied. He insisted they go and lug me back dead or alive, end of the world or not, screw them if they didn't like it, he'd have their heads for this, who the hell did they think they were? Their concise answer, after a hesitation just long enough to accommodate a shrug, was one more gunshot, followed by blunt silence. Hardly would've occurred to Westcott that his IQ was worth no more than his respect for a change in the wind. Had he felt otherwise last summer, we might none of us, he included, be in our undesirable positions.

His dapper thugs' aversion to stains on the material guaranteed they were staying aboveground. But I plowed forward, equally confident they weren't above some impromptu target practice if I popped up among them. For now, they were engaged in solemn conference, and before I reached the junction with the more cavernous tunnel below Commercial Street, the reverberant splat of a dead bulk into the sewage made plain what they'd been discussing. I didn't bother looking back. For reasons of my own, I'd become as callous as they had about ditching certain corpses.

Before going any distance under Commercial Street, all sense of how far I'd traveled, of any correspondence in my surroundings to street-level landmarks, was null and void. Throwing me off further, the air felt overloaded with the chromatic presence, and I blamed my smothering malaise on its baleful surveillance, weighing on me, pressing more and more of the clarity from my head.

I had no darkness down here to be afraid of, small comfort though that was, especially as the light by which I navigated was painful and fatiguing as it slid erratically up and down the spectrum. How early had the "color" claimed these sewers for a beachhead, an occupied territory, a staging zone? Where better for its rampant proliferation? In miles of neglected catacombs, where water from the reservoir collected after Occam had the use of it, where human hosts of particulate alien disposed of liquid and solid waste, itself rife with alien passenger that didn't care if it parasitized organic matter living or otherwise? In fact, relative to the lurid glare around me, the "color" had been astutely secretive, shrewdly inconspicuous in the "surface world."

My bunched-up handkerchief scarcely filtered out the carrion stench. Had no great faith in its shielding my lungs from any buildup of gaseous organism. No stopping alien sentience if it wanted to convert me into an inert vessel like the sewer workers. The gash in my finger, from days ago on the Blasted Heath, leapt to mind and nearly triggered a panic attack, despite the illogic of judging it a more attractive target than my wheezing mouth and nostrils.

But even my least founded anxieties underscored a valid point. I had to quit the sewers at first opportunity. Except I'd need a ladder to reach the bottom rungs in the concrete wells of manholes, and then how to lift a hundred-pound cover, supposing I did backtrack and fish out that ladder I'd kicked into the filth? Suppose Westcott's body had landed on top of it? One too many stumbling blocks for my beleaguered brain. I trudged lethargically on. Resigned to letting fortune smile on me in her own good time.

Meanwhile, every chance look into the sewage helped vindicate my aversion to going back for the ladder. The muck, as it flowed almost imperceptibly toward some faraway treatment center, was in fine iridescing agitation like oil on a windswept puddle. No breeze down here, of course. Just the infestation, yearning vainly to rise skyward. Preferable to dip fingers or shoe into the mere bacterial poison of any other sewage in the world.

The sewer system, I was discovering, did a poor job of duplicating the street grid, and that was good news. I must've covered several blocks already, but hadn't had to ford any channels corresponding to side streets above, or else turn 90 degrees to stay on dry ledge, at a cost of plodding ever farther from my car. I still had to watch my step as crusty pipes of diameters from tin can to bass drum broke through the wall at haphazard intervals and spewed waste from corroded mouths to splatter onto my walkway and dribble down shallow runnels into the main flow. Couldn't tell if chisels or a century's erosion had carved out the runnels, which sometimes widened into pools where trash formed miniature dams.

I also had to duck or else bang my head against bundles of PVC tubes, the property of Occam's utilities, poking from scraggy holes in brick wall or from canker-like irregularities in the ceiling, and following arbitrary angles into other misshapen holes. This was coming to seem less a sewage system than a stupendous jury-rig, and though well aware of which street was overhead, I harbored a morbid suspicion I was lost. And in the broader analysis, I was. I may have overshot the Taurus already, and even if I hadn't and my intuition started tingling in proximity to the manhole nearest the car, how was I going to break out of here? In the absence of any answers, I shambled on.

Helpless as a sponge, I absorbed ever more of the distressing details around me. On the vaulted ceiling, wispy organic stalactites, perhaps composed of microbes in a matrix of their own waste, strained upward but only had it in them to swing in convulsive ellipses, like a disorganized legion of dowsing rods. Occasionally a scattered handful of these filaments snapped off after too much exertion and plopped into the water beside me or the stones in front of me. I had no urge to learn if they held together and resumed futile skyward wriggling in the muck or on the paving. Just so long as none of them rained upon me.

From the clumps of solid refuse, blessedly unidentifiable, that bucked or drifted in the writhing current, I gathered that the water was only ankle-deep. Something to store for future reference in case I absolutely had to wade in. And no matter how nonviable these pieces of waste were and always had been, they were steeped in alien life, the same as Morgan or the slime on the wall. They contained no anatomy, no means of propulsion, but were moving nonetheless, in a manner as undefinable, as wrong in human terms, as the "color" pervading them. Almost slipped more than once as that unholy motion distracted me in passing till I was looking backward, unmindful of my treacherous path.

Also preying on my attention was the mystery of what should've been here but wasn't. Where were the rodents, the possums, the raccoons, all those skulking members of subterrene ecosystem, or their carcasses any-way? Those hardiest of goldfish flushed down the toilet? The roaches, the bugs in general? Never dreamed I'd be distraught over a scarcity of vermin. Might they have staged their own underground exodus in the same hours as Occam's dogs in the streets overhead?

Nothing to hear in this domain outside the squelching of my shoes upon the tainted stones. Might as well be listening to the void. But then through tarmac and earth, as if from another dimension, penetrated the squall of widely dispersed sirens and a coarser momentary racket, as of a helicopter touching down, and shortly the stop-and-go grind of a heavy vehicle. Not at all farfetched to envision freaked-out commuters calling the Staties, the Na-tional Guard, the CDC on their cells as they sped along the outbound by-pass, regretting now they hadn't made more of everything awry in town the last few weeks. Hell, wouldn't put it past the Third Floor to throw up cra-ven hands and pawn off this crisis on a higher authority. Typically, for them, after the point when any human agency could do any good.

Again, survival dictated I keep a low profile, forget about stepping into daylight except where the coast was expressly clear. Went without saying, personnel in uniforms and hazmat suits would take no kindlier to me than cops and other officials usually did. To see me rise in ambulatory shape from the depths would hand them a red-letter excuse to detain or dissect me, de-pending on the captors. Was I bordering on paranoiac here?

On reflection, I could only be thankful my first symptoms of delirium weren't making me more dysfunctional. I also had to begrudge these first responders some sympathy, considering their reward for fulfillment of duty, if they lingered too long, would be a uniquely hideous death. Nor would I fare any better unless my path connected soon with an escape hatch beyond earshot of armed patrols and Westcott's enforcers. Yes, my life hinged sim-ultaneously on staying hidden and burrowing out. A contradiction that latched onto me and gnawed at my grip on coherence.

And so my feet adjusted before my awareness did as the paving began to slope more and more pronouncedly. When I did notice, it startled me off-balance. I toppled backward and slid down what had become a chute as much as a channel. Let out an indiscreet bellow as the slime smeared and impregnated my trouser seat and jacket. No stopping me till the incline ended at a junction with a brick-lined passage, where the heel of my right shoe dug into the gunk beneath the shelf. My plunge had taken a second or two but felt more like an eon. Wrenching out my foot used up a great deal less subjective time. Still not soon enough to save my sock from getting drenched. Managed to keep my hands dry and stand up by using my knees and elbows. Bravely putting all my weight on left foot, worked my right loafer off and tipped it on its side with my toes, to drain it of sloshing muck.

Was grimacing at the amount of liquid that remained to meet my instep, then stiffened like any small species near the bottom of the food chain. Voices from the sunlit world! "Hello? Hello?" Indistinct conversation then passed between speakers who may not have wished to be overheard, who were on to me because of my outcry at the wrong place and moment. I wasn't about to gamble that these searchers were benign. Or break my pose so long as it felt likely someone might have an ear to the ground. My obstinate hand had not let go of the handkerchief, which I plastered over my mouth again. Primarily now for muffling breaths I could only hold a minute.

In the oppressive hush, the sewage rushing down the sluice into the cross channel gurgled and hiccupped as if meeting obstacles. Curiosity, for the umpteenth time, got the unwise better of me. At first squint, a modest cairn of rounded, polished rocks was blocking the base of the incline and clogging the intersection. A harder survey corrected me. As best the mutable light would divulge, the rubble was of an unclean white or pasty brown, and of a uniformly glossy texture, organic instead of mineral. And it was all a single gnarled, bumpy mass, in which black, twisted impurities were embedded totally or in part, as if in aspic, and ranging from the size of mice to overfed rats. Yes, certainly, because that's what they were. Dead and at various stages of dissolution, and delicately quivering in concert with their glistening matrix, suffused with the same blind, hankering life. The entirety of the thing was immobile but acrawl in a way that made my own skin crawl.

What the hell was I gawking at? The answer was already floating within reach in a shadowy eddy of my mind, but I was reluctant to admit it was more than a joke, an urban legend. The tons of oils and grease that fast food joints and housewives heedlessly poured down the drain were reputed to accumulate as "sewer fat" in cities worldwide, and what else might this be? It was definitely organic inasmuch as the "color" had seized upon it, and rodents had seen fit to feed on it, only to die stuck in the gunk or incapacitated by the presence they'd been ingesting.

So much for the whereabouts of at least some underworld fauna, and when the glow entered into a more translucent phase, I could even discern black specks like currants or raisins that gradually resolved as flies. And some of these flies, in keeping with last summer's hefty mosquitoes at the reservoir, I'd initially mistaken for baby mice. Altogether a relief when the air grew too violet to see through again. It couldn't last. In a rapid swing toward rosy light that made my eyes ache, the tumulus of fat had started quaking more markedly, though the flow of sewage against it seemed unchanged. I felt the same alarm as when Morgan's vestiges proved animate. Had my breathing, my tumble into its vicinity, or my concentration on it activated some hapless tropism, like Morgan's urge to approach me because I was there? Whether budging an inch closer to me was even possible or not, I knew I'd hallucinate something to that effect if I dawdled any longer.

Oh hell! I couldn't pinpoint from where it came, but no doubt about it, the groaning, creaking, scraping of ponderous iron meant a manhole would soon be open. Whoever had heard me and helloed wasn't going to leave it at that. Made no difference to me that these persistent scouts might intend no harm. My choice was exclusively fight or flight, and fighting had never worked before. My choice of direction was also exempt from debate. To backtrack was tantamount to doom, to wade across the squalor was unthinkable. I headed to the right, along the cross channel, as hastily as the slippery bricks allowed.

Seconds were manifestly of the essence. Something steel thunked into the paving stones from that same nonspecific location, followed by the squeaking of feet down a ladder. My two pursuers helloed some more, and to my satisfaction they were more muted by distance than they had been while on the street. I scuffled onward, encouraged. Rewarded myself with a cagey smile.

They evidently had a lot to say about conditions down here, but I could make out no more than inflections of disbelief and disgust. Well, better for everyone if they reconsidered their rash mission and climbed back out. Whether they wanted to assist or capture me, they'd deflected me off my path, ensuring I'd never reclaim my car or my general bearings, and damn them for that. They'd given up on hailing me, but their echoing, agitated whispers from nowhere brought to mind the chittering of mice I'd have heard here before. How would these persons deal with the loathsome but harmless spectacle of "sewer fat"? Horrified exclamations and a shocking burst of gunfire broadcast the answer, with chilling implications for the kind of greeting I might expect. I stepped livelier on my advance to parts unknown, noting ruefully that the bricks were slicker than the fieldstones had been, and the shelf some inches narrower.

Nor had I thrown the whisperers off my trail. No, of course not. The coruscating slime was preserving footprints with the fidelity of wet cement. What kind of fiend was I alleged to be who slunk around in loafers? Had that question concerned the searchers at all, they'd have dropped it the instant an inauspicious change engulfed the tunnels. There was no letup in the air's random, stark chromatic flux. But everything for a heartbeat puckered toward darkness and just as briefly brightened into glare, before fading to baseline pallor. Whatever development this portended, how could it possibly be good for me? Or for anybody?

After a vague interval, the waning and waxing of the glow recurred, independent of any shift in hue. The third instance may or may not have involved a shorter wait. Yes, as the next half dozen pulses proved, a subtle increase in frequency was underway, though with plenty of time between each for me to fret about how infinite this tunnel had come to seem. And much worse, more and more of the missing fauna had begun to show up, bloated in the sewage, littering my trail. Disfigured or in collapse, rats, possums, cats, and others too fragmentary to classify, infused with postmortem life, rallied their piecemeal anatomy to squelch forward. They were oblivious to me as I trod among them, and for the time being, not so numerous that I had to test their tolerance of a brusque shoe pushing them aside.

Meanwhile, the glowering, disembodied surveillance I'd weathered all along had flared up front and center in my head again, exerting more feverish pressure on me as the clutter of animals expanded. The pulsations into and out of darkness were spaced, I estimated, a little under a minute apart, and reminded me unwholesomely of uterine contractions. The men on my trail may not have picked up that similarity as they soldiered steadily on, but their speech had become more subdued, more sporadic, their tone more sepulchral, as my overwrought mood would have it.

The disintegrating bestiary's mushrooming ranks were oriented neither toward the sky nor toward me as their arbitrary focus, but were gravitating like iron filings toward a secret lodestone. What were my pursuers making of this, if they had the composure for careful observation, and what the hell was I to make of it? And what difference did it make, since I had nowhere to go except along with the macabre parade?

The intervals between blackouts had been shrinking almost imperceptibly, with the small blessing that the darkness itself never comprised more than a blink. A soundscape had begun to build around me, ubiquitous but coming from nowhere, and it was slowly blotting out the increasingly hoarse, excited whispering of the men on my trail. Again, human brain and sensory organs were ill-equipped to neatly interpret the "color's" effects. What started as a protracted groan of scraping timbers or millstones became a fugitive arc of voltage, and then the creaking of timbers again. The prospect wasn't encouraging in any case, and the volume from afar had already become grating. Assuming the worst, which had always proved wise, everything around me would soon split asunder.

The tunnel, though, stretched mockingly on and on, and the bombardment of my eyes and ears intensified, with nothing for me to do but shamble along, like the proverbial frog in the kettle as the water came to a boil. After a while the accelerating lapses into darkness verged on strobelike, making it impossible to plant my steps with any precision. And the host of animate carcasses had grown too numerous to sidestep. All the squeamishness had been harrowed out of me by now. The rats, the raccoons, the foxes wheezed and crunched as my feet sank into them like they were wads of carbonized newspapers. No reprisals, no protest, no resistance, but I pressed my handkerchief tighter to my mouth, stuffing up my nostrils, as grey powder billowed up and dispersed like multicolored spangles. An abhorrent mush of bone slivers and flesh clung to the undersides of my loafers, causing my feet to wobble.

Far ahead in the chaos seemed to hang a dim cat's eye of stability, like a hazy moon in first quarter, then half, then practically full as I clumped nearer. This, I took it, was where the mangled animals had been driven to congregate. An oasis of calm earthly light, or an outbound route toward which vestigial reflexes still struggled, or a conduit through which the "color's" victims could reach that much closer to the sky, if they could only climb with demolished limbs? I guessed this cement pipe might have been part of some discharge system for overflow during a flood, or else a remnant of some renovation or extension of the sewers, aborted when funds dried up.

I was wading up to my knees in the flimsy, twitching faunal wreckage, and it was hindering my push toward the opening, which acquired new urgency when that rarity of rarities, a human voice, roared through the electric racket, "You! Stop right there! Stay where you are!"

Naturally I shoved faster through the mass of broken specimens toward the mouth of poorly lit salvation. If gunmen were chasing me, this kaleidoscopic glow would handicap their aim, and even if they'd been trigger-happy earlier, how could they justify their miserable subsurface trek if they killed me outright, without learning anything? Clumsily I kicked writhing obstacles aside and set my feet on the slick, gory bricks. Held my breath, and boosted myself on the heels of my hands into the pipe. Narrow in here. I was liable to scrape my back and scalp unless I crouched carefully, but I had no right to complain. An ill-conceived shot whistled toward parts unknown as I slapped the handkerchief back onto my face and shook my head. Stupid rookies!

But had I necessarily been the target? Or had the warning been shouted at me? Nothing more vital than to scurry like hell toward the tiny coin of daylight at the end of this gloom. Still, I had to pause, one foot in the air, alert for something materializing out of the blue. The glow behind me no longer wheeled haphazardly up and down the spectrum, but stalled at that most cryptic, jarring wavelength. To say it brightened would've been a glib misstatement. More to the point, it blushed or combusted, and instead of giving off heat, projected waves of resentment, of hatred, from which I was only partway buffered in this concrete tube.

If not for the grace of lucky timing, or of alien efficiency snubbing one victim in favor of two, it might have been me and not one of my pursuers who shrieked through the roaring static, "Get it off me! It burns! I'm on fire!"

His comrade was yelling, "Get what off you? What is it?" And then that second man was also shrieking hysterically. I resumed my stooping exodus, grateful now that the caking organic residue under my soles quieted my steps. What few intelligible words overtook me stirred memories of those last sheets in A.P.'s wastepaper journal, when he complained of waking up both raw with sunburn and shivering with cold, and of enduring deep but somehow invisible bite wounds. I pitied those men their agonies, though I couldn't distance myself from them fast enough. Why pretend I could do them a bit of good? I only wished for the feeding frenzy to be over, but was under no illusion it would be quick or merciful.

Previously I'd experienced alien presence as diffuse, insidious, viruslike in its influence. This concentrated, deliberate sentience again reminded me of A.P.'s laments about his consciousness displaced and his body pirated, of sleepwalking to the reservoir shore. It gave the hungry "color" both more vivid identity and more nebulous purpose. Was it consuming these trespassers because it needed every scrap of nourishment to advance in its life cycle? Or did it have to purge impurities in its intangible corpus before transition could begin? Or did it simply despise intact humans? I left off contriving rhetorical questions. They failed wretchedly at drawing my attention from the protracted suffering, and I was disgusted with myself for brooding that the "color" must have been saving the lungs for last.

All right, study the cement just ahead of my scrambling feet, then. It was damp, with streaks of dark or rusty stains, and muddy spots. And at face level hung gritty tatters of old cobwebs that I didn't always dodge successfully. No trace of spiders or millipedes or other typical denizens. The "color" must have summoned them weeks ago. Without the unearthly glow, it was much dimmer in here, yet much easier on my eyes. Might almost have been relaxing, apart from the noise that set my blood to pounding through my veins, and the fear that I'd still be on the menu if and when the noise subsided.

In my stricken state, I wasn't aware the mayhem was over till sometime after the fact, and a shaky glimpse backward established that the strobing had recommenced. Either end of the tunnel now seemed a long way away. I broke into a sprint. Not daring to turn my head again, or to remove the handkerchief from my face.

I alternated every second between expecting that first wave of agony to rake through me, and shuddering with relief when it didn't. The disc of daylight continued to hover tauntingly small in the murk. Tried to ignore a stitch in my side and a scorching sensation in my chest. Fatigue slowed down my aching legs, I got my second wind, and to my amazement I was tottering at the mouth of the pipe, blinking painfully in the afternoon sun, and processing that the Miskatonic flowed about fifteen feet below. The pipe projected from a steep, weedy embankment dotted with hunks of masonry and brickwork. I let my vertigo ease an instant. As escapes went, this one felt simultaneously miraculous and anticlimactic.

Twenty-nine

I squatted and dropped to the ground, crumpled onto my side despite wind-milling arms, picked myself up. Not blind to the irony of owing my life to the kind of scorn for the environment I'd been tilting against these several months. The pipe had certainly been designed to spew sewage straight into the river. And, as I learned when I swiveled around to get my bearings, it was in plain sight some dozen shameless yards upstream from the Commercial Street Bypass. Out here the sound from the sewer spilled tinny and pianissimo from the pipe, like the hiss of surf in a conch shell.

I scuttled across the loose, stony soil of the slope toward the overpass. Like the discharge pipe, an arrant misuse of public funds, in the roadway's case for killing downtown Occam, but for which I also had to be thankful today. Not a soul, catatonic or otherwise, did I meet en route, but I was dis-inclined to look too carefully. The farther ahead I squinted, the more acute-ly I suffered eyestrain, and by peering into the shadows under the bridge I realized that the whole landscape was flickering, as it had in the sewers, but more subtly where direct sunlight dispelled it. The strain was worse as I gazed nearer the city center. As if I needed more incentive goading me to-ward the highway out of town! For whatever it was worth, none of the grass or trash saplings on my path were reaching skyward or tipped with trans-parent flames. I tossed handkerchief, still bunched in my fist, at the water, but the wind sideswiped it and it fell among some masonry.

The embankment merged with the even steeper grade up to the road-way. I was climbing to a height where I might've had a view of downtown, might've found out why the sirens and patrol cars and army trucks had fall-en silent, but I trained my vision on the grass at my feet. No interest in be-coming a pillar of salt. Clambered over the steel guardrail near its juncture with the bulbous abutment at the foot of the bridge.

An unkempt used car lot lay before me. Four lanes wide, and nobody in attendance. Everyone was in their cars, of course, the majority of which were linked in ugly daisy chains of rear-end collisions. At a guess, the damage seldom came to more than crushed fenders because the activating "color" must have repositioned drivers away from their gas pedals. Smoke, steam, alarms would have been history hours ago.

I trotted onto the bridge, peeking into windows though I knew damn well what I'd see. Even with their seatbelts on, some people were bleeding from their ears, their nostrils, the corners of their mouths. And behind tinted windshields, they were softly glowing.

My dear old Taurus was obviously a writeoff, but a hundred replacements surrounded me, of no mortal use to their rightful owners, and home was miles beyond walking range. I was halfway over the river and had scouted few cars yet that weren't smashed together. Took sometime longer to locate any that had coasted to a rest with room between them to maneuver out. Nothing caught my fancy, or to put it more bluntly, seemed worth stealing till I skidded short and had to smirk incredulously, in spite of the grim, if not apocalyptic, situation. The luxurious dreadnought of a late '50s Eldorado, pristine, white and aqua, with fins and all the trimmings, was mine for the effort of displacing a scrawny pensioner. Too grand a temptation. Why not trade up?

October breeze rippled at my back, reviving my awareness of the cold slime seeping through my jacket, and for that matter through the seat of my pants, and drying under my shoes. I shrugged off the jacket, let it sit in a heap on the blacktop, kicked off my shoes, yanked off my socks. Wasn't going to defile my house, or my new sedan, with ugly vestiges of "color." What was the inconvenience of a chilly half hour? Popped the trunk and rummaged a pair of frayed bath towels from inside immaculate spare tire, next to a patching kit and a jack and a first-aid case. Perfect. I unpocketed my wallet, dropped my pants, and knotted the larger towel around my hips.

Swung open the door on the driver's side, tossed my wallet onto the backseat. The codger was maintaining the usual posture at behest of cosmic tenant, and pitted grey complexion no longer gave me pause. He wore a snuff-brown polyester leisure suit and white shirt with overhanging lapels, everything a size or so too big. A snappy dresser in his own mind, I hypothesized. Had a neat, thin mustache and neat sideburns with more hair in them than on his barren cranium. He might have been a retired shop teacher or pharmacist. Aspiring to enjoy his golden years in style.

Did I really have to drag him to the pavement, abandon him to grotesque death in return for supplying me a getaway vehicle? It wasn't decent. It was shitty, in fact. I laid the palms of my hands upon his shoulder and knee and gingerly pushed him across the squeaky upholstery to the passenger side. He could have been a Styrofoam mannequin. I pinned one end of the other towel under my headrest and unrolled it to cover the seat. His glazed eyes behind frogman lenses were as unwavering as the cool flames sprouting from upheld fingertips, his elbows bent in faux Egyptian pose to accommodate cream vinyl ceiling.

What harm in carting the aged gent along? Inert freight, that's all he was. Disembodied death grip might weaken with the passing miles, and I'd have saved one life anyway. A big deal, a meaningful gesture, to nobody apart from him and me, but I had to try.

Settled myself on the terrycloth, winced at dampness in shirt and underwear oozing onto my skin. Could only hope the towel would protect the seat, and I could torch the towels and the rest of my outfit in the comfort of my driveway.

Held my breath and gave the key a deferential turn in the ignition. The engine coughed, revved, rattled, died. My third attempt, true to form, was the charm. I exhaled. Better and better, according to the fuel gauge, the car had conked out this morning with sufficient gas to get me home.

Entertained doubts about making the right choice of vehicle after some cumbersome navigation past vans and SUVs askew in their lanes. Too late for switching now, though. I'd already accepted moral responsibility for Mr. Snuff Brown. Past the bridge, the gaps among entrapped motorists gradually widened, and I took the first exit that wasn't clogged with unmoving traffic. Committed the indiscretion once of gaping at town in the rearview mirror. Dense folds of cotton-wadding clouds had screened out the sun, and helped me distinguish an oily iridescent dome blurring the humble skyline. It immediately hurt my eyes, which was actually good for firming my resolve not to look again.

I had mapped out a roundabout orbit on back roads south of Occam, clockwise up to my address. On potholed divided highways and lesser arteries, my tally of accident scenes, whether pileups or single vehicles in the ditch, hit double digits before I relented. The initial few cars racing from out the "free world" in oncoming lanes were astonishing to me, as were Statie cruisers at some mishaps and towtrucks at others. After my hours in Occam, the spectacle of troopers and Triple-A agents going about their business had a hallucinatory quality, as if this were some sparsely populated frontier between realities. Meanwhile, as housewives and delivery guys and utility workers flashed by, we treated each other to expressions of incredulity, as if nobody should be coming from our respective directions. In their case, they were right.

I rotated the dial of the AM radio with the deliberation of a safecracker, but all the local stations broadcast out of Occam. Nothing but static, except for one jolting blare of Nashville from a channel that proved to be completely automated and based in Armitage.

I clicked off the radio. Mr. Brown had been unreactive to the sharp rise and fall of decibels, but my ears bristled at an infringement in the deceptive lull afterward. It was a faraway quavering hum, subterranean rapids, an ongoing crackle, a rending of tectonic or architectural fabric, the amplified rupture of an eggshell from the inside. Each comparison rang briefly true and then resoundingly false. Shameful that I didn't instantly place it as the protean rumbling in the sewer, finally burgeoning aboveground and expanding toward me with vegetative insistence.

I'd sworn off any more glimpses at town, and had nothing to gain by reneging on that. My eyes didn't care. Of their own accord, they swerved perversely toward a core of brightness beneath the darkening nimbus canopy. Afternoon had been preempted by overreaching twilight, an unscheduled eclipse, except where a colossal, translucent pillar of no precise color, practically the diameter of the citywide dome it surmounted, geysered into the cloudbank. I envisioned the pillar's cohesive ascent beyond the clouds, unhindered by gravity, into the Piscid swarm, though I drew a blank predicting what would follow.

I had this image now of skybound firefall in synch with the soundtrack of fragmentation, and it made me weak and nauseous. Nothing alive stood a chance of escaping callous, essentially incidental massacre. People I could name were immersed in that upheaval, and it was of no consequence that they were enemies, or that the intervening miles spared me every detail. The best I could do was pry my eyes away, empty my mind of vagrant speculation about the hellish end of Nathan Atwood, of the pretty redhead nurse, of everyone. But beside me was Mr. Brown to show exactly how the "color" was disrupting human bodies.

"Color" was migrating from everywhere it dwelt, bursting every earthly chrysalis. Which made getting home by roads south of town my smartest move in recent memory. Though the immolation of Occam blocked my northward view, I was confident that the reservoir, and the facilities to purify and bring the water to town, and the sewage treatment plant were trapped under their own shafts of "color," succumbing to the same transformation as Mr. Brown.

A repellently bright blaze of "color" encased him. I couldn't tell if it were shining right through the vinyl ceiling, or impeded by it with no place to go. An appalling possibility, and no chance to do anything about it before conditions worsened. The pockmarks on his face and scalp ignited into constellations glowing hotter than the aura around him. And something was burning, but what? It smelled most like dust in the radiator when the furnace comes on after long disuse. Seams thin as paper cuts were spreading between the brilliant dots. At arm's length, and across the miles to the Gardners' submerged well, the "color" in aggregate must have been hatching from countless figurative shells. To my joyless credit, I'd been right to liken the swelling noise from town to eggs splitting open. The cracks in Mr. Brown were implacably widening, dividing his head into numerous planes, like a rough-cut gemstone.

What happened to him next was grisly and heart-wrenching, even in the thick of my shellshock. He twisted slowly toward me, with excruciating effort, as if laboring to reverse the inertia of a millstone. Was he reenacting only the witless tropism of corrupted Morgan, of the corruption in the sewers, seeking me out merely because I was there? No, Mr. Brown's filmy eyes homed in on me beseechingly, and his dangling jaw fought feebly to shape speech. An ember of the old man's vitality, of his consciousness, was rallying well past his moment of truth, rekindling in the shadow of eternity. He was pleading for my help. I pulled over.

Meanwhile, the "color" within was gushing out unabated and taking him tainted cell by cell with it. The facets of his outer self were caving inward, rendering him even more shrunken inside his oversized clothes. Flecks of him were coming detached and rising from his cuffs, his collar, through the envelope of "color" and lodging against the Eldorado ceiling.

The glaze dispersed from his eyes, which were bulging with a derangement of revelation, and his mouth fell open in a mercifully voiceless howl. A blackness encroached and soon gaped behind his eyelids and his lips, and my own sensory input then reeled chaotically, and I couldn't say if I were looking into the portals of his crumbling eye sockets or out of them as if they were mine, by virtue of emissions into my mind from his, which was dissipating, radiating like the molecules of his body.

In either case, the outcome was a melding with the "color," and a window onto the intolerable vistas it commanded. I found myself alone among the stars, a grain in the endless gulf, except that space was actually rife with infinitesimal particles speeding along random paths and colliding explosively, and with waves of energy absorbing or bouncing off each other, and with other threads in the cosmic fabric of which I could conceive nothing. And none of this I perceived with sight, but with some inhuman faculty that beggared human understanding, and which some lowly parasite in the universal scheme of things took for granted.

I couldn't have partaken of alien perspective for more than a second when my mind recoiled out of self-preservation, and my body followed its lead. I was back in the Eldorado, and my spine was scrunching painfully into the door handle on the driver's side. Mr. Brown, with the last neurons of his identity, had lowered his arms and was reaching shakily for me through the enclosing "color," a dying gesture of supplication, even as the "color," every time his fingers almost brushed my shirt, slammed his fissioning body against the passenger-side door, in rancor, I supposed, at this confinement of its flaking substance within the car.

Those withering mosaic hands thrusting at me and receding and thrusting hopelessly again terrified me more than the "color" itself, and set my fingers groping at the door handle till I tumbled backside first upon the gravelly roadside. That guttering spark of Mr. Brown's selfhood had bought itself a little more time by flaring into full-blown madness, and I'd gotten some crucial distance from those emissions of insanity without an instant to spare. As it was, the impact of his mental overload had to ebb before I had the wherewithal to stand upright.

Muffled by the cascading, electric cacophony from town, the thumping of frustrated "color" in human vessel against unyielding car door goaded me to act, in dread of Mr. Brown shattering and rechristening the Eldorado as a coffin full of luminous, animate carnage. Stranding me out here, with too long a hike home. I staggered around to the passenger side, yanked the door open, used it for a shield as Mr. Brown cannonballed free, rolled without slowing down like a pinwheel, shedding sparks of "color" and confetti of flesh, till he found his footing and scrambled on buckling legs into the woods, toward the siren call of the bedlam in Occam. His sheath of cold flame clung steadfast but had paled in late afternoon sun.

I needn't have taken cover. I was a cipher, meaningless like the sparrows that scattered before his wobbling trajectory through the underbrush. Whatever cinder of humanity lingered, the infestation was in uncontested control, though the odds of that body holding together to cross the town line had to be minute.

Leaden fatigue was catching up with me as I grabbed the wheel and put the car in gear again. To drive, to navigate, were the most I could ask of myself. Any further looks at Mr. Brown, at the maelstrom over Occam, would be too much. Dawned on me that defeat was weighing as heavily as exhaustion, and it wasn't at the hands of the many politicos and their allies who'd stonewalled me for months.

I'd invested my last stores of decency in snatching Mr. Brown out of harm's way, but in his moment of ultimate crisis, his dying appeal for my presence if nothing else, I'd cast him off, like throwing back an undersized fish. Human decency had been devalued into nonsense in this doomsday context, in this peephole upon an astronomic scale where morals had no more role than anything else of this earth, where my survival dictated amorality at best. Maybe that same negation of decency applied in any war zone, except that no armistice would ever repair the illusion of virtue's role in human affairs. Not for me, anyway.

Thirty

If I passed any vehicles or they overtook me, or if any approached on the other side of yellow median strip, I retained no image of them, of nothing but the lane immediately ahead, till I had the sensation of snapping out of a trance. I was parked in my driveway, peering through Eldorado windshield at my house. I left the keys in the ignition, unknotted the towel from my midriff, dropped the rest of my despoiled clothes on the tarmac as I trudged along, numb to the chill of October dusk.

Overhead the first few stars winked dully. They induced a queasiness, a pang of spiritual malaise, a revulsion as if the indifferent heavens had it in them to incite phobia. Had some extremely ancient, recessive mechanism been exhumed in me? How often in prehistory had a night like tonight happened? Those Cro-Magnons whose tribesmen shunned the frigid night sky in sheltering caves, who cast up their eyes and tallied phases of the moon on bones and antlers and so invented astronomy, if not science altogether, had they had to overcome an aversion, already ages old, to the treacherous stars?

I lowered my sights toward town, where glowering nimbus, as sharply circumscribed as mushroom cloud or placental tissue, continued to receive the roaring pillar of "color," which showed no sign of tapering off. Blue lightning zigzagged constantly across the overcast, but the rush of alien departure drowned out all thunder.

My house keys I'd stupidly discarded on the bypass bridge, along with my trousers. I chose a rock and matter-of-factly busted the narrow pane beside the doorknob and undid the lock, as if I let myself in like this every day. The electricity still worked, at which I marveled after flicking on the hall light. Grateful for the first time ever that some swinish conglomerate had bought up utilities statewide, resulting at least in a power grid independent of Occam's existence. Time for the hottest shower I could endure with the undefiled water from my artesian well.

Afterward, as soon as I turned off the faucets, I seemed to hear brutal demolition going on in the next room. Warily pushed bathroom door wide enough for steam to billow into the corridor, and for me to certify that the house was intact. Put on fresh underwear and went to a north-facing window in the kitchen. The ripping, crackling upsurge of "color" had been no more intrusive from here than a neighbor mowing his lawn. Now it was like a nuclear detonation on my doorstep, but slowed down to 16 rpm, in which the uprooting of individual masonry foundations, the evisceration of street after street, the cyclonic uplift of everything and everyone broken and loose reverberated in exquisite clarity. Everything that the "color" had possessed, everything organic it had tinged, everything in contact with that organic material had been recruited into the starbound migration. The pillar of "color" blackened with the bricks and people and trees and soil of Occam, vortexed into slurry.

I was numb to the hellish suffering beyond caring that I was numb, maybe due to general exhaustion, maybe due to permanent moral impairment after the incident with Mr. Snuff Brown. In either case, my one recurring concern was hardly steeped in compassion. After tonight, I wondered, how long would it take for the Gorman County Reservoir to refill?

To lessen the ear-splitting volume of catastrophe, I resorted to the cellar, with minimally worthwhile results. I gravitated right away to the plastic ficus in my former *OGAM Chronicles* studio. Regarded it fondly from my shabby wicker chair. It was no less cheap, dusty, bogus than on the day I'd borrowed it from Pabodie Cable, but here was greenery that wouldn't iridesce, fade to grey, or collapse into powder.

My thoughts began to slip their moorings of the present, to meander among loose ends, unfinished business bobbing to the mental surface, even as my drowsy eyes roved among the chintzy foliage. Aha! I bounced up, grabbed some paper from the eMac's printer tray, and hunkered down again to jot thank-you notes to Gerard Heroux and the others who'd humored OGAM's appeal for folklore about the reservoir. And why not? Time lay before me like an empty prairie out to the horizon. No clocks to punch for the foreseeable future, and no pressure to earn income. The house was paid for, and nobody would be around to collect property taxes any time soon. Even if the state disallowed me Unemployment, my savings could support my frugal lifestyle for months, and my account was in a bank with branches all over the northeast, in no danger of joining the updraft to the Piscids. I let the sheaf of papers, and the top sheet reading "Dear Mr. Heroux," drop between my outspread knees to the floor. Since time was henceforth a boundless plain, what was my rush?

I braved the insane decibels upstairs to settle a mostly academic point. Clamped the phone to my ears and found a dial tone, like a lifeline from otherwise estranged normality. Just to see what would come of it, I went through Wil's and every other cell number off the top of my head, and was shunted without fail, and without a single preliminary ring, to voicemail. Moreover, after the sixth ring at City Hall, Wil's place, the Metcalfe residence, and every other landline I could think of, a recorded message explained that the number I had dialed was "temporarily out of service." Vetoed trying calls to a different area code. Conversation in this din would be ridiculous.

Plus, it was getting worse outside. Was that even possible? I gaped out the living room window. Tried kidding myself that some non-Euclidian kind of optical illusion was taunting me. The "color" wasn't really burning with blinding new ferocity, and didn't really loom like a skyrocketing Niagara a mile down the road. But it did, and I had just enough presence of mind to reason why. In the 1990s, the city water system had expanded to help sell townhouse sprawl, irksomely close to "my" wilderness. And whether by oversight or design, the "color" had taken longer to claim its own out here. Reducing me to the hollow consolation that I'd never met any of those neighbors, had no faces to connect with their delayed holocaust. No, the "color" had no further excuse to carve its swath any closer to home. Or so I tried persuading myself.

Then something streaked across the front yard, just outside the crescent of light from my window, and something lower to the ground followed seconds after. Petrifying me, till my underachieving wits grasped that the streaks weren't luminous. An impulse, or possibly an instinct, propelled me out the front door, and if it was an instinct, it was much less sinister and not as age-old dormant as my phobic cringing at the starry void. In the fringe of dark sky around the platter of cloud, meteors raced into and out of sight like shiners breaking the waves. I flinched earthward, and had a second to brace myself as five substantial dogs charged past my legs, and into relative security. They were dirty, matted, trembling, and wild-eyed, and one of them was Elsie. They caromed in sloppy, irregular ellipses around the living room before curling up in neutral corners behind the sofa, under the table, nesting in armchairs, whining miserably.

Enough of the housepet lingered in them to seek any port indoors in this monstrous storm, but I abstained from testing anyone's personal space with friendly overtures till calm prevailed. None of them looked too malnourished, so some of my neighbors must have been feeding rather than poisoning them. At the thought that some of the suburbanites had been humane, I felt my first pangs of sadness for them. Of course the dogs were mine now, or at any rate my house had become theirs, and more might show up. Would dogs eat tofu franks? That was it for protein in my fridge this week, like it or not.

Did Elsie even recognize me from months ago on Ellery Avenue? Had she led the others here on the trail of my scent? Yes or no, I could stop regretting that I'd rescued no one from the scourging of Occam. But of all the Rice household, who'd have believed last July that Elsie would come out the sole survivor in October? That her collar and tags, like those of her pack, would end up the only artifacts of their owners, of their town?

The halogen glare, meanwhile, had dulled to a translucency in which I could read how the black torrent of slurry had thinned to a high-velocity fountain of speckles, like a pixilated roll of player piano music. The noise was still a few notches from dropping below saturation level.

I was going to be all right, in the primal sense of escaping with my hide, with a life to reassemble, and that trumped all more refined considerations. I almost gave in to jubilation, but I couldn't. One small thing wouldn't let me, but what the hell was it? Concentrating was an uphill battle amidst canine whimpers and panting.

My thumb itched as if calling attention to itself. Yes, that was it. A little scar persisted as my souvenir of that excursion to the Blasted Heath, when barbwire had drawn blood and perhaps injected something as well. I felt the psychic flooring drop out from under me. Had to back away from the window, into a wooden chair at the dining-room table, one of the few furnishings without a posttraumatic squatter underneath. Maybe I'd be fine, or maybe my ordeal was far from through with me.

What had A.P. scribbled in his journal? About something tinier than a mustard seed left to gestate at the bottom of a well in 1882, blossoming into something a millionfold more powerful? If a grain of Blasted Heath were in my circulation, it was inert, denatured, I reminded myself, and had it been there at all, the "color" would have scooped me out of existence when it siphoned all trace of itself to the stars. But why then had the ravening, hateful "color" spared me in the sewers, during its hour of sharpest hunger, when it could have harvested me along with those two men at my heels? What did the "color" know about the grey dust that I didn't?

The whining dogs were already getting on my nerves as I watched my thumb tingle, psychosomatically or not, and I pondered how long I'd be able to stay sane. Or whether sanity even offered the best approach for dealing with this. Decided for the time being I'd qualify as sane until the urge won out to go inspect the vast open grave of Occam. Nothing down there but unacceptable reality, a fatal plunge into assimilation with the soulless universe. Behooved me at long last to learn the knack of living day to day, or maybe hour to hour. At the moment, I asked of the future only that the dogs not beg to be let out before I could tolerate opening the door again. And perversely or not, I had to muse that, come what may, at least the "Gorman taste" was history. I must have been imagining that hint of its presence whenever I swallowed.

www.ingramcontent.com/pod-product-compliance
Lightning Source LLC
Chambersburg PA
CBHW061504030726
47503CB00005B/1809